And then...he saw her

His heart fell to his gut when he recognized the crisp, neat hairstyle, the high cheekbones that could belong to no one but Eve, Eve Triopolous. She seemed to float ethereally behind the counter, treading on air, a graceful woman in white who looked altogether too aristocratic to be working in a place like this. But there was no doubt in his mind as he watched her slide a sandwich plate onto the counter that she indeed worked here. He held his breath. He hadn't remembered Eve as being so beautiful.

She turned on her heel and walked around the end of the counter, and it was then that he realized why she'd left. He gasped with the impact, and the room tilted, bent in two. For when he saw her gently rounded abdomen beneath the skirt of her uniform, he knew.

ABOUT THE AUTHOR

Pamela Browning is a former nonfiction writer
who decided to write fiction one cold rainy day
when she was touring a dump for an article
about waste reclamation. She says, "As the
rainwater sluiced down my neck, I thought,
There's got to be a better way to get a story!"
Writing romance fiction was it. The
warmhearted romances Pam loves to write
brought this author in from the cold and into
the hearts of the many readers who enjoy
her books.

Books by Pamela Browning

HARLEQUIN AMERICAN ROMANCE

101—CHERISHED BEGINNINGS
116—HANDYMAN SPECIAL
123—THROUGH EYES OF LOVE
131—INTERIOR DESIGNS
140—EVER SINCE EVE

HARLEQUIN ROMANCE

2659—TOUCH OF GOLD

Ever Since Eve
PAMELA BROWNING

Harlequin Books

TORONTO • NEW YORK • LONDON
AMSTERDAM • PARIS • SYDNEY • HAMBURG
STOCKHOLM • ATHENS • TOKYO • MILAN

This book is for my own two miracles:
my son, Neill, and my daughter, Bethany

————————◆————————

Published February 1986

First printing December 1985

ISBN 0-373-16140-9

Printed in Canada

Chapter One

"I'm really sorry, Ms. Triopolous. You seem well qualified, but we've already hired someone else."

Eve swallowed her disappointment, put up a brave-enough front to shake hands with the employment interviewer, and escaped into the bright spring sunshine. She had hoped that this particular job in the public relations department of a large advertising agency might be exactly suited to her, and, in fact, it was. But she'd lost out on this position, just as she had lost out on so many others.

"You're overqualified," they'd tell her, or, equally exasperating, "Your experience is excellent, but unfortunately we don't have an opening right now." Which could be true, of course. With the competition from foreign imports, local textile mills were closing at an alarming rate. Two people fought for every textile-related job in this textile-oriented city. Even for skilled jobs, like the ones for which Eve, a magna cum laude graduate of the University of North Carolina, applied.

The sound of her heels on the pavement was muffled by the rundown condition of her shoes, a defeated sound that produced no echo, just a dull pounding. She retreated past houses with signs declaring Rooms for Rent.

Well, that was one thing she and Al, her father, hadn't tried yet—renting out the extra room in their tiny mill-owned house. It was, she reminded herself, something she could keep in mind as a last resort—that is, if they weren't evicted first.

By the time she reached the park not far from the ad agency's building, she admitted to herself that she had no other options but to find a lodger, and even the meager rent derived from renting a room wouldn't help much. She wished fervently that she would land a job, but she'd tried every ad in the newspaper, all to no avail. And she'd been searching for a job for months.

Had today's advertising-agency job really been filled by someone else? Or had the fact that she'd been summarily dismissed from her prized job as public relations director at Wray Mills something to do with it? There was an old-boy network in Charlotte; its members had brushed shoulders at the same colleges, communicated through civic clubs, and their lives were inextricably interwoven through their families. Maybe the word was out: "Don't hire Eve Triopolous. She stirred up trouble at Wray Mills."

Eve eased herself down on a convenient park bench next to a bed of purple-and-yellow pansies, their quaint, kittenlike faces upturned toward the sun. She'd always been partial to pansies; she agreed with Emily Dickinson that violets and roses were too flashy, too showy, too intense. I'm like a pansy, she thought with pleasure. Quaint, quiet, calm. Not flashy.

Nearby a small blond boy tossed bread into the water. Three white ducks paddled furiously across the tiny pond, racing each other for the food, furrowing the sparkling blue ripples into shimmering wakes. The boy squealed in delight and ran to beg more bread crusts from his mother, who tousled her son's curly hair before he danced out of reach. Eve smiled and inhaled a breath of balmy, fragrant air. The sun felt warmer than it had all winter and warmer than it would feel any other day of the year. The soft breezes of spring were sweeping away a long, cold winter, and she was glad.

Dire rumblings from the region of her stomach reminded her she was hungry. She shook a solitary plastic-wrapped sandwich from a brown paper bag and unfolded the newspaper to read while she ate.

The ad fairly jumped out at her from the Personals section of the Charlotte *Courier-Express*. In stark contrast to the other ads set in small type, this one captured her eye with bold capital letters:

—Surrogate Mother Wanted—
Couple will pay $12,000 plus expenses to healthy woman to bear their child. Replies confidential. Call 555-4272.

Intrigued, Eve lowered the newspaper to her lap and thoughtfully bit into her bologna sandwich. Twelve thousand dollars!

Did it really say twelve thousand?

She set the sandwich carefully on the brown paper bag from which she had so recently removed it and scanned the ad again.

Yes, it really did. Twelve thousand dollars! That was a lot of money to Eve Triopolous at this low point in her life.

With twelve thousand dollars, she could move her father out of the mill-village house that they had been ordered to vacate by Wray Mills's management.

With twelve thousand dollars, she could pay a hefty portion of Al's considerable medical expenses.

With twelve thousand dollars—but wait. Maybe it wouldn't be that easy.

She'd heard of surrogate mothers. She wrinkled her forehead, trying to remember what she knew about the subject. As she recalled, surrogate mothers were hired by couples when the husband was fertile but the wife couldn't become pregnant. The surrogate was artificially inseminated with the husband's sperm, which united with the surrogate mother's egg. The surrogate's job was to carry the baby to term, surrendering it to its father and his wife soon after delivery.

Could Eve become pregnant? As cautiously as she would test her footing on a crumbling red-clay bluff, she tried the word on for size. *Pregnant*. She'd never been pregnant, but she didn't see why she wouldn't be fertile. Eve met the only qualifications stated in the ad. She was a woman, and she was healthy.

Oh, she was very healthy. She had not caught so much as a cold in the past five years. Her body hummed along, breathing, digesting, doing all the things a body was supposed to do, even when she fueled it on a diet composed largely of cheap bologna sandwiches, peanut butter and junk food. Presumably, her body could become pregnant, too. Pregnancy was, after all, just another bodily process. And bodily processes were nothing to be afraid of. They were natural, normal.

And she'd might as well face it; Eve had tried everything else. Today, basking in the warm sunshine, sliding her tired feet surreptitiously out of her shoes because they were sore from walking from job interview to job interview to save gasoline, Eve was feeling truly desperate. Desperate, and to some extent hopeless. She remained unemployed even after applying for every job that seemed within the range of her wide capabilities, and her responsibilities at home weighed heavily on her narrow shoulders. And not the least of all, she was sick of bologna sandwiches.

Eve didn't stop to think about what Al, with his Old World ways, would say. And at this point she didn't care what anyone else would say, either. She wasn't afraid of being pregnant, and she didn't look for reasons why she shouldn't be a surrogate mother. At the moment, desperate as she was, there weren't any.

Twelve thousand dollars could be hers, but first she'd have to produce a quarter for the phone call. She fished through her purse, digging into the lining, scrounging for loose change. Then, recklessly tossing the bologna sandwich in a nearby trash can, she raced lightly on tiptoe across grass spring new with green, her tread bright with renewed hope, her short black hair gleaming with blue highlights in the spring sunshine. She dropped her quarter in the public telephone with a resounding *clink*.

Wombs for rent, she thought wryly to herself, and then she dialed the number.

IT WAS ONLY FIVE DAYS after she made her phone call that Eve met the Langs.

A nervous Eve, still surprised to find herself there, waited in the cool, crisp, air-conditioned reception room of the Queen City Infertility Clinic, leafing distractedly through an elderly copy of the *Ladies' Home Journal*. She tapped her foot impatiently. She had polished her shoes that very morning, using the last of the navy-blue polish. She'd dressed conservatively in a navy-blue suit and her best white blouse with the lacy frill at the neck, the same suit she had worn to all those job interviews.

Who were the Langs, anyway? That was the first question she had asked Diane Holtman, the clinic counselor, when Diane had called with the news that an infertile couple was interested in Eve and wanted to meet her.

"Mr. Lang is a textile executive," Diane told Eve over the phone, "and Mrs. Lang is the holder of a degree in music and a volunteer for several of the city's worthwhile charities." Other than that, all Eve knew was that like all couples who consulted the Queen City Infertility Clinic, the Langs were desperate to have a child.

Of course, Eve hadn't dreamed that she'd be called back so soon after taking a comprehensive psychological test and filling out the interminable eight-page form, a form that had made her squirm with its in-depth questions.

"Why do you want to be a surrogate mother?" had been one of the questions. Eve thought about that one for a long time. Finally, she'd written, "For the money." And then, because it was equally true, she added, "Because I want to help somebody." Eve liked the idea that she and the couple for whom she would carry a child would be mutually helping each other.

"Eve?"

Eve looked up. The receptionist beckoned.

"Follow me, please."

Eve did, twitching surreptitiously at her skirt, worrying that her slip showed. She wanted to be perfect. She wanted the Langs to like her. And because her future, if they chose her, would be inextricably intertwined with theirs for as long as it took to create a baby, she wanted to like them.

Diane Holtman was waiting for her at the door to her office.

"Eve," Diane said, clasping her hand warmly. She drew Eve inside.

"This is Eve Triopolous," Diane said to the couple sitting on the couch. "Eve, Derek and Kelly Lang."

With a nervous smile, Eve turned toward the couple, and the moment she saw them, her nervousness melted away, and she thought, *They're beautiful!*

For the Langs were, if any couple could be said to be, a golden couple. Derek Lang was poised and perfect in his well-tailored pin-striped suit. Kelly Lang was blond but not brittle, *au courant* without being annoyingly so. Derek's coarse butternut-brown hair was combed back from his face in a conservative style, neither too long nor too short. Kelly had that indefinable look of the well-to-do, the jewelry and clothes and bearing of the typical Junior Leaguer.

While she was taking their measure, the Langs were taking hers. Kelly Lang thought in surprise, *Why, how sincere and open she looks!* Kelly had been initially concerned about what kind of woman would volunteer to be a surrogate mother. But thirty-four years of living had taught Kelly to trust her native intuition, and Eve's natural dignity reassured her.

Diane Holtman began to guide the three of them skillfully through the crucial interview, but all the while Diane was talking, Derek Lang paid little attention to what she was saying. His eyes were summing Eve up. Unlike his wife, who was thinking of the internal woman, Derek dealt solely in externals. He was uncommonly pleased with what he saw.

Eve Triopolous's black hair was straight and sleek and shiny, and above all, it looked healthy. She wore it in a haircut shorter at the nape than at the sides, as precise and neat as the haircuts of Japanese schoolchildren. In fact, everything about Eve Triopolous was neat and precise. High cheekbones. Milky-white skin. A small nose, honed to a fine point at the end, with nostrils that did not flare or spread even when she smiled. Eyebrows naturally dark and smooth and kempt, feathering across her brow like the tips of ravens' wings. Huge brown eyes, eyes you could burrow into, they looked so soft. He'd read on her personality profile that she was twenty-eight years old and had never married.

"The thing is," his wife was saying earnestly to Eve, interrupting his perusal of her, "that the child would not be yours at all. We would be using my egg and Derek's sperm, which would be fertilized in a laboratory, and then the resulting embryo would be implanted in your uterus."

"I didn't know that was possible," Eve said. "I had assumed that it would be my egg and the husband's sperm, and that the embryo would result from artificial insemination."

"Often artificial insemination is the way it's done when perhaps for some reason the wife isn't producing a viable egg," explained Diane. "But in the case of the Langs, their infertility problem is that Kelly has had a hysterectomy—she has had her womb surgically removed. She still has ovaries, and she can produce the egg. Kelly's egg can be fertilized with Derek's sperm in vitro, but Kelly, of course, cannot carry a child because she has no uterus. That's where you come in, Eve."

"The embryo would be implanted in my uterus?" asked Eve in surprise.

"Yes. The baby would be what is often referred to as a 'test-tube baby.' The implantation in your uterus would be done at a hospital by a local gynecologist who is an expert in infertility. And you would carry Kelly and Derek's child to term.''

Eve's head spun. But this was even better than she had thought! The only misgiving she had harbored about this whole idea involved her mistaken assumption that the baby would result from her egg, would be half hers, part of her, and that she might very well develop emotional ties to it before it was born.

Now, because of the Langs' unusual situation, even that worry faded away. It would not be Eve's baby at all. She would shelter the test-tube child inside her body for nine months, she would bear it, she would turn it over to the Langs. And she would walk away from the experience virtually unscathed, pleased that she was doing a good deed, and not only that, but she would be twelve thousand dollars richer.

And then she would pay their bills, buy a little house where she and Al could live, and she would find a job.

Eve swung her head around to study the Langs. She watched them thoughtfully, studying every detail.

Derek Lang leaned slightly forward in his seat, his clear gray eyes fixed on her in silent entreaty. Eve took in all aspects of him—the broad shoulders, the fine fabric of his suit, the ready intelligence of his expression. He must be a very special kind of man, she thought, to go through this painstaking process in order to have a child. A spark of empathy passed through them in that moment, unmistakable to the two of them. In that moment, Eve recognized the qualities she always looked for in a man—but never found. How fortunate his wife was to have him for a husband!

Kelly Lang gripped her husband's hand so tightly that her knuckles shone white in the glare of the overhead fluorescent light. And Kelly was special, too—several cuts above the ordinary. It was clear to Eve that the Langs were a fine couple, the kind of people who deserved to be parents. Any child of theirs would be a fortunate child indeed. And she knew that all their bright hopes of having a child of their own were pinned on her.

Her decision was made. She didn't have to think about it twice.

With an air of impeccable calm, Eve smiled at the two of them and said softly, "I'm willing if you are."

She was immediately gratified by Derek's beaming smile and the happy tears pooling in Kelly's sky-blue eyes.

So WILLING were the Langs that Eve found herself in a gynecologist's office that afternoon. After a routine physical, Dr. Perry informed Eve and the Langs that he had discovered nothing to indicate that Eve could not carry a child to term.

"I'm so happy," Kelly Lang confided, impulsively hugging Eve when they said goodbye in the parking lot.

Eve hugged Kelly back. She'd only met Kelly that day, but with all their talk of fertility and infertility and babies and bodies, she already felt that unmatchable woman-to-woman closeness that often develops between dear friends. Eve knew instinctively that Kelly was the kind of woman who would be a wonderful mother, who would tirelessly chair committees on the PTA, who would make sure that a child saw the pediatrician regularly and had all the right inoculations.

Moreover, Kelly was a woman who loved her husband; Eve could see that in the way she reached for his hand from time to time, resting her fingers trustingly in his. She was capable of loving a child deeply, the way a child should be loved. And Derek—well, Derek was obviously the kind of man to whom everything came easily. So would fatherhood.

"I'm happy, too," Eve said slowly and with some surprise. She had not expected to feel so delighted. She had expected to feel emotionally removed from the situation. But the Langs were so warm and enthusiastic that their happiness was infectious. Eve already felt as though the three of them were inexorably bound together as they set off upon an adventure of the first magnitude. She drew a deep breath. Having this baby was going to be a wonderful, uplifting experience; she just knew it was.

"I'll have my lawyer draw up the papers," Derek Lang said, smiling widely and shaking her hand briskly in farewell. His hand was firm, his grip reassuring.

"And I'll call you and let you know when the papers are ready," Kelly said with a cheerful smile before folding the crisp white linen of her exquisitely cut dress around her and ducking into their silver Mercedes sedan.

It's almost too easy, Eve thought in amazement, watching their Mercedes until it was swallowed up in the rush-hour traffic on Independence Boulevard.

And then, still slightly stunned by the staggering events of the day, she drove her own unassuming Volkswagen Beetle fifteen miles home to Wrayville, the level of her optimism falling lower and lower with the passing of every mile.

Because now she was going to have to explain this whole strange business to Al. And telling her father, Eve knew, would not be easy at all.

"OH, DEREK, Eve is everything I had hoped," Kelly Lang said later in their bedroom, twining her fingers together behind her husband's neck. She gazed at his handsome face, at his wide eyebrows, which were a bit too short, at his nose, which would be ordinary if it were not blunted at the end.

He nuzzled her forehead. "She's perfect," he said, slapping his wife affectionately on the rump before moving to the closet and removing his tie. He hung the tie on the specially built rack, straightening it until it hung neatly.

"She has a matter-of-fact look about her, doesn't she?" Kelly offered. "As though she wouldn't go into a dither over anything. And that's good, Derek, because I've been reading about babies before they're born, and the experts think they can hear while they're still inside the mother. I wouldn't want our baby to be carried by somebody who was noisy and quarrelsome and—"

"I don't think you have to worry about that with Eve Triopolous," Derek said, picturing Eve's intelligent face in his mind. And not only her face but the rest of her, too—the white skin, the narrow shoulders, the waist not as small as it might be. And her hips, wide hips, hips that would spread to bear a child with no trouble at all, from the look of them. Wide hips swelling gently from waist to thigh, fertile-looking hips, hips that could easily accommodate a baby for nine months, and no doubt a pelvis that would cradle that baby in comfort until the time of birth.

His eyes softened on his wife. Kelly glowed, she sparkled, she looked happier than he had seen her in a long, long time.

Slowly, he unbuttoned the top button of his shirt, and then he unbuttoned the next.

Kelly caught the meaning in his eyes.

"Do you think we have time to make a baby before dinner?" Derek asked softly, moving to take her in his arms. It had been too long since the last time; with his busy work schedule, he was always so rushed.

Kelly lifted her lips to his. So many times Derek had initiated their lovemaking with those very same words back in the days before she had had to have her hysterectomy. The words brought back fond memories of a time when she had still hoped that they *could* conceive a child of their own, and today that hope had been rekindled in the person of Eve Triopolous.

"Oh, darling, this time let's pretend we're really making a baby," she breathed, because in her heart she knew—she *knew*—that soon, soon their baby would be conceived, not inside her body but in a dish in a laboratory, but that didn't matter; it didn't matter at all.

The important thing is that there would be a baby, hers and Derek's, and in her heart she would hold close the comfort that it *could* have been this act of physical love that created their baby; it *could* have if things had been different.

AT THAT MOMENT, Eve was parking her VW under the chinaberry tree in front of a white frame house with a green shingled roof, a house that was identical to every other house in what was known as Cotton Mill Hill, the mill village of Wray Mills. She spared a quick glance toward the cotton mill itself, a sprawling brick building with two tall smokestacks that dominated the scene from its location on the hill. Dominated the scene, the people, the town government, the police force, everything, by virtue of its employment of at least one member of every family in Wrayville. Wrayville would not have existed if it were not for Wray Mills.

But because of her agreement with the Langs, the mill would not dominate the Triopolous family any longer. Eve rejoiced at the thought of it.

The odor of fatback hung in the humid air. Mrs. Quick across the street was boiling up a mess of collard greens, no doubt, for that big family of hers. The smell of food cooking, even the greasy smell of fatback, made Eve's mouth water. She had skipped lunch again today.

"Al?" She swung inside, her heart sinking. She hoped he'd had a good day. But there was no sign of her father in the small comfortable living room, a room that Eve had delighted in furnishing in soft restful colors with her own salary from the mill.

"Al?"

"In the kitchen," she heard, and Eve peered around the door frame to see her father, in his customary chambray work shirt, standing in front of the sink, washing salad greens.

"Thought I'd get a start on dinner," he said, his voice wheezing. "Have any luck looking for a job today?"

Eve paused. "Let me do that," she said gently, taking the lettuce from him. "You sit down and rest."

"Don't boss me, daughter," he said playfully, but she noticed that when he sat in the kitchen chair, he sank into it as though he had little energy. Out of the corner of her eye she noted the sallowness of his skin. She'd thought his breathing had sounded more labored than usual last night, and it worried her.

What to tell him about her day? She'd never answered his question about looking for a job. With luck, maybe he wouldn't ask it again. Yes, that was the thing to do— ignore the question. She still didn't know how to tell her family-oriented father, so set in his old-fashioned ways, that she had hired herself out as a surrogate mother. He worried about her too much as it was.

Which was what he was doing at the moment. *Poor Eve,* Alexander Triopolous thought as his daughter blended lemon juice and olive oil for salad dressing. *She tries so hard.*

"Eve, you know, I can sympathize with you being out of work," he said, thinking she might want to talk about it. After all, he himself had been a long time without employment in his own youth.

Eve swished the salad dressing in its cruet before answering. "It's different now from the way it used to be," she said carefully. "This isn't 1947. It's not a postwar economy. I thought I'd have an easier time getting a job."

"This area depends on textiles," he said. "And with all the foreign imports—well, foreign imports are kind of like the red tide. They're killing jobs around here."

He meant it to be a joke. But after he'd returned from France in World War II, when he'd gone back to his family home in Tarpon Springs, Florida, and expected to resume his profession of harvesting sponges like many of the other members of families of Greek heritage who lived there, red tide had been no joke.

Red tide, a microscopic malady, began destroying the sponges on the floor of the Gulf of Mexico in 1947, and sponge fishing died out. The Greek-American spongers in Tarpon Springs moved on to other lines of work as bankruptcies flourished and stores closed their doors. In desperation, Al had contacted his army buddy, Joe Rigby. Joe hailed from Wrayville, North Carolina. Did Joe know of any jobs there?

"Yes," Joe had enthused, phoning long distance over a crackling wire. "Get up here. The cotton mill is hiring."

And so Al Triopolous had hitched a ride to the little town outside Charlotte, and best of all, he had landed a job in the card room of Wray Mills, a cotton mill that manufactured gauze and diaper fabric that was much in demand because of the postwar baby boom.

The handsome Greek-American had appeared breathtakingly exotic to the local girls, who were entranced by his un-Southern accent and his flashing brown eyes. Still, he had managed to elude all of them for seven years until he met blond, petite Betty Simpson. And then he had fallen, and he had fallen hard. It wasn't the austere, restrained courtship it would have been under the stern Greek traditions in Tarpon Springs. Al married Betty within three months of meeting her.

Al Triopolous never left his job in the card room, the place in the mill where cotton, straight from the bale, is fed into carding machines whose wire teeth separate and straighten the fibers. He grew accustomed to the cotton dust hanging thick in the air, leaving an ever-present coating on his clothes, on his wavy black hair and in his lungs. There was nothing unusual about the coating of cotton dust, because loping down the hill after work to the little house he and Betty rented from the company, Al looked like most of the other mill hands. Covered with lint, they were called "lintheads." Al never minded being called a linthead. What he would have minded more was being unemployed.

He hated to see his daughter going through the same hell he had gone through back in '47. Coming home day after day after looking for work, Eve looked exhausted. It had been going on for months now, this job search of hers. It was all his fault she had lost her prime public relations job in the mill.

Eve would have held that job forever if it hadn't been for him. A high school honor student, Eve had attended the University of North Carolina on a scholarship provided by Wray Mills. And when she'd "made trouble"—the mill's words—about Al's workmen's compensation claim, they had fired her with angry diatribes about being an ingrate after all the company had done for her. Eve was not one to compromise her principles, and that made Al proud. But he'd filed the claim, and then she'd felt she had to stand behind it. He'd never get over the feeling that it was his fault that Eve was out of work.

"Did Nell Baker stop by today, Al?" Eve asked him casually as she dished up their dinner, leftover lamb stew, from a pot on the stove.

"Can't you tell? She dusted and vacuumed, and she drove me out of the house. It was good for me, I guess, because I managed to walk down to the corner and back." He shook his head. "She's a whirlwind, that one." But Eve noticed that he was smiling.

"She likes you," Eve said teasingly. She smiled and flipped her short hair back from her face as she sat down beside him. "In fact, I think she has a crush on you."

"Ha!" her father said. "Nell Baker just wants somebody to push around. I remember how she used to treat poor old Bud. 'Do this, do that,'" he mimicked. "Drove the fellow to his grave, if you ask me."

Eve's smile faded. Bud Baker had died over a year ago of what was termed "acute chronic respiratory disease." Bud had worked in the carding room, too. He'd displayed the same symptoms her father had.

"Say," her father was saying, realizing it was time to change the subject, "I heard a rumor today when I was out walking. Somebody told me the mill's going to be sold.''

"Sold?"

"That's right. Nobody's saying who the customer is yet, but the word is that it's a big conglomerate that owns several mills. What do you think of that?"

"I wonder how the sale of Wray Mills to a big textile conglomerate will affect your claim," Eve said darkly, unable to eat any more stew.

"No telling. I'm not saying I believe the talk. There've been rumors before."

"That's true," Eve said, the tension easing in her stomach. "Lord, I can't wait to get out of Wrayville."

Al shot her a shrewd look. "How can you say that?" he asked. "You've never known any other home."

Eve shoved her plate of stew away. "On the day they fired me from the mill, I was glad, *glad*, because I knew I'd be leaving," she said fervently.

She got up and rinsed her plate off in the sink, willing her heart to stop pounding. She couldn't help the resentment that she felt against the mill. Not after what the management had done to her father and to her.

Al began to cough, and she turned in alarm. She should have known not to talk about getting fired; whenever Al became emotionally upset, he coughed.

His skin looked papery and old, and the coughing was wearing him out. Eve rushed to her father's side and held his hand until the coughing spell had spent itself at last.

"Ah, Eve," he said, his voice no more than a whisper. "Maybe you're right. You need to get out of Wrayville, away from the mill. You'll get a job soon—sure you will—and then maybe in a couple of years you'll meet a nice man, get married and have babies. You know, that's the one thing that would comfort me in my old age. Some grandchildren, Eve. I've always loved kids. Wanted more of my own. You'd be happy, Eve, settled down with a husband and some babies.''

He smiled at her wistfully, and Eve pressed her cheek against his so that he couldn't see the despairing expression in her eyes.

As old-fashioned as his hopes for her were, she knew he wanted only the best for her, and the best for Al Triopolous since his Betty had died had been his relationship with Eve, his only child. Eve couldn't tell Al now—she didn't dare tell him—that she was going to bear a child, that the child wasn't even going to be hers and that she would have to give it up in the end. He wouldn't understand. He wouldn't even appreciate the irony of the situation.

The anguishing question tormented her; if she couldn't tell her father she was going to be a surrogate mother, how in the world was she going to manage it at all?

Chapter Two

Charlotte, North Carolina, is named after Queen Charlotte of Mecklenburg-Strelitz, wife of King George III of England, and the city bills itself today as the Queen City. If Charlotte is truly the Queen City, thought Eve as she steered her Volkswagen down shady tree-lined streets on this unseasonably warm May afternoon, then Myers Park must surely be the many-faceted jewel in her crown.

It was a section of town where big houses sat far back from the street, so far back that all Eve could tell about them was that they were large, and in some cases palatial. Here the very air was rarefied, and the breeze slipping through the leaves overhead whispered ever so discreetly, "Money, money, money."

The Langs' house turned out to be a Georgian structure of old brick with an imposing front door, a neatly manicured garden and a look of old money. Textile executive? Derek Lang must be the scion of one of the area's well-known textile families, the product of prep school and Davidson College and Harvard Business School for his MBA. This wasn't the home of any middle-management type.

Eve didn't know why Kelly Lang had insisted that she sign the papers relating to their employment of her as a surrogate mother at their home. She would have preferred the cool formality of the lawyer's office. But it was too late now to insist upon that.

Eve smoothed her hair and checked her face in the mirror before walking swiftly up the brick walkway to the front door. As she raised the brass lion knocker and let it fall, she realized how hollow her stomach felt. She wasn't sure if the hollow feeling was due to nervousness or if it was because she hadn't been able to face the thought of another bologna sandwich for lunch and so hadn't eaten anything since breakfast.

"Come in out of the heat," bade Kelly, answering Eve's knock, wearing a rose-red sundress and dangling white hoop earrings. When Eve hesitated inside the door, Kelly immediately put an arm around her waist and drew her across the hall to the study.

"This is Harry Worden, our attorney," Kelly said, indicating a florid-faced white-haired man who spread papers on the desk. He looked up as they entered, gave Eve a curious once-over, and apparently deciding that she passed inspection, he stumped over to shake Eve's hand.

"And of course you know Derek," Kelly went on.

Derek nodded. Today, in the face of a hot late May day, Eve wore a simple white short-sleeved cotton dress of some soft, petallike material, severely tailored except for white embroidery on the collar. With her coloring, the effect of the white fabric against her pale skin and dark hair was stunning.

"If you'll just sign here . . . and here," Harry Worden told her, and without a word, but gripping the pencil tightly in her nervousness, Eve signed and sat back in the big wing chair.

The papers were shuffled to Derek, who scrawled his name quickly and with a flourish, and then to Kelly, who signed and then flashed her husband a radiant smile.

It's legal, Eve thought with a sense of amazement, *just like that. Three signatures and I get pregnant. When I pass go, I'll collect twelve thousand dollars...twelve thousand dollars...twelve thousand dollars....* The sum throbbed inside her head with each beat of her heart.

The attorney handed each of them a copy of the contract and snapped his briefcase closed. "Now if you'll excuse me," Harry Worden said with a brisk nod, "I'll be going back to my office." Kelly left with him, presumably to see him to the door.

Eve rose from her chair. She had just signed away at least nine months of her life, but the reality had not hit her yet. The enormity of what she was doing, the impact of it—when would she believe it? When the embryo was implanted in her uterus? When her body began to change from the effects of pregnancy? When her pregnancy was so unmistakable that she finally had to tell Al, or worse yet, that he guessed? She grabbed the back of the chair in sudden dizziness as Kelly returned.

"Eve?" Kelly's worried face wobbled in front of hers; Derek's strong arms held her up and then eased her onto a nearby couch.

"I—I'm all right," Eve said.

"Are you sure?" Kelly felt her forehead.

"It's just the heat. Or something," Eve said, struggling to sit up.

"Umm," Kelly said uncertainly with a quick glance at her husband, "there was something Derek and I wanted to talk over with you. If you feel up to it, that is. Are you hungry? That is, would you join us for lemonade and a snack?"

Eve's stomach manufactured unseemly noises at the mention of food. She managed to look mortified.

"Yes," she said with as much dignity as she could muster. "Actually, I forgot to eat lunch today."

"Oh, in that case," Kelly said, summoning a sweet-faced black woman wearing a gray-and-white uniform, "we'll have some of my aunt's chicken salad sandwiches. Louise, make sure some of Aunt May's sandwiches are on the tray, will you, please?"

"Now, wouldn't we be more comfortable on the terrace? It's shady there this time of day." This was Derek. He regarded Eve seriously and with concern as Eve passed a hand over her face, trying to brush away the light-headedness.

At Derek's suggestion, the three of them naturally gravitated without discussion through the French doors to the adjoining terrace overlooking a tranquil rose garden and sat down at the small wrought-iron table. Eve tried to restrain herself from eating too many of the delicately assembled chicken-salad sandwiches, but they were so *good*.

"Are you feeling better, Eve?" Kelly inquired after Eve had polished off at least half a dozen of the little triangles, and Eve smiled and nodded and reached for one last sandwich.

"Then perhaps we should talk about—" And here Kelly looked at her husband for help.

Derek cleared his throat. "Kelly and I thought that— or rather we *hope* that—you will consider moving in with us after the baby is conceived. That you'll live here, with us, until the baby is born."

Wide-eyed, Eve looked from Derek to Kelly, who nodded to corroborate the invitation.

"Our contract stipulates that we take care of your living expenses," Kelly reminded her.

"But—"

"We would still pay you a generous allowance," Derek interrupted, mindful that she had replied in part to the form's question "Why do you want to be a surrogate mother?" with "For the money." It hadn't escaped Derek's attention that Eve had looked hungry when she arrived here, looked as though she were used to being hungry, and he didn't want his child to be deprived of the proper nutrients while it was *in utero*. If she lived here, she would eat properly; Kelly and her Aunt May would see to that. He didn't mind paying her an additional allowance, not at all. Kelly had convinced him that it would be worth it to ensure a healthy baby.

"Please say you will," Kelly said softly but persuasively. "It would be fun for me to watch the baby grow, to go with you to Dr. Perry for the checkups."

Still undecided, wondering if Al could manage without her, if Mrs. Baker would look after him, Eve only stared.

"Would you like to see your room?" Kelly stood up, taking Eve's answer for granted. Eve found herself being propelled up the wide stairs, past the majestic grandfather clock on the landing, down a hall carpeted in jade green, to a guest room that was a charming vignette of antiques. A French needlepoint armchair waited elegantly before an English lady's writing desk. Pink Scalamandré velvet print swooped into graceful swags over her window. A Schumacher print covered the walls, and the same print cunningly adorned the coverlet on the dainty brass bed.

"It would make my wife happy if you'd stay with us," Derek said, sliding an arm around Kelly's shoulders and pulling her close.

Eve loved the room. It was beautiful. "I'll think about it," she said, feeling as though she'd been inserted unawares into a fairy tale of her own imagination. She felt like a princess, and a bogus princess at that. What had she done to deserve such beautiful surroundings? She peered into the corners of the room and regarded the closet door with trepidation. She fully expected a frog to leap out wearing a sign demanding Kiss Me.

"You wouldn't have to move in, you know, until you're actually pregnant," Kelly said anxiously, totally unaware of Eve's feelings of unworthiness.

"When—when will that be, I wonder?" Eve asked as the three of them walked downstairs together.

Kelly's face shone. "That's the other thing I wanted to tell you. Oh, Eve, I spoke with Dr. Perry this morning," she said. "We're going to try next week." She smiled lovingly up at her husband.

Next week, Eve thought with wonder. *I might be pregnant next week. Pregnant. Me!*

The thought awed her.

THE PROCEDURE had been simple. An egg extracted surgically from Kelly's ovary united with Derek's sperm in a Petri dish, and in an incubator set previously at the temperature of body heat, the fertilized egg shivered and shuddered and clove in two. In sudden bright bursts of energy, nuclei split, chromosomes energetically aligned themselves, and the unique design of a new baby was irrevocably created. And once again, in a process as ancient as the ages but no less miraculous for all that, a fertilized egg became a new human being, child of Kelly and Derek Lang, citizen of the universe.

When it was several cells in size, the tiny embryo was injected into Eve's uterus by Dr. Perry, using a syringe with a soft plastic tip. Kelly had been present in the room when it was done, clinging tightly to Eve's hand.

"Are you all right?" she'd kept asking Eve, her blue eyes intent on Eve's face.

Eve, lightly sedated, barely felt the embryo when it entered the mouth of her womb. "I'm perfectly all right," Eve reassured Kelly. She was glad that Kelly was with her, holding on to Eve's hand for dear life. Kelly's presence made the tiny morsel of life in her uterus seem more like Kelly's baby. And she must remember, Eve told herself fiercely, that it *is* Kelly and Derek's baby. She, Eve, was merely providing a temporary home for it.

If they were lucky, the embryo would embed itself in the lining of Eve's womb, and Eve would be pregnant. *If.* That one little word with its myriad possibilities had never seemed so big to any of them before now.

Afterward, the three of them settled down to wait, Kelly and Derek in their big Georgian house in Myers Park, and Eve, nervous despite her calm front, at home in Wrayville with Al.

If the pregnancy didn't take, they would try again. And again. They would try every month for a year, if necessary.

But an elated Eve knew by the end of the first week that they had been successful. Her breasts began to swell, and she knew from her recent reading that this was one of the first signs of pregnancy. Eve understood her own body too well to believe that this new swelling and tenderness was a sign of anything other than what it was.

Eve cautiously told Kelly, who called every day, that she thought she was pregnant.

"On the first try? Oh, Eve, I can hardly dare to hope!" Kelly's voice quavered with emotion.

"Neither can I," Eve replied, her heart in her mouth. She wanted this to be the real thing, hoped for it more than she ever thought she would.

Al answered the phone one day when Kelly called. "Who's that?" he asked when Eve had hung up.

"A new friend of mine," she said casually.

"Oh," said Al, who was engrossed in a tired rerun of *Gomer Pyle* on television. "I didn't think I recognized her voice." And he said no more about it.

Eve agonized. She almost wished Al had been more curious, because she'd never kept secrets from him before. When would she tell her father what she was doing? What would he say? How would he react?

For Al Triopolous was the product of an old-time Greek culture where marriages were arranged, where husband and wife didn't kiss in front of the children, where girls did not date, where old traditions were preserved. True, he had broken those traditions himself when he had left Tarpon Springs, never to live there again, and when he had subsequently married Eve's mother. But what would Al think of a woman, his own daughter, who deliberately impregnated herself with the child of a couple she hardly knew? And for money, at that? Though her motives were pure and would benefit both of them, Eve dreaded telling Al with all her heart.

Nights, lying awake and listening to Al's labored breathing next door, Eve stared into the darkness and worried the problem in her mind. She hugged her secret close in the dark, running her hands over her breasts, her midriff, her hips, searching for some sign that her body was betraying her to Al. But no, her stomach was still flat. And so she still didn't tell him.

"WELL LADIES, how does February sound for your baby's due date?"

Kelly and Eve, side by side in Dr. Perry's office after his examination of Eve, turned to each other in glee. Eve never knew who held her arms out first, she or Kelly. She only knew that she was happy, joyful, ecstatic, on behalf of Kelly and Derek.

Kelly pulled away from Eve and wept into a daintily embroidered handkerchief. "I can't help it," she said sobbing, "I'm just so *happy*! And oh, Derek will be, too!"

Eve was happy, too, but that wasn't why she wept. She wept because she still didn't know how she was going to tell Al.

"AND SO THEY WANT ME to move to Charlotte," Eve said carefully.

"This 'textile executive' you're going to work for—he doesn't mind that you were dismissed from Wray Mills?" Al asked sharply.

"We've never actually discussed it," Eve said, moistening her lips and hating herself for being so evasive.

"Ah," Al said, and he paused to cough. "It must be a pretty good job, eh? What exactly will you do?"

"I'm going to be a sort of personal assistant," Eve said, getting up and rummaging in a drawer for her father's inhaler. "Have you been using your inhaler, Al?" she asked. "I don't like the sound of that cough."

"Don't worry," he said.

"I'd worry a lot less if I thought you were taking good care of yourself while you're living here alone," she told him firmly, setting the inhaler within Al's reach.

"Mrs. Baker will be glad to take care of me," he retorted. His dark eyes sparkled at her.

"Oh, Al, you know what I mean," she said.

"I'll miss you, daughter. But we'll still have the weekends."

"Yes," Eve said, trying not to wince as her swollen breasts chafed against the fabric of her too-tight bra. "We'll still have the weekends."

But for how long? she wondered. *How long will it be before I start to show?*

IT TOOK ONLY A WEEK of living with the Langs to turn Eve's act of self-survival into an act of love.

Yes, the hefty allowance that Derek gave her made it possible for Eve to tackle the tall stack of Al's medical bills. Yes, the contracted agreement that she would receive twelve thousand dollars when the baby was born ensured a brighter future for her and Al. But after being with Kelly and Derek and Kelly's Aunt May, who lived with them—well, Eve would have been an emotional cripple if she hadn't loved them.

"Eve," Kelly would say, popping into her room after breakfast, "I'm going shopping. Won't you come with me? Oh, please say yes," and Kelly would bear Eve away in the Mercedes, drive to Eastland Mall or Southpark Mall or any of the other wonderful shopping places Kelly knew, and they would shop for baby furniture or baby clothes or maternity clothes for Eve, giggling and carrying on like two teenagers.

Or Eve would say after she had been there a few days, "Kelly, play something on the piano, will you, please?"

And Kelly would sit dreamily at the piano, playing tune after tune while Eve listened attentively and with admiration for Kelly's considerable talent.

Eve loved Kelly for her lack of pretense. Kelly was easy to be around; she was a good conversationalist; she possessed a voice that rolled forth rapidly at times and at other times proceeded in fits and starts as she stopped to catch her breath and then rattled it out in words.

The two of them talked and talked, Kelly of her upbringing in upper-crust Charlotte, Eve of her childhood in a cotton-mill town. Their backgrounds were dissimilar enough to be interesting to each other, and they had the common ground of the baby now growing in Eve's womb. After only a few weeks, Kelly was the sister Eve had never been privileged to have.

Aunt May was nearly seventy, a spry type with a great cloud of curled white hair sheened with lavender. Her plump figure, because of her addiction to frivolous shoes with absurdly high heels, reminded Eve of a pouter pigeon wearing stilts. A box of chocolates was never far from hand, and Aunt May was deplorably hard of hearing and kept misplacing her hearing aid. She pronounced herself "tickled pink" about the baby.

"I don't think much of space flights and laser weapons and all that," she confided loudly to Eve on Eve's first day in the Myers Park house. "But I do approve of modern technology that lets somebody have a baby for somebody else. Now that's progress. Here, dear, have a chocolate-covered cherry. No? You're not into bean curd and health food things, are you? What's that? What?"

Eve, who had only been trying to tell Aunt May that she was determined to eat properly for the baby's sake, gave up. It was enough that Aunt May liked her.

And Derek. The unfailingly methodical Derek, who rose at the same time every day, dressed in a well-cut three-piece suit before going outside to retrieve the paper and then read it carefully front to back before driving off to work at his job in one of the new gleaming glass-and-chrome office buildings on Tryon Street. Who always kissed his wife as soon as he walked through the front door, whose love for Kelly beamed from his gray eyes, which could sparkle with humor or darken with empathy.

Was there ever so perfect a husband as Derek? Did he ever fail to compliment his wife on her appearance or neglect to hold her chair for her at dinner or listen when she spoke? Eve's admiration for Derek grew day by day. *If I ever marry,* she thought more than once, *let it be to a man like him.* But this was only daydreaming. Such men, Eve had decided long ago, were few and far between. Even the one man she'd ever been serious about, and that was more than two years ago, had had a few rough edges. And Derek had none of those, at least none that Eve could see. *I'm glad Kelly has Derek,* Eve thought on several occasions. The best part was that Eve knew that Kelly understood her own good fortune.

A thoughtful host, Derek even took time to inquire gravely after Eve's health.

"You need to eat regularly," he had chided her one day when she admitted that she'd skipped lunch.

Eve shrugged. "It's an old habit."

"Seriously, Eve, the baby's health depends on what you eat. Or drink."

"I don't drink. Not even wine with dinner."

"I know." His eyes, slate-gray now, rested on her fondly. "That's one of the things that Kelly and I picked out of your personality profile. You don't drink, and you don't smoke. That was important to us.''

"I never cared much for drinking. And smoking— well, I tried a cigarette once. I hated it.''

Derek laughed. "I tried it once, too. And hated it.'' He smiled warmly.

"Now junk food's something else again,'' Eve admitted with a grin. "I love to fill myself full of potato chips, pretzels—''

"Have you ever eaten cheese doodles dipped in Pepsi?'' asked Derek with a rare look of mischief.

"Don't tell me you're a junk-food junkie, too!'' said Eve, shocked to amazement. Junk food simply did not fit in with what she knew of the ultraconservative Derek Lang.

"Don't tell anyone. It wouldn't be good for my image,'' he whispered.

"I won't,'' Eve whispered back conspiratorially. "If you won't tell anyone that I still occasionally snitch a potato chip behind Kelly's and Aunt May's back.''

Derek laughed again. Then he became more serious. "I can keep a secret. *If* you'll promise me not to skip any more meals.''

Eve sobered. "I promise,'' she said, meaning it. "I want this baby to be healthy, too, Derek.''

It was shortly after that when Derek intercepted Eve on one of her secret solitary forays into the pantry at midnight.

"Aha!'' he said, flicking on the light. "Caught you!''

Although she was startled, Eve's mouth curved upward in a smile, which made her look like a happy chipmunk, for she had just crammed it with a double handful of caramel corn.

Derek relieved her of the bag of caramel corn and stuffed his own mouth, and they stood solemnly munching until Eve swallowed hers and burst into laughter.

"Do you raid the pantry often?" Derek asked curiously when he could. He had just returned from an eighteen-hour day at the office and was wearing his customary three-piece suit; Eve was clad in her nightgown with an old bathrobe over it. He stared down at her bare feet.

"Umm—well." She curled her toes under so that the hem of the long robe covered them.

"The truth, Eve," he said sternly.

"No," she said boldly, looking him straight in the eye. "Because if I did, you would have caught me long before this."

He stared at her, then threw his head back and laughed long and loud.

"Shh, you'll wake everyone up," Eve said in consternation.

"And that would be a terrible mistake. They'd eat all our caramel corn."

The episode had ended with their sitting at opposite ends of the breakfast-room table, coconspirators passing the caramel corn back and forth until it was all gone. When, at one in the morning, yawning, they both traipsed off to bed, she and Derek were friends.

Eve was pleased that Derek cared about her. And she was happy that, like Kelly and Aunt May, he had accepted her temporary presence in his home as part of his life.

Yet despite the easy camaraderie, on the third week of Eve's residence in the Myers Park house Kelly confided that Derek was distracted by problems at work.

"I just thought I'd mention it, because we don't want you to think he's not interested in you and the baby. But Lang Textiles is going through growing pains." And Kelly shook her head ruefully. "Derek feels responsible, because since he took over as president after his father retired, it's his management concept, and he wants it to work. Anyway, Derek's job is going to gobble up a lot of his time for the next few weeks," Kelly said. She lit up with a brilliant smile. "That's why I'm so glad you're here, Eve," she said, linking her arm through Eve's and making Eve feel more a part of life in this house than ever.

Eve knew without a doubt that this baby she carried, this baby who was now no more than the size of Eve's thumbnail, was the luckiest baby in the world, being born to Kelly and Derek.

Still, even the most perfect couple were bound to have disagreements. Nevertheless, for Eve it was a surprise when she finally encountered one.

On a warm summer evening five weeks into her pregnancy, Eve lingered alone in the study, thumbing through a book Kelly had suggested she might like, when she heard Kelly and Derek talking on the terrace. She started to leave; it was almost dusk, and if she had stayed, she would have had to turn on a light, which would draw attention to herself.

"But Derek, I just thought if you felt like talking about it, I—"

"Kelly, no. I'm tired when I get home at the end of the day, and as for talking about the mills, well, I'd rather not. We're so bogged down in negotiations that I wonder if I ever should have been so hardheaded about acquisitions, if maybe the others were right." Derek's voice was tight with worry.

"With the baby on the way," Kelly said slowly, "I know I haven't been exactly attentive to you, and that worries me. I haven't meant to ignore you. It's just that I'm so excited, and I love having Eve here, and maybe I've been spending too much time with her. I have to confess that I—I was lonely before Eve came, with you so busy."

"Lonely?"

"Yes, Derek. There are so many things I've wanted to talk about, and—"

"Don't I talk with you? Don't we do things together? Didn't I call you this afternoon and ask if there were any errands that needed doing downtown so that you wouldn't have to go out in the heat?"

"Of course, but that's not what I mean. Oh, Derek, with the baby coming, we should be closer than ever, and we're not. You know we're not." Her voice lowered a half tone. "We haven't made love in weeks!"

"You know how tired I've been!" Derek snapped. Then, wearily, he said, "Oh, hell, Kelly, I'm sorry. I love you—you know that—and I'm happy about the baby."

"I know," Kelly said, sounding anything but happy herself.

A long silence. Then Derek said tenderly, "Come over here," and that was when Eve, very disturbed by this time that she had eavesdropped on this highly personal marital discussion, crept quietly out of the study and upstairs to her room. It was nothing. Of course it was nothing. So why did she feel so unsettled by it?

Naturally there was no mention of Kelly's discussion with Derek when Kelly knocked gently at Eve's bedroom door the next morning.

"Eve?" Kelly said.

Eve, still wearing her bathrobe, lay on her back on the brass bed, fighting nausea. Eve hadn't told Kelly that she'd begun to have morning sickness. It would only worry her. The nausea only lasted for a short time right after breakfast, and besides, it was just a slight queasiness.

"Come in," Eve said, sitting up. She wondered, a little guiltily, how Kelly and Derek's discussion had ended last night. She hoped—but then, it was none of her business.

"You're not sick, are you?" Kelly asked in concern.

"No, no. Just a little tired. You know, I asked Dr. Perry about it, and he said it's usual to be tired during the first couple of months."

"I was going to ask you if you wanted to come with me this morning," Kelly said with a grin. She looked normal and happy and also very pretty in her pastel plaid skirt with the sky-blue blouse that matched her eyes. "But I've just changed my mind. If you're tired, you'd better rest."

"No, I—"

"I'm going to the printer's. My music club is staging that benefit concert next month, and I'm going to order the programs this morning. I'll only be gone for an hour or so, so it's hardly worth your getting up and getting dressed. I'll be back before you know it." Kelly cast a look out the window. "Anyway, it looks like rain. One of those summer storms is probably brewing. We can't have you traipsing about in the wet, little mother!"

Eve fell back upon the pillows with a wry grin. "Well, as long as you put it that way," she said.

Kelly laughed. "See you later. And if for some reason I'm not back before lunch, look after Derek for me, will you? In his present frame of mind, he's not able to take Aunt May for more than fifteen minutes at a time.''

"Will do," Eve said, and Kelly jingled her car keys at her as she cheerfully waved goodbye.

Moments later, Eve heard the Mercedes backing out of the garage, and shortly afterward the pitter-patter of raindrops began. A distant rumble of thunder rattled the window. Soon the melody of the rain on the roof lulled Eve to sleep, and she slept until almost twelve.

When she awoke, she was amazed that she'd slept so long. She went downstairs to ask Aunt May or Louise if Kelly was home yet, yawning in spite of her long nap. She'd be glad when this phase of her pregnancy was over, she thought. She'd never expected to be so tired.

A car reeled recklessly into the driveway, and Eve peered out the hall window at it through the steady downpour. Oh, it was Derek. He was home for lunch as usual, and she, slugabed that she was, hadn't even dressed yet. She turned to go back upstairs.

But something about the way he angled out of his low-slung Corvette stopped her. He hurried through the rain without a raincoat, which was peculiar in a man as meticulous as Derek. Derek was never without an umbrella; when it rained, he always wore a tan Burberry raincoat, even for the slightest shower. His shoulders seemed oddly slumped.

And now he was striding toward the house, his suit coat flung open, his tie flying up against his shirt, and his face was the face of a man demented.

Something was wrong, terribly wrong. Eve froze, unable to move.

Derek threw the front door open and saw her standing there, cringing now like a frightened rabbit. His eyes were rimmed in red, and in a heart-stopping moment, Eve was positive that the water on his face wasn't rain.

His face, his handsome face, crumpled before her very eyes. He held his hands out to her in supplication. They trembled, flinging raindrops on her feet.

"Eve," he said, his voice hoarse with anguish. Petrified, in horror, she didn't know what to do.

"Eve, there's been an accident. A terrible accident. Eve, oh, Eve, Kelly is dead."

And then Derek collapsed in her arms.

EVE NEVER KNEW afterward how she got through the next few days. The turgid July heat clamped down on the house in Myers Park even more oppressively than usual, and the heat intensified the smell of the flowers, the flowers that were strewn everywhere, disgorged by florists' vans and florists' trucks until it seemed that all the flowers in the world had converged upon this spot.

Aunt May was literally prostrate with a grief that, for the first time in her life, she could not assuage with chocolates. Derek was unable to function, and this so surprised and angered him that he wasted no time on the usual bromides or niceties required by the occasion. Heartbroken, he moved through the rituals stony-faced, rigid and uncommunicative. And so the bulk of what needed to be done fell on Eve's shoulders.

Derek's father came from South America, accompanied by his elaborately bejeweled wife, who was young enough to be his daughter, and Derek's mother arrived from Virginia and remained glassily tranquilized throughout the ordeal. Derek's sister, an angular woman with no warmth to her, who was quite clearly there only because she felt it was an obligation, flew in from Grosse Point on the morning of the funeral and rapidly flew out again that evening. Kelly had only one relative, Aunt May. So when people wondered who Eve was, she merely said she was a friend of the family. No one knew, no one guessed, what her true mission in the household was.

Eve's main concern was for the baby she carried. Her mourning was for the baby's mother. And for the baby's father she felt compassion. She had never seen anyone as grief-stricken as Derek Lang.

But she—she must remain strong. For the baby's sake. For Kelly's sake. And for Derek's sake.

Because when all this was over, when the mourners had gone home, the baby would be all that Derek had left of Kelly.

And so the night after the funeral, when the house was finally silent, when darkness fell, when the only sound in the house was the muted tick-tock of the grandfather clock on the stair landing, Eve knocked on the door of Derek's study.

He didn't answer, so she pushed the door open.

Derek sat at his desk, one small lamp lit, and the green-shaded light picked out the golden highlights in his butternut-brown hair. His face was buried in his hands, and he didn't look up when Eve walked in.

She cleared her throat. "Derek," she said softly, "I don't mean to be a bother. But we need to talk."

He raised his head, and his face seemed engraved with new lines of tragedy, his gray eyes reflecting the agony of his loss. He didn't speak for a long moment, just stared at her as though he had never seen her before. For a moment he wondered who she was, what she wanted. Then he remembered, and with the memory came even more sorrow.

"Eve," he said, and his voice was raw. She saw his throat muscles working, and she thought he would break down. But he didn't.

She felt a foreshadowing of doom, but she knew she was headed straight for it and that it was too late to stop.

"Eve," he said, more clearly now that he had regained control of himself. "I've been thinking about it. I think the best thing for you to do under the circumstances would be to have an abortion."

Chapter Three

The air felt leaden. Eve couldn't breathe. Her eyes dimmed, and she had to grip her hands together tightly to keep them from shaking. She sank into a chair across the desk from Derek. Had she heard him correctly? No, she couldn't have! But from the way he was measuring her reaction, she knew she had.

She was taking it calmly. He might have known she would. Hadn't Kelly said that Eve wasn't the type to go into a dither about anything? Eve sat squarely in the chair, her hands folded neatly in her lap, and his eyes lingered for a moment on her hands. Her fingernails had wide half-moons at the base and were cut sensibly short and unadorned by anything but clear nail gloss. Everything about her was neat and precise; she was a symmetrical person. Eve. A symmetrical name, even. He liked symmetry in furnishings, which is why he had chosen this Georgian house, but also in people and in life. Only life wasn't always symmetrical, was it?

"No," she said firmly.

He closed his eyes and reopened them. He was not in the mood for an argument.

"It would be best," he repeated. "Best for all of us."

Eve shook her head. "I can't believe you mean that."

"I do."

"Derek, you're very tired. You're overwrought. I can understand. In fact, it would be better if we talked in the morning." She started to get up, groping for the support of the chair arm. She was falling apart with weariness.

"Yes, I am tired," he acknowledged heavily. "In fact, I'm exhausted. But I assure you that I'm thinking clearly and that I am not drunk or stoned or under the influence of anything else that would distort my thought processes."

"But to destroy the life that Kelly wanted so much, to destroy part of her and part of yourself—"

"That's enough!" he said sharply. And then, more kindly, he said, "Look, it's not your fault. You were dragged into this by us, and I apologize for that. You—"

"I was not dragged into anything!" Eve protested, her temper flaring. "I wanted to have this baby for you and Kelly. I wanted to help you and—"

"You wanted the money," he said wearily. "I read the application. Look, you'll get your twelve thousand dollars. I'll pay you, anyway."

Eve swallowed. Her mouth felt dry. "I did it partly for the money," she said slowly. "But that wasn't the whole reason. Derek, I loved Kelly. She was like a sister to me."

Derek leaned back in his chair and blinked at the ceiling. A sigh tore from his body, a sigh of anguish. "Don't talk about her," he said brokenly. "I can't stand it." He pressed the heels of his hands to his eyes for a moment, then lowered his head to look at Eve.

Tears dampened Eve's lower eyelashes. She looked so hurt, so vulnerable. God, what a scene to put her through! First Kelly and now this. Eve had suffered too many shocks lately. Derek knew in that instant that he could have handled the matter more sensitively, and he wished he had.

He stood abruptly and walked to the window, gazing out over the moonlit terrace with its memories of his wife. Just a few nights ago the two of them had stood there.... He clenched his hands and stuffed them deep in his pockets before he turned to face Eve, who was surreptitiously brushing at her damp cheeks with the edge of one hand.

All through this whole ordeal, Eve had been a quiet, comforting presence, handling all the small details that he and Aunt May had been unable to manage. Derek hadn't seen her cry at all until now. Too late, his heart flooded with gratitude. He was ashamed of himself for hitting her with this at the wrong time.

He walked slowly to where she sat staring down at the carpet.

"Eve, look at me."

Slowly, she raised her eyes to his, those soft brown eyes. Deep inside them he saw the hurt.

He spoke gently. "Eve, this isn't the time to discuss this. I'm sorry. I shouldn't have startled you with it. But time is important. If it's going to be done, it should be done soon. You're how far along?"

"Six weeks," she whispered, sick at heart.

"Six weeks."

She squared her narrow shoulders, and looking down at her, he noticed that one was slightly lower than the other. Her shoulders looked so fragile, as though any burden would be too great for them. But when she stood up, he realized suddenly that he had miscalculated her reaction.

"There will be no abortion, Derek," she said, looking him straight in the eye. "Even if I have to raise the child myself."

Now her shoulders rose in anger, like hackles, and she reminded him of an angry swan he had once seen, a fierce black Australian swan that had spread its wings and attacked him with a frightening hiss when he wandered too close to its nest. But Eve simply stared at him, her gentle brown eyes glinting with determination, and then she turned swiftly and walked out of the room.

Bring the child up herself? He couldn't believe she would even consider it. It was out of the question.

Slowly, Derek returned to his chair. He had made a mess out of this; no doubt about it. He asked himself in anguish, *What would Kelly do?* And because he knew the answer right away, he let his head sink to the desktop, the cool polished walnut surface soothing his hot forehead.

Oh, Kelly, Kelly, he thought. And then, finally, now that everyone had gone, he felt alone enough to loose the floodgates of his own grief.

"NEVER," Eve muttered to herself as she flung off her clothes and slipped into her nightgown. "Never."

She slid between the sheets of the dainty brass bed and stared up at the ceiling. She knew she wouldn't sleep tonight.

There was no way Derek could make her get rid of this baby. Ultimately, it was her body; feverishly, she had examined her copy of the contract with the Langs. Although their attorney had not foreseen this contingency, as far as Eve could determine, the contract they had all signed gave Derek no right to insist that she terminate the pregnancy.

Abortion was against Eve's principles. It would always be against her principals. She would never, as long as she still drew breath, allow anything to hurt this baby, the baby Kelly had wanted so much.

For now Eve knew that she wanted the baby, too. The baby was part of Kelly, and that part of Kelly deserved to survive.

Tears trickled out of the corners of her eyes, and she pressed the palms of her hands to her abdomen as if to shield the unborn child. In wonder she realized that her abdomen was beginning to swell ever so slightly with the baby's presence. Suddenly she was overcome with an emotion that she recognized as unmistakably maternal: she loved this baby, this baby that was part of her and yet not, and this baby needed her. As much as Kelly and Derek, she was responsible for its existence. Without Eve, this baby could not have been.

No matter what Derek said, the baby would be born.

Even, as she had told Derek, if she had to raise the baby herself.

"DID YOU SLEEP WELL, Aunt May?" Eve asked Kelly's aunt the next morning.

Aunt May trickled another spoonful of sugar into her coffee and stirred it lackadaisically. "Need curls?" she replied. "I should say I need curls. In fact, I have a hairdresser's appointment this morning."

"Not need curls, Aunt May," Eve said more loudly. "I asked if you slept well."

"Oh," Aunt May said in a slightly disappointed tone. "That pill the doctor gave me put me right to sleep. Do you have anything to take at night, dear? You're looking tired."

Eve hadn't slept last night, not a wink. "I wouldn't take any medicine, because it might affect the baby," Eve reminded her gently.

"Oh, I hadn't thought of that. You do have to be careful, don't you?" Aunt May raised blue eyes to Derek as Derek entered the breakfast room. "Good morning, Derek. Did you know Eve can't take any sleeping pills because of the baby?"

Derek shot Eve a sharp look, which she returned levelly. Eve *did* look tired, he thought. But she wasn't taking sleeping pills because of the baby. What was the point when soon the baby wouldn't exist anymore?

Louise, her eyes downcast and swollen with crying, brought a serving dish of scrambled eggs and retreated to the kitchen. Derek helped himself before passing them to Eve, who passed them on to Aunt May without taking any.

"Aren't you eating breakfast?" Derek asked sharply.

"I'm not hungry," Eve hedged. She was barely managing to keep morning sickness at bay.

"I'm not hungry, either," Aunt May declared, pushing her chair away from the table. "I don't have any appetite. Anyway, Louise is driving me to the hairdresser in an hour or so, and I want to get dressed." She smiled wanly at Derek and Eve before weaving off down the hall in a pair of impossibly high heeled satin bedroom slippers.

"Eat something," Derek ordered, pushing the scrambled eggs in Eve's direction.

The very sight of eggs sickened Eve.

"I—I can't!" she managed to gasp before lurching to her feet and running for the powder room nearby, where she slammed the door closed and, with a peculiar sense of retribution toward Derek, proceeded to be sick to her stomach.

"Eve? Eve!"

Eve ran the water in the sink and dashed some over her face. She stared at her reflection in the mirror. Her face looked back at her, a chalky gray-white. If only Derek would stop making that ungodly racket outside the door, she would feel much better. Trembling, she threw the door open and with a great deal of effort walked out with her head held high.

"Are you all right?" Derek didn't like the look of her, and he didn't want to worry about her. Didn't he have enough to worry about with his wife dead and the mills to run and poor old Aunt May? And yet he *was* worried about Eve, her normally pale skin so white that he could see the minute blue veins threading her eyelids like a natural eye shadow. Did her eyelids always look like that? He couldn't remember.

"Morning sickness," she explained unnecessarily. It surprised her that he was so upset. It gave her hope that he was so upset.

"I didn't know you were having morning sickness."

"It just started about a week ago." She forced a smile.

"Can I get you anything? Are you all right?"

Surprisingly enough, she was hungry—ravenously hungry.

"I think I'll eat breakfast, after all," she said, sounding stronger than he had expected. And then she sat down, and to Derek's utter disbelief, she devoured not only a huge mound of eggs but also sausages and biscuits complete with butter and orange marmalade.

"You said you didn't want me to skip meals," she said by way of explanation.

"That was before—" And then he stopped because of the warning look in Eve's eyes.

A biscuit and its accompanying marmalade sat heavily on her tongue. With effort, she swallowed. "Before you decided that this baby wouldn't be born?"

Derek nodded. "I'm hoping you'll come to your senses about this, Eve."

"No, Derek, I meant what I said."

Louise, sniffing loudly, came in to clear the table, and they remained silent until she left.

"Eve, you're only adding to my grief by being stubborn."

"And you're adding to mine by being stupid."

No one had ever, in all his life, called Derek Lang stupid. He flushed, and then he rose from the table and threw his cloth napkin on the table. With one last unfathomable look at Eve, he slammed out of the house, and in a few moments Eve heard the Corvette roar out of the driveway.

Eve sat in the toile-papered breakfast room and stared grimly out the bow window at the woodpecker that was finding its own breakfast in the bark of the tree outside.

She managed to remain numb for five minutes. Then the phone rang.

STUPID. Was he being stupid?

As he drove to work, Derek forced his mind to flip through the gut-wrenching scene in his study last night.

I was stupid, he realized with a start. Stupid to have thought that Eve would fall right into his pattern of thinking, stupid to have flattened her so suddenly with the idea of an abortion. Well, maybe not stupid. He was grieving for his wife, and perhaps he hadn't been thinking as clearly as he thought he had. If he'd been thinking clearly, he never would have approached Eve in that manner, never.

He parked his Corvette and fielded the startled gaze of the parking attendant as he set off at a swift walk for the nearby entrance to his office building. Probably no one expected him to come to work the morning after his wife's funeral. Well, why shouldn't he? There was nothing to stay home for now.

"Good morning, Mr. Lang," was the subdued but surprised greeting of the receptionist.

Derek nodded briskly and proceeded with what he considered appropriate speed down the gray-carpeted hall to his office. Returning to work was turning out to be an ordeal of the first magnitude, he thought to his chagrin. But then, it would have been an ordeal no matter when he did it.

A group clustered around the water cooler murmured morning greetings, which he returned a bit too heartily. He walked on, aware that they were all staring at his back. He clenched his teeth.

"Good morning, Derek," said his secretary, Maisie Allen, hanging up the phone. Obviously she had been forewarned that he was on his way, probably by the goggle-eyed receptionist.

He nodded, less briskly this time, and fairly ran into the sanctuary of his office, shutting the door firmly behind him. He stopped for a moment, feeling oddly out of breath as he stared at the wide-window view of Charlotte below, and wondered why there was no fresh cup of coffee on his desk. Maisie always had coffee waiting on his desk when he arrived.

"They didn't think I'd come in," he said out loud, and then he jumped when the door behind him opened unexpectedly.

"Just delivering your coffee," Maisie said, trotting briskly to his desk and setting his cup down on it. An inadvertent picture of Maisie's moon face surmounted by a tall and pompous hat at the funeral sprang into his mind. They had all been there, though, taking part in his tragedy. All the employees. His office manager must have given them yesterday morning off.

"Thanks," he said in as normal a tone as possible, though to himself his voice sounded as though it were pitched incredibly high.

Maisie, a no-nonsense matronly woman with an immense bosom and an equally huge derriere, trotted back out again. Derek walked slowly to his desk and sat down at his chair with a sigh.

Well, why shouldn't he come to work today? Work was the only thing that would take his mind off Kelly and the accident. Work and its attendant problems—the worry about what foreign textile imports were doing to the industry, the acquisition of the new mill—would occupy his mind, if not assuage his grief.

He ventured a tentative sip of the coffee. It was very hot. He set the cup down on his desk again. In the summer the weather was too hot to drink coffee. That's what Kelly always said. Kelly....

With difficulty, he forced himself not to think about her. Think about something else instead. Perhaps he should give up coffee; someone else had given up coffee recently. His brain fogged up like a windshield on a rainy night, and when the fog cleared, he could hear Eve, as distinctly as though she were sitting beside him. In fact, when she'd said it, she'd been sitting beside him at the dining-room table. "I'm giving up coffee until after the baby's born, because I'm worried about the effect caffeine will have on its growth." Kelly had smiled in approval, and so had he. Eve had smiled back, revealing that one bicuspid, turned slightly sideways, the only feature that offset the symmetry of her face but only showed when she smiled.

Eve smiling, Eve crying. Eve crying the way she had cried in his study last night, the glistening tears drooping momentarily from her lower eyelashes before spilling down her pale cheeks.

He knocked his coffee cup over and jumped up before the brown liquid could stain his navy-blue suit. Swearing, he blotted at the mess with a monogrammed handkerchief. He could have called Maisie to clean it up, but— well, he didn't want to talk about anything right now. He snatched the oval gold picture frame up before the coffee inundated it, then dabbed ineffectually at the desktop and replaced the picture frame. The picture, of course, was of Kelly, an exuberant Kelly on the day they had climbed Mount Mitchell, the highest peak in North Carolina. It had been one of the happiest days in their lives, the first day of a wonderful vacation they'd taken six years ago, right after she'd found out for sure she was pregnant. He had snapped the picture himself.

Six years ago. That baby would have been almost five and a half by this time if it had lived. Five years old and no mother. But would Kelly have been in her car at that precise time four days ago, in the path of the other driver, if she'd had a five-year-old child at home? Maybe not. Then again, maybe, and maybe the child would have been with her, in which case he would now be mourning both his wife and his child. Who was to say what would have happened had some turning point in life arranged the choices differently? Who knew beforehand what twists of fate would affect us? The myriad possibilities loomed before him in a kaleidoscope of combinations:

you travel this road, and other roads branch off it; you select a different road, and you're presented with other roads, other choices.

It was what he would have to make Eve see, he knew. That the road he had chosen when Kelly was alive was not the road he would choose now. That it wasn't too late to backtrack and start over again, taking another route.

Was Eve capable of comprehending?

He pictured her soft brown eyes, her intelligent face. Yes, she was capable. He was sure that eventually he could make her see the folly of continuing this pregnancy.

Who would have thought that Eve could be so stubborn?

"AL, DON'T BE PIGHEADED!"

Eve's patience with her father was wearing thin. She didn't want him to get upset; if he did, he'd only have another coughing spell, which would sap his fragile energy. And it was obvious to her that Al was going to have to muster all the energy he could. Today, this very morning, the management of Wray Mills had ordered them to vacate their house by the end of the week. They'd known they'd have to move eventually. But by the end of the week? Impossible.

"Eve, dear, I'm going to walk over to the mill first thing in the morning and talk to them. I'll ask them for a month's extension. I've lived in this house for thirty years; another month wouldn't hurt. Anyway, they don't have a waiting list. No one wants to move in. I think they'll listen to me."

Eve shook her head dubiously. "You're a thorn in their side. They want to get rid of you, probably so they won't have to find your 'lost' workmen's compensation claim before they sell the mill. You know, every time you walk past the mill, they probably feel guilty for what they've done to you."

"Done to me? You mean this lung problem? I know, I know, but Wray Mills gave me a job when I was desperate. I've never forgotten that."

"Oh, Al. They gave you a job that made you sick in the end. And they say that the disease you have can't be proved to have been caused by conditions in the mill. That's hogwash, and you know it!" Eve paced the floor of the small living room, wrapping her arms around herself in her agitation. On the floor a fan hustled the stale heavy air of a Piedmont summer, but it wasn't the fan that chilled her. It was her father's unwarranted respect for Wray Mills.

"Let me talk to them tomorrow," Al insisted. "You're staying the night?"

Eve gestured toward her small overnight bag. Al's phone call with the news that he was about to be evicted had brought Eve back to Wrayville immediately, and she had packed enough clothes so that she could stay for a few days. Anyway, she had needed to get out of the Myers Park house. She hadn't wanted to talk to Derek, because she knew he'd only pressure her.

"I'm glad you're staying," Al said, his features brightening with his first smile since Eve's arrival that morning. "It'll be like having you living at home again."

But of course it wasn't. Could you ever go back home? Eve wondered as she walked down the narrow Cotton Mill Hill street after dinner, waving to the neighbors, most of whom she had known all her life, and stopping now and then to chat with those she knew well.

Yes, she said over and over, she was enjoying her new job. Yes, she told an interested Nell Baker, she liked living in Charlotte. She sensed that their friends were being cautious about what they said about living arrangements, perhaps because everyone knew by this time that Wray Mills had ordered them to vacate the company-owned house. People sympathized, Eve knew. It was just that they were wary of saying much about the situation for fear of reprisals from the company, especially now that everyone's job was in jeopardy because of the rumored takeover of Wray Mills by a large textile conglomerate.

At the bottom of the hill, she recognized the lanky jean-clad figure of Doug Ender. He hailed her with enthusiasm, smiling as she approached. Doug was one of the few people in Wrayville who was not dependent on Wray Mills for a living.

He'd grown up here, and his family had been mill people, but they were all gone now. Doug, a bachelor, had worked his way through law school at the University of North Carolina and had returned to Wrayville to start his modest practice. He handled wills, lawsuits, and defended local toughs who got into trouble with the law. He and Eve had known each other since they were children, and he had done her a favor by agreeing to take the case in Al's claim for workmen's compensation.

"Eve," Doug said, his face lighting with pleasure. He looked genuinely happy to see her, and she was happy to see him. "I heard you found a job." He fell into step beside her.

Eve nodded. She was unsure whether to discuss her "job" with Doug; she worried about his reaction. She and Doug were close—close enough, she'd thought on various occasions, for their relationship to deepen into something more. But it never had, mostly because Eve had always held back, waiting for that special chemistry to happen. And now, with her pregnant—well, if the chemistry was going to happen between them, it would have to wait.

"Any news about my father's claim?" she asked him, partly to change the subject but partly because she wanted to know.

Doug's expression became serious. "No, I'm afraid not. The mill management is in chaos, not knowing if the mill is going to be sold or not."

"Then it's true? Somebody is talking about buying Wray Mills?"

Doug nodded. "It looks like it. Eve, I don't know what that would mean in regard to Al's claim."

"I suppose it depends on the buyer," Eve replied. "Whether or not they have a record of settling byssinosis claims or not."

"Some of the textile companies deny that it's a legitimate disease. They say they're not sure conditions in the mills cause it."

"No one who has ever seen the inside of a card room at the mill could say that all that flying dust isn't detrimental to the people who work there."

"Not everybody has seen the inside of a card room," Doug said with irony. "You and I never would have if we hadn't grown up here."

"We're just lucky, I guess," Eve said ruefully.

"Yeah," he said. Then, quickly, he suggested, "Say, Eve, let's have dinner together tonight."

She looked up at him, surprised. It was entirely natural that he ask her out, and a few weeks ago she would have accepted. But now, with her mind in a turmoil about Derek's demand that she have an abortion and with her worry about Al's possible eviction, how could she say yes?

"Oh, Doug," she said, "I can't. I'm only here for a few days, and I should spend my time with Al. He hasn't been feeling well at all."

"I understand," Doug said evenly, and Eve could tell at a glance that he really did understand. He was a nice-looking man, tall and dark, with hazel eyes that crinkled at the edges when he laughed; she'd always thought Doug was attractive.

They reached her house, and he walked her up the front path.

"I'd like to see you some other time," he said, looking down at her and smiling that wide comfortable smile of his. "Maybe we could go to a movie. Or we could have dinner together in Charlotte. I have to go into the city sometimes."

"Okay," she said carefully.

She told Doug goodbye and hurried inside the house, feeling a little sad. She hadn't really counted on this apprehension about Doug's attitude toward her pregnancy. Did her feelings mean that she cared more about him—and in a deeper and more meaningful way—than she'd ever admitted to herself?

She peered into the mirror over the bathroom sink. Despite the sorrow of the past week, she looked better than she'd ever looked; her cheeks had rounded with this pregnancy, and her swelling breasts strained against the fabric of her simple cotton blouse. She wondered if Doug had noticed. If he had, he hadn't let on.

After dinner, Eve said to her father, "I'll clean up the kitchen while you rest." Al gratefully went to sit on the rusty green metal glider on the front porch where he watched the fireflies and chatted idly with a few old cronies from the neighborhood.

Eve couldn't help feeling nostalgic as she worked in the familiar kitchen. How many of these blue-willow-patterned dishes had she washed in this sink as she was growing up in this house? She traced one of the willow-tree branches with a fingernail and thought she had washed more dishes than most little girls, because her mother had died when she was eleven. She'd taken over the responsibility of running the house at an early age, arranging the dishes in shining rows in the kitchen cabinets, taking pride in managing the household money, seeing that the mops and buckets and the Electrolux were lined up neatly in the broom closet.

But of course the real responsibility hadn't hit her until Al had to quit his job prematurely at age sixty, when his doctor had diagnosed him as totally disabled due to chronic lung disease. Then, at the age of twenty-six, financial responsibility had fallen squarely on her, but she'd been proud of her ability to support the two of them and support them well.

By that time, she'd progressed through the mill's manager-trainee program into which she'd been hired after receiving her B.S. in business administration at UNC. She'd been handling the coveted job of Wray Mills's public-relations director with considerable aplomb for over a year. Eve Triopolous was one of the few salaried women managers employed at the mill. The year she'd been fired was the first year she'd drawn an executive bonus. Oh, she had loved her job, all right. But that was in the past. Right now she had to figure out what to do about her future.

Sighing, she declined to watch television with her father and went early to bed where she ran her hands over her abdomen again, exploring the expanding world of the baby who remained a secret to most of the world, to her

father, to Doug, to everyone who didn't live at the house
in Myers Park. Eve couldn't help smiling into the darkness. It was exciting, feeling her body change shape to
accommodate a new human being. Never again would
Eve wonder why some women seemed to revel in their
pregnancies.

The next morning, over Eve's worried objections, Al
walked, huffing and puffing from the effort, up Cotton
Mill Hill. She couldn't go with him; she was *persona non
grata* around the offices of Wray Mills since her dis-
missal. And besides, Al's absence would give her a
chance to get over her morning sickness in private. Eve
stood edgily on the tiny front porch, arms folded tightly
over her stomach, anxiously watching Al and worrying
about him as she watched his tortured progress up the
hill.

"Don't do this!" she'd begged in vain. To her, con-
fronting the very officials who had decreed that they
move was too much like throwing himself at their mercy.
Where was her father's pride, his self-respect? But she
hadn't figured on his misplaced loyalty to the company
for which he had toiled for thirty-eight long years.

"Don't worry," Al had insisted, patting Eve awkwardly on the shoulder. "I have to talk to them. I have to.
I'm sure as soon as they realize what a hardship it is for
us to move in a week, they'll soften their attitude."

*Like they softened their attitude when you filed a claim
for compensation and they fired me?* Eve was tempted to
ask, giving way to shrewishness.

But she held her tongue. She knew as well as Al that he
didn't have any place to go if they were evicted. So she
stood by helplessly, wishing there was some other course
they could take, while Al labored his way up the hill to
beg for time from the management at the mill.

"EVE! EVE?" Derek stomped through the lower hall, calling up the stairs. Where was she, anyway? He had expected her to be right there, the way she always was, standing silently in the background, a gentle presence watching him greet Kelly with a kiss.

"She's not here," Aunt May's voice quavered. "She's gone home for a few days." Aunt May came and peered down at him, her round, wrinkled face hanging over the upstairs banister. "Is everything all right?" she ventured.

"Yes. I mean, no, how can it be all right?" he shot back impatiently. What a question to ask someone whose wife had just been killed! The old girl didn't have much sense, never had. But she was Kelly's aunt, and he'd always been polite. It was going to be difficult without Kelly to act as a buffer between them. Well, perhaps Aunt May hadn't heard his remark.

It was too much to hope for. "Oh. Well, I see," Aunt May said, sniffing. She pulled her head back in from the stairwell, like a turtle. Now he knew he had hurt her feelings. He could hear her retreating down the hall toward her room. She was probably in tears. Oh, God, was anything ever going to be all right again?

He ran upstairs and burst into their bedroom, the pale blue haven he had shared with Kelly. He had to find Eve, and he'd forgotten where Eve said she lived before she moved in with them. He sat down at Kelly's small secretary desk and started pulling out drawers and digging in cubbyholes. Where the devil was Kelly's tan leather address book?

He dragged a bunch of papers out until they all sat in a heap in front of him. Bills for Kelly's charge accounts, a bunch of personal correspondence, but no address book. The book would have Eve's address in it, neatly inscribed in Kelly's round handwriting; he knew it would. But he couldn't find it.

Kelly's raw silk jacket, the one she had worn when they went out to dinner last Saturday night, hung over the back of the chair where he sat. When he'd decided that the address book wasn't in the desk after all, he fingered the silk fabric for a few moments, lost in memory. A hint of Kelly's favorite fragrance wafted from it, bringing her back to him in a strangely haunting way.

"When does the hurting stop?" he asked himself brokenly, and then he buried his face in the raw silk, wishing he had Kelly, wishing he could find Eve, wishing that he could still look forward to fatherhood, wishing without hope that everything could be the way it was before the accident.

"AND SO THEY GAVE ME a week to stay here while I look for another place to live!" Al declared triumphantly, but never had Eve heard so hollow a victory. What had the mill management so graciously bestowed? Just another week. And after that, then what?

"I'll look for a place in Charlotte where we can both stay," she told him. Al thought she was living temporarily with a girl friend while searching for an apartment for herself in the city.

"Evie, I never wanted to be a burden to you," Al said quietly, his expression clouding over. Eve knew what a blow to Al's Old World pride it was to have the woman of the house taking care of him. In Greek families, it was customarily the other way around.

"You're not a burden," Eve told him firmly and with a smile that she hoped did not look forced. She patted him awkwardly on the shoulder, like a parent comforting a child. When had he become the child and she the parent?

Eve knew she could remain at the Myers Park house with Derek and Aunt May for the next week. She needed that time to bargain with Derek, to talk him out of this idea he'd had about her getting an abortion. Surely when the first pangs of grief had faded, he'd realize what he was doing and agree that the baby should be born and that he should be its father. He *was* the father, after all; nothing could change that.

But it was going to be difficult. And she couldn't stay at the Myers Park house with Derek after she'd convinced him that the baby must be born; it would be better for everyone if she moved out. She and Al could find a place to stay in Charlotte.

There was one problem, though. Money. She had a couple of hundred dollars in her savings account, a cushion against hard times, and if these didn't qualify for hard times, she didn't know what did. Her small hoard probably wasn't enough to rent a place, and she knew that Al didn't have as much saved as she did. If she could get a job—but she'd already tried that, and she hadn't been pregnant at the time.

Actually, there was more than one problem. If she and Al lived together, she'd have to tell him even sooner about her pregnancy. It would be very hard to hide so telltale a sign as morning sickness from her father.

"Don't worry, Al," she said, trying to sound more confident than she felt. Even as she said it, anxiety gnawed at her stomach. She knew, in that moment, that in trying to alleviate their problem, she had only added to it. Things had been bad before; their future had been bleak. But now, now! They were being evicted, and she was pregnant besides. She still didn't know how she was ever going to tell Al.

And yet, given the same chance all over again, Eve knew she would do exactly what she had done—contract to bear a child for Kelly and Derek Lang.

That was what, despite everything, she still intended to do.

Chapter Four

Eve, dragging her feet but determined to tackle Derek once more, went back to the Myers Park house on Monday.

"Oh, Eve, it's so good to see you," said a mournful-eyed Aunt May when Eve tentatively tapped on her bedroom door and announced that she had returned. Aunt May pursed her lips. "I know how hard it is for Derek right now, but he's been absolute hell to live with."

Eve smiled a sad smile. "I can imagine" was all she said.

"Well," Aunt May said, rallying. Today she wore her hearing aid; that was a relief. "I'm glad you're here, Eve. I wanted to bake some cookies today. Will you help?"

Eve was surprised, then glad. Baking cookies with Aunt May would get her mind off her own problems, and it would give her something to do until Derek came home and they embarked on their inevitable discussion. She knew that Derek would not postpone it; he would want to get it over with.

"I'll be glad to help," she told Aunt May warmly.

The two of them chased Louise out of the kitchen, and Louise gladly relinquished the space, smiling, Eve realized, for the first time since Kelly's accident.

"What kind of cookies are we making?" Eve asked as she helped assemble the ingredients.

"Chocolate chip," Aunt May said. "They're Derek's favorite. Now Kelly, she always prefers—" And then Aunt May stopped, her round pink face dissolving into distress.

"That's all right, Aunt May," Eve said, choking up herself. "It's hard to realize that she's really gone, isn't it?"

Aunt May nodded before turning her back and busily sifting the flour. Eve allowed her the privacy of silence for a while.

"Here, Eve, you measure the chocolate chips," Aunt May finally said, and Eve did.

"Does it bother you to talk about Kelly?" she asked Aunt May.

"Some," Aunt May said. Her faded blue eyes rested on Eve's face, and there was sorrow in their depths. "You know, Kelly was always so *good*. She let me mess around in the kitchen. She made sure Louise wouldn't mind my cooking before she hired her. Kelly turned down three perfectly fine maids because they didn't want to allow an old lady in their kitchen. Considering how hard it is to get good help these days, that shows how much Kelly cared about me, don't you think?"

Eve nodded, unable to speak.

Aunt May relieved Eve of the cup of chocolate chips and dumped them into the stiff dough. She stirred the dough rapidly, then stopped in mid-stir. "Kelly kept me from being a lonely, dried-up old woman. Now I don't know what will happen to me. I really don't know." After a moment she smiled shyly at Eve. "But with you here, I won't be lonely, will I?" she continued with forced briskness. "Now hand me that spatula, will you, please?"

Eve put the spatula in Aunt May's wrinkled hand, sorrow welling up inside her. This wasn't the proper time to defeat Aunt May's expectations. And yet she doubted that she would be living at the Myers Park house much longer.

In midafternoon, Derek called to tell Aunt May brusquely that he wouldn't be home for dinner and to go ahead and eat without him, only Aunt May thought he said he had his feet about him and hung up, vaguely puzzled, the thought never occurring to her that Derek hadn't given her a chance to tell him that Eve had returned.

That was why Derek was surprised to stumble upon Eve unawares at nine-thirty that night when he arrived after several hours of misspent time at the country-club bar. Eve was sitting in the comfortable wing chair in his study, knitting what appeared to be a yellow bootee. The sight of her, looking so domestic and content in the pool of light from the desk lamp, irritated him.

"Knitting little garments, I see," he said with annoyance. He was more than a little drunk.

Eve started at the sound of his voice. She hadn't heard him come in. The color drained from her face. This wasn't the Derek she knew; he was in his shirt-sleeves and had tossed his suit jacket carelessly on his desk, and his eyes were bloodshot. He didn't appear to be in a good mood.

"They're for the baby," she said firmly, knowing that this would be a perfect lead-in for the conversation that was to follow. She didn't see any sense in postponing it no matter what kind of mood Derek was in. It was a problem that needed to be confronted head-on, full-out and immediately.

"There isn't going to be any baby," Derek said just as firmly.

"Derek—" Eve began. She drew a deep breath and rested her knitting in her lap. "Now that you've had a few days to think it over, you must see that you can't destroy Kelly's and your baby. It's part of both of you, and there's no reason why you can't approach fatherhood with the same eagerness you had when Kelly was alive. You wanted this baby. You know you did."

Derek set his lips in a grim line. "I wanted it then. I wanted it because of Kelly. But I don't want it now."

Eve spoke slowly, and her voice flowed, mellifluous and unafraid, into what had been a menacing silence.

"I think you do, Derek. You're denying it right now, but I think you want this baby."

She was wise and so sure. He resented her intrusion into what should be his decision and his decision alone. "It wouldn't be fair to bring a baby into this world without two parents," he said gruffly. It was what he truly believed.

Too late, she realized from his slurred speech that he'd been drinking, but she didn't see anything to do but go on with it. "Derek, it's all you have left of Kelly," she reminded him gently. "This baby, this child, that she wanted so much. You know how she longed for a baby; she spoke of her yearning to have a child so often. She was overjoyed about the baby. I'm sure that after you think it over, you'll change your mind."

A lump rose in Derek's throat, choking off words. Why did Eve insist on making this so difficult? Why didn't she just have the abortion and be done with it? It was cruel of her, cruel and heartless, to remind him of his beloved wife's longing for a child. Damn, damn, damn! Why didn't she just go away, this woman who was gazing at him so implacably, gazing with soft brown eyes as gentle as a gazelle's, the black pupils so large that they gave her face a kind of openness that Kelly had remarked about, that Kelly had liked.

"Oh, God," he said, clenching his hands into fists and throwing a look of pure anguish in her direction. He wished he'd had more to drink. To Eve's despair, he threw the French doors to the terrace open and flung himself out into the night.

Eve dropped her knitting and ran after him. She didn't trust him now, didn't trust the misery he was feeling, didn't know what the misery would make him do. For she knew that he was mourning his wife, and she knew that if she missed Kelly, Derek missed her a hundred times more and in many more ways. It was pathetic, seeing this strong man, to whom everything had apparently come easily, in pain over this. She wanted to help him. She wanted him to be the way he had been before Kelly's death, neat, methodical and organized, not sad and disheveled and drunk. In a burst of suffering, she realized that she had not only lost Kelly; she had lost Derek, the *real* Derek, the one who had joked with her and laughed with her and been her friend, too.

Cautiously, she tiptoed out into the night, expecting Derek to be on the terrace. But he wasn't there.

Where was he? She peered into the gloom. It was a dark night, and there was no moon. Finally, she saw his white shirt—at least she thought that's what it was—in the rose garden. Her heart beating rapidly, she descended the brick stairs and walked briskly toward the rose garden, where the sweet and heavy fragrance of the roses made her stomach lurch. Her morning sickness was threatening to become morning, afternoon and evening sickness. Any strong odor seemed to bring on the nausea, and Eve had no earthly idea what to do about it.

"Derek?" she said softly.

"Leave me alone," he said gruffly, and she could tell from the roughness of his voice that he was either in tears or perilously near them.

"No," she said, her stomach churning so that she could barely speak. She tried not to smell the roses, tried to ignore their cloying fragrance. "Leaving you alone would be the worst thing I could do," she said. "You don't have to lock your grief inside you. It helps to talk about it."

"How the hell would you know?" he said, his back toward her. He was tall, much taller than she, and she realized with a start that she hadn't ever seen Derek in anything but a business suit. He never wore sport shirts, and tonight his white long-sleeved shirt, which he wore to work every day despite the summer heat, displayed his shoulders to advantage, shoulders that Eve now realized owed little to the shoulder pads in his suit jackets.

"I know about losing a loved one," she replied evenly, although her stomach was still roiling. "My mother died when I was eleven."

Silence. Then Derek said in a quieter tone, "I'm sorry. I didn't know."

"It—it was a long time ago," she said.

"When does it stop hurting?" Derek's voice was no more than a whisper.

"I'm not sure it ever does. You go along day by day, learning to live with it, and after a while you're able to think about other things. Time is a healer. It's a trite thing to say, but it's true."

He turned to look at her, to gaze down at her eyes, the whites of which seemed luminescent in the darkness. Her skin, so fair for a brunette, glowed with a dewy freshness, and her cheeks were more rounded than they had been when she first moved in with them. Suddenly his senses were filled with her, with the way she looked as she returned his gaze with so much empathy. But no, he shouldn't be leaning toward her this way, closing the distance between them, wanting to touch her, wanting her to hold him in her arms and soothe away the pain. He shouldn't, and he wouldn't.

Stiffly he said, "Perhaps it is as you say. Maybe time really is a great healer; I don't know. At any rate, I'm not going to change my mind about the baby."

"But—"

"Please don't argue with me. I've opened an account at the bank for you; I've deposited three thousand dollars in it. That's in addition to the twelve thousand I was going to pay you after the baby was born. I'll pay you the twelve thousand when you've shown me evidence that you've had the abortion." He thrust something into her hands; incredulously, she looked down and saw that it was a passbook.

Derek's words gouged Eve's very soul. She wanted to cry out in agony with the pain. What kind of woman did he think she was, to accept payment for the killing of his and Kelly's child? What kind of man was *he*? Had he always been this monster, or had he really been the loving, thoughtful man she had observed with Kelly? Thoughts swam through her mind, swelling and ebbing, churning, churning the way her stomach churned....

With great economy of movement, Eve leaned over and threw up beneath a perfectly shaped rose bush.

"Oh, Eve," Derek was saying in horror, and she closed her eyes so she wouldn't have to look at him. His voice descended upon her as from a great distance. "Eve, you poor thing. Eve?" He sounded stone-cold sober now.

His arms folded around her, and she wanted to die of embarrassment, wanted to sink into the soft mulch at their feet and never see him again. She retched once more, but this time Derek was holding her head; tears streamed down her face, and Derek was wiping them away with his handkerchief.

"Eve, can you stand up? Shall I carry you inside?"

Her head spun dizzily, crazily, on a rose-scented merry-go-round. Only there was nothing merry about it. "No," she managed to say finally, "no." And then Derek was brushing the hair away from her forehead, was gently rubbing the back of her neck, and she realized that they were sitting on the hard ground. Derek was sitting on the ground with utter disregard for his clothes, and she was cradled against his chest.

"Are you sick? Should I call a doctor?" The worry in his voice surprised her. She wouldn't have thought he could surmount his pain to care about her, especially when they had just participated in such an unnerving discussion.

"No, please," she said, "it's just the morning sickness carried over to the evening. Any strong odor seems to set me off, and when I smelled the roses..." Just thinking about it set off a new wave of nausea, and she struggled for control.

"Have you been vomiting every day?" Derek sounded flabbergasted, and when she looked at him, she knew his concern was real.

She nodded. "It will pass soon," she said, not too confidently.

Eve was aware of the crickets in the shrubbery, creaking out their raucous song, and she suddenly felt the smooth, fine cotton of Derek's shirt against her cheek, and she became aware of the warmth of his body close to hers. She struggled to sit up straight.

One lock of Derek's usually perfect hair fell over his forehead. "You won't have to go through this much longer," he said, and if his words were meant to be soothing, they were not. His meaning was unmistakable.

Stunned that he would say this to her when he knew how she felt about the abortion, Eve pushed him away. Shakily, she rose to her feet, brushing Derek's hand away when he tried to help her.

"An upset stomach is a small price to pay for a baby," she said with dignity, and she turned and walked swiftly away. Quick tears stung the inside of her nose, and Eve knew she was dangerously close to breaking down in front of him. But that, after her embarrassment in the rose garden, she was determined not to do.

"Eve," she heard him call, his voice urgent, but she paid no attention. She had meant to change his mind tonight, but she had failed; she had failed utterly.

Late that night, when she was in bed and her light was out, she heard Derek's heavy footsteps in the hall. They paused outside her door, and she tensed, holding her breath, waiting for him to knock. But he didn't knock, and shortly thereafter she heard the door to his room close gently, and then, thoroughly exhausted, Eve slept.

The next morning she realized why Derek hadn't knocked. She found the bank passbook on the floor just inside her door. When she'd heard him pause outside her door, he'd been pushing it underneath. Folded inside was a note.

"Eve," it said in Derek's large but neat script, "take the money. When it's over, I'll see that you get the twelve thousand. I'll be out of town for the rest of the week on business. It would be best if it were over with when I return." He had signed it simply "D."

"It would be best if it were over with when I return," Eve repeated out loud to herself. How unfeeling, how uncaring!

Angry now, she ripped the curt note into little pieces and tossed them in the wastebasket. Maybe it was good that Derek didn't want the baby. Would she really want this child to have a father who was so unmoved, so emotionally detached, that he could write such a note?

Trembling, she sank down on the bed and buried her face in her hands. Derek Lang could keep his three thousand dollars, the bonus he was paying for her to commit murder. She wouldn't touch it. She had told Derek she was prepared to raise the child herself. Well, in spite of everything, she still felt that way. She didn't know how she was going to support her father and herself, and she certainly didn't know how she would support a child. But if she had to, she would.

In the meantime, she required a place for Al to live. For herself and Al, she corrected herself. It was clear that she could no longer stay here. This house was no longer a safe haven.

She squared her shoulders and steeled herself to make the best of these changed circumstances. She went downstairs, found the newspaper where Derek had left it so precisely folded and flipped through the For Rent ads. Before long she had carefully weeded out the ones that were clearly unsuitable for her, which left her with a list of possibilities. After telephoning most of them, she gave up in discouragement. Everything was so expensive!

Landlords wanted the first month's rent and a security deposit. "I'd like to see the house," she said more than once, "but we can't afford it."

Thoroughly disheartened, Eve decided on the spur of the moment to ride over to Wrayville to visit Al. She wanted to check on him, to make sure that he was getting along all right, and besides, she needed the lift that seeing her father would bring. She called a goodbye to Aunt May, who was murmuring things to herself as she puttered around the daylilies on the terrace, and she told Louise not to expect her back in time for dinner.

Before long, she was in her sturdy Volkswagen, heading out of the city. The day was bright and hot, and as the red clay road banks skated past her car window, Eve's spirits lifted for the first time since Kelly's accident. Derek was being unreasonable, and his position on the abortion was unconscionable, but the baby was safe, and the silver lining in this dark cloud was that she and Al would be together again when she finally found a house for them. *When* she finally found a house? *If* she finally found a house. It was proving to be more difficult than she had anticipated. And she still didn't know what she was going to do about a job.

When she pulled her car beneath the chinaberry tree, she was surprised to see Nell Baker peering anxiously out the window. Nell smiled widely at the sight of Eve and ran outside.

"Eve, I'm so glad to see you," Nell confided, sliding an arm around the younger woman's waist. "Did your boss let you off work today?"

"I'm glad to see you, too," Eve replied, ignoring the question. "How's Al?"

"Oh, Eve, not good. Doug Ender stopped by, I understand, and afterward Al had a real bad spell. In fact,

I thought that was why you came home. Didn't Al call you? No? Well, I came over to stay with him after I stopped by and saw he wasn't well, and I can tell you that he hardly slept all night. He's upset about leaving Wrayville, you know. And, of course, his claim against the mill." The little woman, so robust and full of energy, peered up at Eve through silver-rimmed glasses.

Eve concealed her alarm. "Is he all right now?"

"He's asleep, and a good thing, too. Oh, Eve, it worries me. You know how he is. He thinks he can fight this sickness all by himself, but he can't; he can't. I saw it happen with my Bud."

"And the company claims that the disease doesn't exist," Eve said bitterly.

"Maybe if Wray Mills is being bought by that big textile group, maybe it will make a difference in your father's claim. Maybe they'll admit that working in the mill caused Al's byss—byss—Oh, how do you say that word?"

"Byssinosis," Eve replied. "Byssinosis. Just say brown lung. It's easier, and it means the same thing—that a man worked in cotton-dust levels that were dangerously high and that he got sick and may die because of it."

"It killed my husband," Nell Baker said dully. "I know it did." With visible effort, she changed the subject. "Eve, have you found a place for Al to live? I already have one boarder, you know. Al could board with me if he likes."

Eve shook her head. "That's kind of you, Nell. But Al and I want to be together if possible. I've been looking for a place." Today she longed to pour out her story to Nell, who had been wonderful to her ever since her mother died. But she knew that Nell would be shocked if she knew that Eve carried another couple's child, and she thought that Nell might even tell her father. And in his present state of health, telling him would be disastrous.

At Nell's urging, she peeked in on her father. He was lying on his bed, and his breathing was tortured and difficult. He had to fight for every breath he took, for every bit of life-giving oxygen. It broke her heart, as it always did, to see her once-vigorous father reduced to such a painful state.

"If you'll stay with Al, I'm going to walk over to Doug's office," she told Nell. "I have to know what Doug said to get Al so upset."

"I'll be here," Nell assured her.

Eve's nostrils twitched at the customary cooking odors emanating from the Quicks' house across the street. No longer did such aromas stimulate Eve's appetite. She stepped up her speed until she was well past.

Doug's office was located in a small brick building at the bottom of the hill.

"Eve," Doug said, looking uncommonly pleased to see her. He hurried around his desk to clasp her hands in his. His eyes clouded with concern at the expression on her face. "Are you feeling well? You look so pale."

"Oh, Doug," she said, sinking into the chair across from his desk.

"Something's wrong," he guessed, pulling a chair up beside her. Then, with alarm, he said, "You're not sick, I hope?"

She lifted her eyes to his. She could talk to Doug; she could trust him. She'd known him all her life. He was one person whom she could turn to for advice. "I'm not sick, Doug," she told him. "Just pregnant."

His face reflected shock and surprise.

Quickly Eve poured out her story. Doug listened incredulously, then intently.

"Can Derek make me have the abortion, Doug?" she asked urgently.

"Eve, I—" He stopped, then stood up and paced around the room, thinking. He shook his head and smiled at her, but his hazel eyes were troubled.

"I don't think he can make you have an abortion. As far as I know, no case like this has been tested in the courts, and I admit this is outside my area of expertise. But it's your body, and since there are no provisions in the contract you signed, well, I don't think Lang has a leg to stand on."

Relief flooded her. "Thank God," she whispered.

"Eve, if I can help you in any way..." Doug began.

"I'll be all right," she told him. "The best way you can help me is by doing as much as you can for Al. Nell told me you stopped by to see him."

"I had to tell Al that we may have to sue Wray Mills for his compensation."

"Oh, no," Eve said. "Al would hate that." Anger surged through her at this news. Conditions in the cotton mill had ruined her father's health so that he'd had to quit work before retirement age, and then Wray Mills refused to pay back wages and compensation. Yet Al would recoil from the thought of any legal action against the mill, to which he had felt loyal for thirty-eight years. If they were forced to sue Wray Mills, what toll would that take on her father's health?

"It might be a good idea to file the lawsuit before the rumored sale of the mill occurs," Doug said.

"Rumored? You mean it's still not a sure thing?"

Doug shook his head. "The mill management is trying to keep a lid on rumors. So far, I've heard so many big textile names mentioned as possible buyers for the mill—

Spring, Cannon, Burlington—that I don't know what to believe these days."

"Don't file a lawsuit, Doug. Not yet. I don't think Al could take it."

"All right, Eve. I won't. I'll try to think of something else we can do instead." Doug's voice was gentle.

She rose to go.

"And Eve," he said in parting, "keep in touch."

Eve nodded before walking blindly out of his office, through the tiny waiting room and outside. She kept her head down as she walked the short distance back to the house. It had been hard to tell Doug what she'd been through, but she felt better for it. And she knew she could trust him not to discuss her situation with anyone else.

She visited with Al for a short while after he woke up, fighting tears as she watched Al struggle for the breath to talk.

"I talked with Doug," she finally said, feeling it necessary to bring the subject up.

"He told you that we might have to sue the mill to get my compensation?"

"Yes. I asked him not to do that yet. He said he'll try to think of something else we might do."

"Good. Good. I don't want to sue the mill. I just want what's rightfully mine."

"Well, don't worry about it," Eve said soothingly.

"I won't. It's nice that you have a good job now, Evie. We don't have to worry about money so much."

"I love you, Al," she said, bending over to kiss his cheek before she left, hoping he could not read the despairing expression on her face.

"I love you, too, Eve," Al told her.

Oh, what was she going to do? How was she going to manage? After a quick farewell to Nell Baker, she fled the mill-village house, trying to organize her thoughts.

Riding along the country highway toward Charlotte, Eve thought, *I've got to get a job.* If she had a job, she'd know how much rent she could afford. It was pointless to continue searching for a place to live if she didn't know how much money she'd be making. At the moment, everything seemed to be caving in on her at once. Al's obvious setback made her ache inside, and then there was Derek and the baby and even Aunt May to worry about.

She'd filed a job application at the big computer plant in northeast Charlotte, but that had been months ago. They'd never called her, but it would be a place to start. She could go by and check on the status of her application today. She glanced at her watch. It was past one in the afternoon, and she hadn't eaten lunch.

I promised Derek I wouldn't skip meals, she told herself. Then she realized that Derek couldn't care less. It wasn't Derek to whom she had to keep promises now; it was the baby. It wouldn't be good for the baby if Eve fell back into her haphazard eating habits. She checked her face in the small rearview mirror. She looked presentable, but she knew of a small restaurant at Dugan's Crossroads up ahead where she could order a hamburger and use the rest room to make any major repairs to her makeup. She wanted to look her best when she tackled the computer company's employment office.

She slowed in front of the neat clapboard house adjoining the restaurant's parking lot. The parking lot was filled, but Eve finally found a place to park beneath a rusted Coca-Cola sign featuring a woman wearing 1950s makeup.

What is going on in here? she wondered when she stepped inside. The place was packed. It was a small restaurant, once a country store, and every booth was filled. The patrons were mostly men in work clothes. Perhaps there was a big construction project nearby. She worked her way to the counter and edged onto a just-vacated stool.

It was a good ten minutes before a harried fellow wearing an apron appeared in front of her.

"Take your order?" he asked, whipping out an order pad.

"I'd like a hamburger and a glass of milk," she told him, and he disappeared into the kitchen where she could observe him through the pass-through. He seemed to have more arms than an octopus as he slapped a circle of hamburger on the grill, mixed a new batch of cole slaw and shot whipped cream onto a hot-fudge sundae.

Didn't he have any waitress help? Apparently not, because not only was the guy doing all the cooking, but he waited tables, too.

Her hamburger was delicious, and she wolfed it down. She wanted a glass of water, though, and when she tried to catch the eye of the restaurant's jack-of-all-tasks, she failed. Well, she could get it herself. This was hardly the kind of place where it was necessary to stand on ceremony. The glasses and water were on the other side of the counter. She got up and poured water into her glass, only to be confronted by the fellow, whose shirt was embroidered with the name Lenny.

"Gee, thanks," he said, breaking into a broad grin. "Mind getting some water for those fellows next to you at the counter? Say, you want a job for the next two hours? I'm swamped," he said. "Pay's good, plus you get tips."

"But—" she started to say, and then stopped. Nell Baker always said that a bird in the hand is worth two in the bush, and this would be a way to pick up some extra cash. "I've never waitressed," she said uneasily.

"Come on; it's no big deal. Here," he said, thrusting the order pad into her hand. "Got to get the orders of those people who just came in. Sure, go on!" With a challenging grin, he bustled away.

Instead of being annoyed, Eve found herself amused. A waitress! Well, it was a job, if only for the next few hours, and at this point she wouldn't turn down anything that would bring in money. So she obediently wrote down orders, carted food to tables and cleaned them with a Clorox-soaked towel after the customers left. It was four o'clock before the restaurant cleared out enough for her to talk with Lenny.

"Say, you're good," he told her admiringly. "Thought you said you never waitressed before." He was the possessor of a jaunty smile and a mobile mouth; it would be hard not to like him.

"I haven't," she said. Coins weighted her skirt pocket. She'd made out pretty well in tips.

"Want a job? Permanent. I need someone. Got this construction job about a half-mile up the road. Big new hot-water-heater plant. Got construction workers coming in for breakfast, break, lunch, another break; then the shift's over at three, and they come in for a snack. Listen, I've never been so busy in my life, and my last waitress quit yesterday to run off to California with her boyfriend."

"Well," said Eve, her mind racing. "This location is awfully far from the city. My father and I are moving from Wrayville to Charlotte, and I *am* looking for a job.

But to drive all the way out here every day to work—I don't know.''

"What kind of job are you looking for?"

"I used to be in public relations. I wasn't counting on being a waitress."

"Public relations? This job'll teach you to *really* relate to the public!" Lenny's grin faded; then he shrugged. "You find a place to live in Charlotte yet?"

"No, I—"

"Look, you want to work here, you can stay in the house next door. It's my house, two bedrooms, but with a wife and four kids it got too small. Inherited it from my folks; this restaurant used to be my dad's store. Built it up myself, doing real good. Anyway, the house is empty. You want to live there, we can work out something on the rent and your salary."

"You'd let us live in your house?" Eve was stunned at the offer.

"Sure. Better for people to live in it. Keeps vandals away, and you'd be close to your job."

She'd like that. She'd be able to keep an eye on Al. He'd enjoy coming to the restaurant, chatting with the construction workers. He wouldn't be lonely.

She didn't have to think twice. Lenny's offer was a solution to two immediate problems.

"It's a deal," she heard herself say, and without further ado, she and Lenny shook on it.

Chapter Five

Derek steered the Corvette around a huge puddle in the middle of the road. Tropical storm Dondi, downgraded last night from a hurricane, had moved in from the coast and was dumping torrential rains on the North Carolina Piedmont.

He shifted uneasily in his seat, his damp shirt sticking to his back, and wished longingly for the cool, crisp weather of October. This was the last week of an unusually humid September; approximately four weeks to go until relief arrived in the form of the first frost.

He slowed the Corvette to a crawl as he approached the L & D Cafe at Dugan's Crossroads. The Corvette's windshield wipers scrambled frantically, barely able to keep up with the deluge.

Believe it or not, there was a woman actually walking alongside the road in this horrendous weather. He noticed her, tried not to splash her, then cast a backward glance toward her in utter disbelief.

She wore a loose, nondescript beige raincoat over a white uniform, and she held an umbrella over her head, which didn't help much to protect her from the rain. But her hairstyle—he'd never seen anyone else with that particular hairstyle, geometrically precise, black hair short in the back but longer at the sides.

"Eve," he muttered, wishing he could get a better view of her. But a van loomed behind him, riding his bumper, and the last he saw of her, someone was holding the door of the restaurant so she could duck inside.

He'd come home to the Myers Park house from his business trip three months ago and found Eve gone. He discovered the bank passbook with its untouched three thousand dollars placed in the exact center of his desk, a silent rebuke.

Still, he'd fully expected Eve to turn up after the abortion and ask for her twelve thousand. When she didn't, he wondered why. But he couldn't find Kelly's address book to contact her, and he didn't want to try to locate her through the Queen City Infertility Clinic—too many unhappy memories there. So he never did. He was sure that after he'd left on his business trip, Eve had seen the light and had the abortion. He figured she'd find him when she needed the money.

But she hadn't. He hadn't heard one word from Eve, not one. After Kelly's death, Derek had fiercely attacked the many problems of adding Wray Mills to the Lang Textile empire, trying to find solace in his work, and so he'd never followed up on his obligation to locate Eve. Moreover, when she'd left, he was wallowing in the depths of his grief, indulging in boundless self-pity. Only recently had he begun to take mild pleasure in the things he'd enjoyed before—a round of golf, a quiet dinner with old friends, and sometimes he couldn't face even those.

Could that have been Eve going into the L & D Cafe? No. Why would Eve be at that little restaurant at Dugan's Crossroads? Still, the memory of her teased him, and the nagging idea that he'd been derelict in his duty toward Eve wouldn't let him rest. A week later, when he had to go to Wrayville for another round of interminable secret negotiations, he stopped at the L & D Cafe. No reason not to stop there, anyway. It was lunchtime, and he was hungry.

He realized as soon as he stepped inside that he was out of his element. His pin-striped suit was clearly out of place among the yellow hardhats and worn blue denim shirts and jeans. But he slid across the red vinyl seat in a vacant booth and scanned the neatly typed menu. From the jukebox in the corner blared the sound of John Denver whining for his old guitar. Derek drummed his fingers impatiently on the scuffed Formica tabletop. The service was slow.

Where was the waitress, anyway? He didn't see one. There was a guy with Lenny written across his chest who seemed to be everywhere at once.

"I'd like to place my order, please," Derek said when the guy breezed by.

"Sure," Lenny said amiably before disappearing again.

And then, and then . . . he saw her. His heart fell to his gut when he recognized the crisp, neat hairstyle, the high white cheekbones, the brown eyes that seemed larger than ever and could belong to no one but Eve, Eve Triopolous. She seemed to float ethereally behind the counter, treading on air, a graceful woman in white who, with her long swanlike neck and her air of calm composure, looked altogether too aristocratic to be working in a place like this. But there was no doubt in his mind as he watched her slide a sandwich plate onto the counter from her tray and favor the man who sat there with her unique smile, that she indeed worked here. He held his breath.

He hadn't remembered Eve Triopolous as being so beautiful.

She turned on her heel and walked around the end of the counter, and it was then that he realized. He gasped with the impact of it, and the room tilted, bent in two. For when he saw her gently rounded abdomen beneath the skirt of her uniform, he knew.

He shut his eyes tight, then opened them again. Eve was still pregnant. She was something like four or five months pregnant; he didn't know which because he had never been very good at determining such things.

The buzzing in his ears reached monumental proportions, and when it stopped, she was standing beside him, marking something efficiently on her order pad, and then she inquired crisply and impersonally, "May I take your order, please?"

His hand clutched her wrist, and her eyes widened in alarm as she looked up, completely unawares. She hadn't paid any attention to him; he was just another customer.

When she recognized Derek, her knees went weak. They stared at each other for a long moment, startled brown eyes converging with steely gray ones. Eve felt her world, the one she had constructed so carefully in the past few months, crumble slowly to dust.

"What are you doing here?" was the best he could manage.

She wrested her arm away. "Working," she said evenly. "Did you want to order something?"

"My God, Eve, how can you be so blasé?" he said tightly.

She lifted an eyebrow. "I'm not. Now are you ordering or aren't you? I have a job to do."

"We have to talk."

"We don't have anything to talk about."

"You can stand there with my baby in your belly and say that we don't have anything to talk about?"

A curious glance from one of the construction workers made him lower his voice at the end of his sentence.

Eve flushed. "Please, Derek. Don't embarrass me."

That brought Derek to his senses. He didn't want to embarrass her; it was embarrassing enough, he was sure, to have to work in a place like this, with all these men looking at her day in and day out, watching her pregnancy progress.

One thing he knew—he couldn't eat anything. "Look," he said wearily, "can I come to the place where you live?"

"No," Eve said quickly, thinking of Al. Her father was still struggling to understand the forces that had compelled Eve to volunteer as a surrogate mother. His attitude toward her unmarried pregnancy was touchy enough without the baby's father appearing on the scene.

"Then you come to my house," he told her. "Please."

"Why? Have you had a change of heart?" Her tone was sarcastic. Maybe he deserved it.

"If you don't agree to meet me somewhere, I'll be back here again and again until you do," he said through clenched teeth.

"Eve? Eve!"

It was Lenny, calling her from the kitchen.

"I can't have you coming here," Eve said, glancing worriedly over her shoulder toward the kitchen and feeling something akin to panic. "You'll jeopardize my job."

"You shouldn't have a job like this, on your feet all the time; it's not good for you. And the work's hard."

Her features stiffened into an impenetrable mask. Her eyes were full of disdain. "This job is going to enable me to support your child, Derek," she said tightly, flipping the pages of her order book over and stuffing the book in her uniform pocket.

He tried to avoid looking at her bulging abdomen, but it was right in his line of vision. Guilt washed over him.

"My office," he said with effort. "Tomorrow. Eleven-thirty?"

"Tomorrow is my day off," she said. She wondered at the bleakness in his voice, the pain in his eyes. What was she getting herself into? She would be a fool to agree to see him, to risk upsetting her life again for him.

No, said a voice deep inside her. *Do this for Kelly.*

It was what Kelly would have wanted; Eve was sure of that. If there was any chance that Derek would accept his child, any chance at all, Eve would have to take it.

"Eleven-thirty," she said quietly. "All right, Derek. I'll be there."

He nodded slowly. There was a faint dusting of dark hair on her forearms. He'd never noticed that before.

Without speaking, aching inside, he handed her his business card in case she didn't know where he worked. Then he got up and walked out of the restaurant. He knew she was watching him from the window as he unlocked the Corvette and slid inside. As he drove onto the highway from the gravel parking lot, he couldn't remember feeling this despondent since the day Kelly died.

It was clear to Derek as he drove back into the city that something had gone terribly wrong with his life. He'd always had a plan for everything. Things came easily to him, he was convinced, because he had made an overall plan for his life when he was still in his teens.

This was the result of having a mother who would say to him when he was six years old and on the way out the door with his playmates, "Derek, what's the plan?" Early on, he got the idea that there must be a plan for everything. Get an education, find a suitable wife, get married. Have two children, a boy and a girl, who would go to prep schools and then to good, prestigious colleges, not the state university, and who would grow up to have plans that would include summer visits to their parents who would by then be stooped and gray haired and retired according to plan.

All was guided by the plan. But then Kelly had the problem about not being able to have babies. That had certainly not gone according to plan. After Kelly's hysterectomy he'd thought, *Oh, well, sometimes you have to alter the plan; we'll adopt.* And so Derek had consoled Kelly with that. He hadn't realized how much she wanted his child, his and hers, a child of their very own, until she'd come up with the surrogate-mother plan.

Derek hadn't known much about surrogate mothers. Oh, he'd heard something about it on a television news show once. But then Kelly had presented the surrogate-mother idea to him as a plan, and that is what convinced him. There was a plan. They'd find a suitable surrogate, Kelly's egg and his sperm would unite, and not too long afterward, the baby would be born. Kelly would, of course, manage the whole thing in her own efficient way.

And then, most inefficiently, she had died. It wasn't fair, leaving him with all of it; it wasn't fair for Kelly to disrupt the plan. He felt a quick stab of anger toward Kelly, which subsided immediately, leaving him feeling foolish about being angry about something over which she had no control.

The only thing to do, thought Derek unhappily, was to make a new plan. His grief had prevented that until now. But since he had seen Eve, had come face to face with her unmistakable pregnancy— Oh, damn. The situation was preposterous. How the devil was he going to make a plan that would accommodate it?

EVE'S MIND was not on accommodation as she dressed to meet Derek the next morning. It was on her pregnancy and what she might do to convince Derek, in one more last-ditch effort, to shoulder responsibility for the child he had fathered.

"Daughter," Al said as she leveled steady brown eyes at her reflection in the mirror beside the door of Lenny's little house. "Are you sure you know what you're doing?"

"No," she admitted, fluffing out the silken strands of her straight dark hair with her fingers. "But I have to take the chance."

Al heaved a wheezing sigh. "Stay home, Eve. Derek Lang has shown the kind of man he is. He never even tried to find you."

"You'd understand if you knew what kind of shape he was in after his wife died," Eve said firmly.

"But Evie—" Al began, but Eve refused to listen. She pecked Al quickly on the cheek before escaping out the door. She didn't want any more advice.

Al was better now, but it had been rough going when she'd had to inform Al of her pregnancy and the circumstances surrounding it. She never wanted to deliver a blow like that again, ever.

She had chosen a quiet moment a few days after she'd started work at the L & D Cafe. She'd prepared Al's favorite Greek dish, moussaka, and had even spent precious money on a bottle of the imported resinated wine that Al loved so well. When Al was mellow with good food and spirits, she'd taken the plunge.

"I have something to tell you, Al," she'd said gently, in her most direct manner.

Al had had a good day. He was feeling expansive, and his brown eyes glowed with fondness.

"Eh? So what is it, Evie?"

She swallowed the lump in her throat.

"I—" She could not continue.

"Something that's hard for you to tell me?" A shadow of foreboding passed across Al's face.

Eve drew a deep breath. "I'm pregnant, Al. I'm going to have a baby."

Al stared at her. His face fell. He looked old, tired.

"It's not what you think," Eve hurried on. "I'm not involved with anyone. I hired myself out as a surrogate mother."

"A surrogate mother," Al said in disbelief. "I've heard of such a thing. But you—" And he stopped and stared at her again in disbelief. "You let your body be used that way?"

"I wanted to. They were going to pay me twelve thousand dollars. And they were a lovely couple, Derek and Kelly Lang, and they wanted a baby." Tears sprang to her eyes as she remembered Kelly's longing for a child.

"Ah, don't cry, Eve," her father said, his voice breaking. "I can't believe you let them do that to you, but don't cry about it."

Eve blinked back the tears. "There's more," she whispered.

"More? What more could there be?" Al's eyes flashed with anger, but when he saw the effect this had on his daughter, he clamped his lips tightly together.

"I was going to bear the child for the Langs. There was no job in Charlotte, Al. I wasn't living with a girl friend; I was living with the Langs. I'm sorry I lied to you, but I lied because I didn't want to tell you about it. I shouldn't have lied—I wish I hadn't—but at the time I thought it was for the best.'' She stopped and swallowed. ''Mrs. Lang—Kelly—was killed in an automobile accident. It was awful, Al. She was my friend. And then—and then Derek said I should have an abortion.''

Al sank back in his chair. He had paled, and his breathing was labored.

''Al, are you all right? Shall I get your inhaler?''

Her father shook his head grimly. ''Go on,'' he said. ''Tell me the rest of it.''

''I refused to have the abortion. I ran away instead. I'm going to have the baby, Al.''

With a curse, Al struggled to his feet. Eve followed him as he paced heavily into the living room.

''We needed the money,'' she said desperately to Al's back as he stood, his shoulders heaving, his head resting against one arm raised against the doorjamb.

''We needed the money,'' he repeated, his voice barely audible. ''But we didn't need it so much that you had to sell yourself.''

''I wasn't—'' But she couldn't go on. She'd known all along that her father, with his Old World ways, would see it that way.

''Come sit down, Al,'' she said, going to him and turning him gently by the shoulders. He let her propel him to his favorite chair.

''I know how you must feel,'' she said, clasping his hand in hers. ''But it will be all right. I've got a job, a real job this time, and I've found a place for us to live.''

''The man,'' her father said. ''This Lang. He won't help you?''

She bit down hard on her lip and shook her head. ''I'm afraid there's no chance of that.''

"He must be a real jerk," Al spat out contemptuously, "to leave you all alone with this responsibility."

"He was so devastated by the loss of his wife—" she began.

"Don't tell me that! He fathered a child and walked away from it! What kind of a man would do something like that! If I ever got my hands on him— Don't expect me to have any sympathy for the man." Al stuck out his lower lip belligerently.

"Aren't you glad I found us a place to live? Don't you want to hear about my job?"

Al regarded her balefully. "Tell me," he had said.

And so Eve had told him haltingly about the little house Lenny had offered, about her job at the restaurant.

"A waitress? You, with your college degree, are going to work as a waitress?" Al began to cough.

"It's a job, Al. A way to live. And I like working for Lenny. He's a nice guy."

Al had had no choice but to let Eve remain in control. He had moved out of the mill-village house where he'd lived all those years and had made an effort to be happy in Lenny's little house. He'd made friends among the construction workers, who jollied him along, and if they weren't the cronies he'd had in Wrayville, well, at least they were company for him. He liked Lenny, too. Eve, maneuvering now through downtown Charlotte traffic, supposed Al's adjustment was the best she could hope for.

She found a place to park in a lot not far from Derek's office building and hurried inside. At the front desk, she gave her name to the receptionist.

"Mr. Lang is expecting you," the receptionist informed her in dulcet tones.

At the receptionist's direction, Eve stepped into the elevator and rode to the twelfth floor. She walked down the gray-carpeted hallway, her eyes wide. Lang Textiles, the sign on the door had said, with a list of mills in smaller gleaming gilt lettering underneath. The executive suite occupied the whole twelfth floor of this building.

"Ms. Triopolous?" said the secretary when Eve presented herself at Derek's office. Maisie Allen was openly curious, but she cut short her stare. "Mr. Lang is expecting you. Walk right in, please."

Hesitantly, Eve pushed open the door to Derek's office.

He sat at his desk with the wide window at his back. Outside, the air looked heavy with smoky mist, blurring the blue of the sky.

Derek was on the phone, but he looked up when he saw her.

"I'll get back to you on it," he said into the phone, and then he hung up abruptly.

Eve stood, her chin held high, regarding him with that cool expression on her face. Her hair swooped into the hollows beneath her cheekbones, hollows that had filled out since her pregnancy but were hollows nonetheless. Her eyes watched him warily from beneath eyelashes short and straight as the bristles in a blunt paintbrush, the kind of eyelashes that were too short to cast a dusky shadow on those perfect high cheekbones, a fact for which he was suddenly and absurdly grateful, for it occurred to him in a flash that those cheekbones should never be hidden in shadow but splendored in light.

"Please sit down," he bade her, only to discover that his heart was hammering in his chest like a wild tom-tom, making a jungle creature of him, and he'd never been anything but civilized in his whole life. While he was recovering, she spoke.

"Derek, I agreed to meet you because I hope that there is some chance that you'll accept the baby as yours," she said.

His eyes rested for a moment on her breasts, so full above the mound that was the baby. Her breasts were round and full, not cone-shaped as they had been before.... But how had he known that her breasts were supposed to be cone-shaped and widespread? He must have noticed at some time in the past, but he had no recollection of it.

He pulled his eyes away from her body, poised so carefully in the chair across from him. He cleared his throat. "You're how pregnant now?" he asked.

"Four and a half months," she said, and he thought he detected a trace of pride in her voice.

"Too late for an abortion?"

"It was always too late for that," she shot back.

His eyes flew to meet hers, and he was surprised that there was no animosity in their brown depths. He sighed and decided to be direct.

"Eve, why? Why did you run away? Why didn't you have the abortion? I thought you had. I thought—"

"Didn't you believe me when I said I wouldn't?" Her voice was deeper now, stronger.

He didn't take his eyes off her face. "No," he said quietly. "I guess not." Then he was silent for a moment. "I should have guessed when you didn't take the passbook with the three thousand dollars with you. That should have tipped me off."

She crossed her legs, and Derek found himself mesmerized by the exposed white skin on the inner part of her calves.

"No amount of money could convince me to get rid of Kelly's baby," she said.

"It's my baby, too," he said before thinking.

Her gaze was level. "That's exactly what I hoped you'd say. The baby belongs to you when it's born. I told you I'd take care of the baby if you won't, and that's still true. I love this baby, have grown to love it, carrying it under my heart all this time—" Her voice broke off, and he was amazed to see that her eyes glistened with tears.

Poor Eve. She'd been through so much. He got up and walked around his desk until he stood in front of her.

"How long have you worked at the L & D Cafe?" he asked, and his voice was low.

"Since I left your house." She dared not look at him, or she would begin to sob. She hadn't minded the work, the feet that swelled until she wore a shoe a size larger than she had before, the lower back pain that had become almost constant now that her center of gravity had shifted forward. It hadn't been easy, although she'd never complained, not even once. But now, with Derek Lang standing before her, so handsome and unchanged by the series of events that he and Kelly had set off, events that had changed everything for Eve, the burden she carried seemed heavier than it had ever felt before.

"All that time you've been working at the L & D Cafe so you could afford to have my baby?"

He had called it his baby again. "Yes," she said, staring down at his wing tips.

He touched a finger to her face and slid it under her chin. Her skin felt like velvet. He tipped her face toward him.

"Eve, let me take care of you," he said gently. "I'm ready to accept responsibility for getting you into this fix. Let me."

"I'm not sure what you mean," she whispered.

He reluctantly allowed his finger to fall away from her face and walked back around his desk to hide his pain at the situation that should never have happened. He fiddled with his letter opener to hide his unaccustomed confusion. He and Kelly had ruined Eve's life, perhaps ruined it permanently. Now that she sat so quietly in his office, asking nothing for herself, the fact was brought unavoidably home to him. To be blunt about it, he felt like a cad. He had to think what to do about it, and it wasn't easy. He didn't have a plan.

He shot Eve a glance of assessment. She looked as though she were concentrating on keeping herself pulled together, maintaining a stiff upper lip. Something about her in that instant seemed very courageous. For some reason another picture of her leaped to his mind, a picture of Eve sitting at the opposite end of the breakfast-room table from him as they both gobbled caramel corn.

"Do you still eat junk food?" He shot the question at her, not knowing why he asked.

The shadow of a smile tugged at the corners of her mouth. "More than I should. But since I've been working in the restaurant, Lenny sees that I eat the right things. He and his wife have four children."

She shrugged, finding it impossible to explain how the gregarious Lenny had taken her firmly under his wing the day she'd vomited at the smell of bacon sizzling on the grill. It was the second day she worked there, and Lenny had sized her up shrewdly and said, "Pregnant, huh?" She'd wanted to die of embarrassment, but all he'd done was pat her on the shoulder and say, "Let me know if you need time off to go to the doctor or anything," and he'd asked no questions. After that she'd tried even harder to do a good job.

"You're not still skipping meals, then?" Derek's gray eyes were unfathomable; she couldn't figure out what he wanted.

"No, it wouldn't be good for the baby," she said.

"Good. Then you'll go to lunch with me." And he picked up the phone and said, "Maisie, call the Versailles Room and make reservations for two for twelve-fifteen."

Eve gasped. "I can't. I'm not dressed for it. I didn't—"

"You're dressed just fine," he assured her, noticing for the first time what she wore. Her tent-shaped dress was fashioned of a light nubby material in a sort of rose-beige; the print scarf at her neck was folded artfully into the vee where two buttons were unfastened.

Derek tried to remember what kind of clothes Eve had worn before, but he couldn't for the life of him recall any of them. She'd favor something unobtrusive, no doubt, the kind of clothes that might have come from anyplace from Belk's to K mart. He was reasonably sure that she'd never worn anything of the superior cut and quality you found at Montaldo's. Kelly had bought most of her clothes at Montaldo's. Suddenly, he had the rash urge to hustle Eve over to that particular store and buy her something, anything.

"Well, come on, let's go," he said, suddenly wanting to be out of the office and in the fresh air.

Eve stood up, wishing she knew how to get out of this situation. She felt bloated and big and definitely not up to walking into the Versailles Room, the fanciest restaurant in downtown Charlotte, with Derek Lang looking so suave and debonair in his executive suit. People would think—but then, did it really matter what people would think? She'd stopped worrying about what people would think when she decided to become a surrogate mother.

She trudged doggedly after Derek down the gray carpeted hall until he slowed his step to match hers and tucked a proprietary hand under her elbow. His hand there made her skin jump; she didn't know how to react.

They walked to the restaurant, which was only a few doors away from the office building. Eve sent halfway-frantic glances at Derek, who kept his hand firmly cupped around her elbow. Once she tried to shake his hand away, but he demurred.

"In case you should stumble," he offered by way of explanation, waving at some nearby sidewalk construction.

The restaurant was crowded, but they were ushered quickly to their table by a maître d' whose attitude toward Derek could only be described as obsequious.

Derek gave their order to the waiter, hesitating over the wine list as his eyes seemed riveted on Eve's stomach.

"No wine for me," Eve said, and when Derek didn't shift his eyes away immediately, she blushed.

After the waiter disappeared, Eve tried to regain her customary composure. So she wouldn't have to look at Derek, so sophisticated and handsome across the white linen tablecloth, she looked around. She'd never eaten in the Versailles Room before, with its inverted waterfalls of glittering crystal shimmering with light and its creamy gold-rimmed china and its fresh flower centerpieces on every table. The room was filled with well-dressed matrons dripping with real pearls and with dapper executives in stylishly tailored suits conversing earnestly over martinis.

"It's not much like the L & D Cafe," she explained when Derek's quizzical glance intruded on her observations.

His expression darkened at that, and she knew she had said the wrong thing. "It can't be pleasant working there," he said, looking uncomfortable.

"It's not so bad," Eve retorted, her defenses up now. "Lenny has been good to me. He lets me stay in the house nearby. It's his house, and he could rent it, but it's mine now for practically nothing, and—"

"You live there alone?" he asked sharply. He and Kelly had talked about Eve's private life, but it had been so long ago. He didn't remember much about her family. Or about her, really. Memory had been lost, set adrift on the sea of grief in which he had been floundering for the past three months.

"My father lives with me," she said.

"I see." He was immensely relieved. What if she had been living with a man, a boyfriend? At the moment he couldn't have imagined anything worse, although he supposed that for Eve at this time in her life, such a situation was unlikely.

Eve said, "How's Aunt May?"

"Lonely, and as daffy as ever."

"I never found Aunt May daffy," Eve objected seriously.

Derek raised his eyebrows. He hadn't expected Eve to stick up for Aunt May. Eve's defense reminded him of Kelly; that was something Kelly might have said and which Derek would have attributed to family loyalty.

"Really?" he said thoughtfully.

"Aunt May's lonely, as you say. And her hearing problem makes communication difficult. But that's no reason to put her down. She was nice to me," Eve said reflectively and with more than a little sadness. She'd hated not saying goodbye to Aunt May. She'd left a fond note, because she couldn't have faced Aunt May's questions.

"She misses you," Derek told her. "It was a mean thing you did, running off like that. Aunt May cried for days. And on top of Kelly—"

"Stop," Eve said fiercely. Her eyes flared with a brief spark of anger; then, like a snuffed candlewick, it went out.

"Sorry," Derek said, looking down at the tablecloth. He paused. Lately his wife's aunt had been rubbing him the wrong way more than usual. It felt good to be able to open up about it to someone who might understand.

"Aunt May drives me crazy," he went on a little desperately. "Remember how Louise used to serve roast beef on Sunday and things like chicken breasts and veal cutlets on weekdays? Well, Aunt May buys oddments like hot pickled sausages and Twinkies and something called tofutti and expects Louise to make a meal out of it. Aunt May says she sees people eating these things on her favorite soap opera. I never get a decent meal anymore."

"That shouldn't pose a problem for a closet eater of junk food," Eve pointed out.

"But it's not fun to eat junk food if you don't have regular food to compare it with," Derek said. "Actually," he went on in a more controlled tone, "I think the old girl needs something worthwhile to do with her time. Planning for the baby gave her that. Did you know she sewed a complete christening gown by hand, all daintily embroidered? The gown, the bonnet, everything. She showed it to me after you left. She worked on it in her room every night. She'd wanted it to be a surprise for Kelly, she said. And after—afterward, she wanted me to have it. I—I had to tell her that you'd had the abortion, because I thought you had.''

"Oh," Eve said in a small voice, feeling as though the breath had been knocked out of her. She ached at the thought of Aunt May thinking that she, Eve, would have actually allowed such a thing to happen to this baby.

"I was wrong to have told her that," Derek said heavily. "But at the time..."

"Oh, Derek, please tell her—tell her the truth," Eve said, her voice breaking.

"You could tell her yourself. *Show* her yourself. Come back home, Eve," Derek said softly. "Come back where you belong."

His eyes, so compelling, would not release hers.

"I can't," she said, wishing he wouldn't look at her like that.

The waiter served their food, providing an untimely interruption.

The waiter left. "Why can't you?" Derek asked just as Eve, striving for normalcy, was about to delve into her fruit salad. His tone of voice was so commanding that she didn't think she'd be able to eat a bite.

She set her fork back down on the table. She inhaled a deep breath, trying to be as rational as possible. "Aunt May aside, it would be wrong of me to accept your hospitality, Derek, when you don't even want the baby. Besides, my father lives with me now, and I can't leave him. I'm his sole support." She picked up her salad fork again, only to find that her hand was shaking.

"Eve, I'm reassessing this whole situation, but I need time. I'm sorry, but I still don't think I can take the baby, for more reasons than I want to go into right now. But, Eve, you shouldn't be working that waitress job. I want to take care of you. I feel responsible for you and for the baby; you must understand that.''

''You didn't feel too responsible for us three months ago,'' she pointed out.

A white line bisected the space between Derek's eyebrows. ''Do you know what it was like for me then? Losing my wife and then faced with rearing a child all by myself? Don't you have one iota of understanding for how I felt?'' His expression was agonized, and with a shock Eve thought, *Why, he's felt this more than I ever dreamed,* and her thought was followed with a rush of unexpected compassion for this man who spoke with such anguish and such passion. Never had she expected to feel so sensitive to Derek Lang and his heretofore incomprehensible emotions.

''Maybe I do understand,'' she said slowly and with great surprise.

''At least if you were under my roof I'd have the comfort of knowing you were eating properly—''

''I am eating properly,'' Eve insisted. ''I told you that.''

''Knowing you were eating properly and that you didn't have to work in that restaurant. And it would be so good for Aunt May to have someone around the house; you got along with her well.''

Eve remembered the two of them baking cookies together; it was the kind of thing she had always imagined she would have done with her mother if her mother had lived. She would like showing Aunt May how to make Greek pastries. Aunt May would like it, too. It was true that she had missed Aunt May.

''I have my father to think about,'' she reminded Derek doubtfully. ''I can't just up and leave him, you know.''

"Your father could come with you. There's plenty of room in that big barn of a place, plenty of room for all of us. It's so empty now, so empty."

Eve picked at her lunch, nudging morsels of broccoli quiche around her plate. Al, feeling as resentful as he did, would never move into Derek's house.

"Will you think about it at least? Will you, Eve?" Derek couldn't understand why she didn't jump at this chance to make things easier on herself. The world was filled with women who would hang on to a man as though they had a problem with static cling—and not in their panty hose, either. Obviously Eve Triopolous was not one of those women.

Thoughts whirled through Eve's head. If she lived at the Myers Park house with him, wouldn't he begin to feel a curiosity about and perhaps an affection for the baby she carried? She'd pegged him as a warm, caring person—or at least as one-half of a warm caring couple—before. Couldn't Derek Lang become that person again if he were given the chance? Didn't he deserve that chance, for the baby's sake as well as his own?

Again she thought of Kelly, of this much-wanted baby who was the product of a union of Kelly and Derek. Eve loved the baby, did not doubt that she loved it enough to take care of it for the rest of its life if need be. But a child belonged with its biological parents if possible; she utterly and with all her heart believed that, and she, Eve, would never be this baby's biological parent. It was Derek, only Derek, who was the sole surviving biological parent of this child, and father and child belonged together.

The piece of broccoli quiche she was toying with broke apart. She lifted her eyes to his once more. "I'll think

about it, Derek,'' Eve said slowly. "I'll think about it."
It was all she could promise at the moment.

Derek smiled, the slow smile lighting up the depths of
his silvery eyes, illuminating his handsome face. She
didn't know how it happened, but his hand found hers on
the tablecloth, was warm as it covered hers, and as his
fingers curved around her hand to press against her palm,
her back stiffened, and she uttered a single involuntary
"Oh!"

"Eve," he said, not yet knowing the import of what
had just happened. His voice was warm honey flowing
over and around her, and all at once she wanted to get up
from the table and throw her arms around his neck, to
laugh, to sing, to let everyone in this big fancy restaurant experience her boundless joy.

She smiled, a big smile that revealed her quirky bicuspid, and it was a smile that brightened her eyes and
warmed his heart quite unexpectedly.

"Eve, what's wrong?" he said in alarm when he saw
the moisture collecting in the corners of her huge brown
eyes. But she was smiling; she was smiling with such
brilliance that she couldn't be in pain.

"Derek, oh, Derek," she said, pressing her free hand
to the gentle mound only partly concealed in the folds of
her flowing rose-beige dress in a gesture that he found
strangely endearing. "I think I just felt the baby move.
For the first time!"

And he couldn't breathe with the wonder of it, he
couldn't speak, he couldn't do anything except squeeze
Eve's small white hand tighter and tighter, and she was
squeezing back, their energy flowing back and forth, one
to the other, conveying their awe and reverence and
amazement at this irrefutable evidence of the baby's existence and its reaffirmation of life. And they sat like

that, unaware of clanking silver and glassware, of passersby brushing the sides of their table, unaware of anything at all, clasping hands across the linen tablecloth and clearly shaken at their sharing of this special moment.

Chapter Six

"And so your mind is set, daughter?" Al regarded her over the apple cobbler that reposed on their dinner table that night courtesy of Lenny at the L & D Cafe.

"Yes," she affirmed. "I've given Lenny notice, but he says you can live here as long as you please. I'm moving into the Myers Park house, and Derek is very happy. Al, please understand—this is something I have to do." She watched him anxiously, hoping that this new direction wouldn't send him off into another coughing spell.

"I'm sure Derek is 'very happy,'" Al huffed. "You moving into his house like that. In my day it would have been a scandal, and I still think it's highly improper. I never thought to see the day that a daughter of mine would be pregnant with a man's child and not even married to the man." He fixed her with a baleful look. His blatant disapproval broke her heart.

"Al, Al," she said, running nervous fingers through her short hair. "Nothing improper has ever taken place between Derek and me. You know that. You know how I contracted to bear a child for him and his wife; you know everything. I haven't done anything wrong, Al. And now I'm convinced that moving into the house with

Derek would be *right,* the right thing to do under these very unusual circumstances. Please understand!''

Al shoved his chair back from the table and walked to the window. It looked out on the highway, and down the road the neon lights of the L & D Cafe were just flickering on.

"Understand? You ask a lot, Eve. You've always been a good girl, taking care of the house when your mother died, getting top grades in college, then being hired on as public-relations director at the mill. I've always been proud of you. And you've been loyal, and you've taken care of me. You never ran around with men or acted wild like some of the girls we knew. But Eve, this surrogate-mother idea is out of character for you. I don't know why you ever did it. I can't believe you didn't ask me first.''

"Ask your permission? Oh, Al, I'm a grown woman. I didn't require your permission. And we needed the money.''

"In the old days, the daughters in Greek families didn't date, didn't marry, without their fathers' permission.''

"In the old days, there was no such thing as *in vitro* fertilization,'' Eve reminded him gently. "Couples who wanted babies had to do without them, because infertility could not always be cured. Isn't the new way better?''

Al looked sad. "Maybe.'' He reflected on this for a moment. A car's headlights illuminated his face, and then Eve drew the curtain across the window. She sat down on the sofa and beckoned Al to sit next to her. She placed one hand protectively over her abdomen, hoping she might feel the baby move. She sat like that often these days.

"Did I ever tell you, Eve, that your mother and I wanted more children?" Al said so suddenly that it star-tled her.

"You've said you wanted a bigger family," she told him.

"Well, we did. A big, big family, as big as the Quick family who lived across the street from us in Wrayville. We never had any children after you. Your mother never became pregnant again."

"Do you know why?"

"No. Her doctor couldn't tell her why. It just never happened. I've often wished we'd had more children, lots of children, like the big Greek families I knew when I was growing up."

"So you see, Al," Eve said, encouraged by this reve-lation, "what I'm doing is a sign of progress. Of mod-ern medicine. There's no stigma attached to being a surrogate mother, at least not among people who are well-informed."

"Still, you're going to live with this man, the father of your baby." Al was stubborn, just as she was. His lower lip stuck out, underscoring his implacability.

"Only until his baby is born. And you could come live with him, too," Eve said. "You're perfectly welcome. In fact, you and Aunt May would be the perfect chaper-ones."

"No," Al snorted. "That's where I draw the line. I'll not go with you, Eve. I cannot stop you from doing what you will do. But I needn't put my seal of approval on such goings-on."

She'd known he'd react this way, but she'd felt bound to repeat Derek's offer. "If you're going to be that way, well, I know you'll be happy here in Lenny's house. You can still go over to the restaurant and talk with the construction workers. And I can visit you a few times a week if you like.''

"No," Al said obstinately. "You have taken matters into your own hands once too often. You assume too much, daughter. I won't live in Derek Lang's house but I'll not presume on Lenny's generosity, either!"

Eve was dumbfounded. She'd thought she'd arranged everything so perfectly; if Al wouldn't go to Derek's house, he'd stay here at Lenny's. She couldn't believe he wouldn't go along with it.

"What will you do?" she asked.

"I'm going," Al replied loftily, "back to Wrayville. I'll rent a room from Nell Baker. She offered it, you know. She rents a room to one other widower, Vernon Platts, so I won't be lonely with the two of them around. My social security check will cover the expense."

"But Al—"

"I miss my friends from the mill. I miss Wrayville. I didn't want to tell you that before because it tore me up to see you working so hard so that we'd have a place to live and food to eat—" Al's voice broke.

"Oh, Al," Eve said, on the verge of tears herself. "Oh, Al."

"Anyway," Al went on, recovering, "maybe this is for the best. I can go back to Wrayville, and you won't have to work so hard in the restaurant, eh?" In that moment Eve sensed how difficult it had been for her father to be so absolutely dependent on her.

"I wish you'd go with me," Eve whispered, knowing it was hopeless."

"No, that I cannot do, Eve," Al said, heaving himself up from the sofa.

"I'll miss you," Eve said, trying not to burst into tears, which seemed to be precipitated these days by any little emotional crisis.

"I'll miss you, too, daughter," he told her, but his face was set in an unyielding expression, and she knew that however much Al loved her, he was not going to change his mind.

"Eve?" It was Derek, home from work for the day. Tonight, her first night back, he was early.

In her room, Eve set aside the book she was reading and pulled herself to her feet with the aid of one of the brass bedposts. The bigger she got, the harder it was to stand up on her own. The baby turned a somersault; with a grin she patted the hard mound of her belly.

"We're going to go see your daddy," she whispered to the baby.

Derek saw her as she rounded the landing, the big grandfather clock chiming six times in welcome as Eve slowly made her way down the flight of stairs, her white hand barely skimming the banister. She looked so beautiful that she took his breath away.

There were two spots of color high on her cheeks, which was unusual in itself. But it was her eyes, her eyes sparkling in her bright, intelligent face, that captured his attention. And she was smiling in welcome, showing those tiny white teeth, so perfect except for the one bicuspid, and she was rounder in places than she had been just a couple of weeks ago. He was so happy to see her that he felt like scooping her into his arms and whirling her around, which of course would never do.

He fell back on the mundane for something to say.

"You're all moved in? Everything is comfortable?"

"Everything is lovely," she said honestly. "Lenny helped me move my things in his truck, and Aunt May was so happy to see me that she baked my favorite kind of cookies. Peanut butter."

"My particular favorite is chocolate chip. But should you be eating cookies? Are cookies junk food? Don't you have to watch your weight or something?" He looked so boyish despite the dignity of his conservative but elegant suit. He looked like a suitor come to call, which was ridiculous, considering that it was his foyer in which they were standing, gabbling like idiots about inconsequentialities, and she was the guest, not he.

"Peanut butter is very nutritious, Derek," she assured him solemnly. "So I'm sure it's okay to eat peanut-butter-cookies."

"Ah," he said, rocking back on his heels. "Will you join me for a drink before dinner? No, you won't. Bad for the baby."

"I could have tomato juice," she suggested, suddenly wanting very much to sit down with Derek, to watch his face as his expression changed in response to her.

"Tomato juice," he said with satisfaction. Louise appeared in the hall.

"Please get Eve a glass of tomato juice, and a bourbon and branch water for me," he instructed.

"I'm so glad you're back," Louise whispered, squeezing Eve's arm as she passed her on the way to the kitchen. She flashed Eve a wide white-toothed smile. Louise's reassurance made Eve feel good, as though her presence here was desirable in and of itself, not just because she was gestating the Langs' child.

"Your father never changed his mind about moving here with you?" Derek asked carefully once their drinks had been served and they sat in the living room, Derek on a Chippendale couch, Eve in an armchair with her feet resting on a footstool upholstered in needlepoint.

She shook her head. "I'm afraid not. He's renting a room from a former neighbor, and he seems happy with his decision."

"Why didn't he want to live here?" Derek asked, wrinkling his brow.

Eve shrugged. She didn't want to offend Derek. "You have to understand my father's background. He's very Greek, very Old World. He doesn't approve of my being unmarried and pregnant. He doesn't approve of our living together."

"Good God," Derek said before tossing down a long draft of his bourbon and branch water. He stared at Eve. "And so he thinks you're some kind of scarlet woman? Letting your body be used for pay?" There was irony behind Derek's voice, and something more, too.

"More or less," Eve said, and she couldn't look at him. Why did she always cast her eyes down when caught in his intense gaze? Why couldn't she return his look with one of her own, one that told him she was proud and strong and could handle any circumstances that came along? Was it some Old World ploy, learned subconsciously from her black-garbed grandmother so long ago on those lengthy family visits every summer to the Greek community in Tarpon Springs?

"How awful," Derek said. "How terrible that this should come between you and your father." His words were heavy and oppressive, falling as they did like dead weights into the tightly strung atmosphere of the room.

Eve tried to speak around the lump in her throat. She would never understand how she managed to cope when she was on her own, and then when Derek came along and put his thoughts about her situation into words, she always choked up.

"It's not your concern," she said unhappily. "It's not your worry. Anyway, my father and I are on good terms. I'll visit him often."

"But he'll never understand why you did this," Derek offered.

"No. Probably not."

"Eve." She couldn't avoid his eyes when he spoke in that authoritative tone of voice. And when she looked at him, his expression was tender and compassionate.

"Eve," he went on, speaking slowly and distinctly and watching her with total absorption, as though he wanted to get inside her head and hear his words from the inside out, as though he wished he could *be* her for this short moment in time and therefore hear what he had to say solely from her point of view. "Eve, please accept my apologies. I am sincerely sorry that Kelly and I ever started this, that we ever got you into this—this mess. If I had it to do over again, I would never agree to it. Never."

"But—"

"Never, Eve," he said with heart-stopping earnestness.

"Let me say what I was going to say," she said softly. She became aware of the glass in her hands, of the dampness from it running down her palms. She set it carefully on a coaster on the burled-walnut cocktail table in front of her. She stood and walked to the fireplace where she stared at the huge gold-framed oil portrait of Kelly over the mantel, summoning the words she wanted to say. She drew strength from the sweet expression in Kelly's blue eyes.

"I'm glad that I'm pregnant," she told him, turning to look at him. "I love the feeling of a child within me. And if I hadn't decided to be a surrogate mother, I might never have had the chance. So don't feel sorry for me. I'm happy, Derek; I'm really happy."

Derek shook his head and lifted his eyebrows in disbelief. Her pear shape was starkly outlined against the white of the wall behind her. Eve was absolutely, unmistakably pregnant, her neat, compact body forced into new lines by the baby. He couldn't imagine that she actually enjoyed the process. Though he had to admit that from the healthy look of her, pregnancy seemed to agree with her. Still, he said in a quiet voice, "Don't be silly. You would have eventually married some nice fellow and settled down to raise a bunch of kids."

Eve shook her head vigorously. "I'm not so sure. I'm twenty-eight, Derek, which is closer to thirty than I like to think about some days. I've never dated much—only one serious romance, which ended when the man left Wray Mills for another job far away—and after that I concentrated on my job. I was a good Greek daughter, taking care of my father, never planning to do much else. I might never have borne a child. Now I will. I'm not sorry."

"This man of yours—did you want to marry him?" He was way out of line, asking. But somehow he had to know.

Eve took her time answering. She and Burke Whitlaw had gone through the manager-trainee program at Wray Mills together. What they'd experienced was more a commonality of interest than anything else. They had shared some good times. Yet when Burke had left Wrayville, there'd really been no great sadness. In fact, Eve had been aware only of a sense of moving on, of growing. Marry Burke? She'd never considered it seriously. They hadn't been right for each other.

"No," she said slowly. "I didn't want to marry him. Or anyone."

"But you're so pretty, Eve. A woman like you—" he left his sentence unfinished, thinking about men competing for her warm smiles, wanting to touch her body, to kiss her slim and elegant neck, the nape of it where the hair was so short and sleek, to kiss the insides of her milky-white wrists. Oh, there should be men flocking around Eve Triopolous. He couldn't believe that there weren't.

Eve blushed slightly. She was glad when Aunt May chose that moment to descend upon them in a fit of unbecomingly girlish enthusiasm, and Eve sat down again so that she could prop her feet up.

"You know what I did today?" Aunt May asked, bounding without pause into the conversation. "I planted the pansy beds. Oh, they're going to be so pretty in the spring! I planted lots of those big yellow ones with purple petals. Do you like pansies, Eve?"

"Oh, yes," said Eve. "They always remind me of little faces, upturned toward me and smiling."

"Now that's a sweet thought. I never thought of them as faces. My grandmother used to call pansies heartsease. They do kind of ease the heart just to look at them, don't they?"

Aunt May prattled on, but Eve welcomed her ramblings. She was irked that Derek looked as though he could barely tolerate them, and she was uncomfortable under his frank and undisguised gaze, but it was only a short time until Louise announced dinner.

Aunt May insisted on lighting tall candles, which cast the wainscoted dining room in a mellow glow, and Eve took her customary place to Derek's left, with Aunt May at the foot of the table. Eve was conscious that the three of them avoided looking at the place to Derek's right, where Kelly used to sit. Other than that, dinner was unremarkable except for a warm, familiar sense in Eve's heart that she was happy to be back.

"AND HOW DID YOUR VISIT to Dr. Perry go today?" Derek asked when he came home the next night.

"Fine. I'm fine, the baby is fine, and when the weather is fine, I'm supposed to do lots of walking." Eve smiled at him as she pulled on a loose cardigan that she kept hanging in the foyer closet.

"You're going for a walk now?" Derek seemed surprised.

"Of course. The leaves are changing color, and the neighborhood is beautiful."

"I'll come with you. That is, if you don't mind."

For one long, terrible minute she seemed taken aback, and he was afraid she was going to say no. But then she nodded briskly. "All right," she acceded.

They stepped out into the crisp, cool air. Derek inhaled deeply; this was the kind of weather he liked.

"Let's stop and look at Aunt May's pansy plants," Eve said on impulse. Aunt May had not only planted huge beds of them but had bordered a long brick walkway alongside the house with little green plants, flowerless now.

"They seem so fragile," Eve said, staring down at the tiny green sprouts. "As though they won't make it through the winter."

"Oh, they'll make it," Derek said confidently. "Aunt May has a wonderfully green thumb. I employ a gardener, of course, but she loves to work with the flowers herself. She's the one who created the rose garden for Kelly, you know. Those pansies will come up blooming in the spring; wait and see.''

Wait and see? It was not likely. The baby was due in February, and she would be gone by the time the pansies bloomed. But the baby, if Derek kept it—surely she could persuade Derek to keep it—would be able to see the bright colors of the pansies, their nodding little faces.

''Heartsease,'' she murmured, wondering how her heart would be eased if she had to leave the baby. She didn't dare think about it, not now. She turned and walked swiftly down the path, so swiftly that Derek, with his longer strides and without the handicap of being off balance, could barely keep up with her. She didn't slow down until she reached the sidewalk.

They strolled down the tree-lined street. Dogwood leaves had already turned various shades of red—carmine, ruby, scarlet. Lagging just behind were the leaves of the ginkgo trees, bright bursts of yellow now.

''What else did the doctor say today?'' Derek's eyes fixed on her with interest.

''I'm gaining too much weight. And I should remember to take my vitamins.''

''Gaining weight? How dangerous is that?''

''Not as dangerous as they used to think it was, but if I gain a lot, I'll have trouble losing it after the baby is born.''

''I see.''

''I didn't know you'd be so interested,'' ventured Eve, casting a curious sidelong glance at him.

''Of course I am,'' he said quickly. He shoved his hands down in the pockets of his suit trousers. A little girl in a smocked dress ran out of one of the houses across the street and stood staring at them.

"I wonder what she's staring at," Derek said, amiably.

"You, probably." Eve smiled. "You strolling down the street for a casual before-dinner walk, relaxed and comfortable in your three-piece suit."

Derek pulled his hands out of his pockets and looked down at himself. "Honestly? Do I look out of place?"

This brought a peal of soft laughter from Eve. "Yes, Derek. Most people take off their ties and vests and suit jackets when they come home from work, and then they put on something more comfortable."

"Comfortable? You mean a sweater?"

"A sport shirt, a sweater, a turtleneck. Don't you have any?"

"Well, of course," he said, sounding miffed. "People give them to me for gifts. But I feel perfectly comfortable in what I'm wearing."

"Don't you ever unbend? Have fun?"

"Well, I don't openly cavort, if that's what you mean." He had stopped sounding miffed and was looking down at her with laughter in his eyes. "It's sort of like eating junk food. Bad for the image."

"Oh, Derek. Is the image so all-important?" She spoke in a teasing tone, but he chose to answer her seriously.

"I became the president of a Fortune 500 company when I was only thirty-one. I never thought people would take me seriously if I showed up at the office looking less than dignified."

"And at home?"

There was a long silence, and then he said very quietly, "I wasn't home much."

The way he had spoken made her bite back the light retort on the tip of her tongue.

"I'm getting winded," Eve said after they had walked another block in silence. "Do you mind if we sit on that wall for a minute?"

"No, of course not."

She rested her hand on the stone of the wall for a lingering moment. It was cold, but she sat down anyway, and Derek sat beside her, staring moodily into space. Leaves freed by a stirring breeze overhead drifted down. One landed on Derek's shoulder.

Without thinking, Eve reached up to flick it away. So did he. Their hands touched.

Eve quickly pulled her hand away and clasped it with the other in her lap. The buoyancy of their mood had vanished, fading during their conversation, disappearing entirely when their hands had brushed each other. Eve shivered.

"It's getting chilly now with the sun going down," Derek said abruptly. "We'd better be getting back to the house."

Unhappily, Eve stood up, avoiding his eyes, and they headed toward home. Derek didn't speak, and neither did she. In the houses along the way, lights were winking on, and it was dark enough for windows to cast geometric shapes onto the spacious grounds of the houses they passed.

"I had so much responsibility at work," Derek said suddenly. "There was always so much to do."

With a start, Eve realized that Derek was talking about his absences from home, the effect they had had on his life with Kelly. Her cheeks colored when she recalled the conversation she had overheard when he and Kelly had been on the terrace and she had been in Derek's study.

"I—I'm sure there was," she said, wondering why he was telling this to her.

"Most of the time she understood, I think. If only I hadn't become president of the company when I was so young! But there wasn't any help for it. Dad groomed me to be president from the time I was a boy, in the manner of all the old textile barons. If you had a son, he would one day take over the mills. I never dreamed that my father would decide on early retirement and run off to Rio de Janeiro with a woman younger than I am."

"Is that what happened?"

Derek nodded grimly. "And that left me holding the Lang Textiles bag. Not that I didn't relish it at first. Putting my ideas to work was—and still is—a challenge. But I should have known what a toll it would take on my marriage."

What was he telling her? That his marriage hadn't been as perfect as it seemed? That he and Kelly weren't really the "golden couple" she had imagined? Eve groped in her memory for something Kelly might have told her that would help her to understand. As close as she and Kelly had grown, Kelly had never revealed any problems with her marriage. Kelly had always been cheerful and smiling, delighted about the baby, supportive of Derek. The only sour spot Eve could remember was that scene on the terrace when she had run away before they'd detected her presence, and even that had ended in tenderness between Kelly and Derek.

Derek's words bewildered Eve. But she knew by the deeply etched line between his eyes that he was tormented by something, something she knew very little about and perhaps never would. She didn't need to know, really. It was enough to know that Derek was flagellating himself for some real or imagined problem in his marriage and that he needed someone to talk to.

"Do you want to tell me about it?" she asked softly, forgetting her chill, forgetting everything but the human being who walked beside her and who seemed so lost and alone.

The faraway look in his eyes disappeared and was replaced by one of guardedness. He studied Eve's face, upturned toward him in the dusky shadows of early evening. Then his eyes dropped to the round protrusion of her belly, more noticeable than ever now that her hands, tucked into the cardigan's pockets for warmth, pulled the sweater fabric taut. He seemed to come to his senses.

"Not now," he said unhappily.

A chastened Eve walked faster, trying to keep up. Had she overstepped her bounds by asking Derek if he wanted to talk? But she could have sworn he'd been asking her, in his own oblique way, to listen!

Eve knew that only if Derek felt whole and well would he take this baby. *Let me find the best way to help him,* Eve thought fervently as she preceded him into the brightly lit foyer. And inside her, his child stirred, reminding her that time was growing short.

Chapter Seven

The telephone rang bright and early on this Saturday morning. Eve, who had been awake since seven and had just come in from retrieving the newspaper from its accustomed place beneath the boxwood hedge, scooped the ornate gilt receiver off the hall phone.

"Eve?"

She recognized the male voice immediately. "Doug! How in the world are you? I haven't talked with you in weeks!"

"I know, and we're going to remedy that. How about dinner tonight?"

"Nothing's wrong, is there? Al's not sick?"

"No, no. He's looking chipper, in fact. I think living at Nell's house agrees with him. But, well, do I need an excuse to see an old friend?"

Eve sank down on the bottom step, then regretted it. How would she get up again?

"Eve?"

"You don't need an excuse to see me, Doug, but I'm very pregnant. I'm not sure—"

"I have nothing more strenuous in mind than sitting in a quiet restaurant and lifting our forks to our faces.

Anyway, you can't turn me down. I have something important I want to talk with you about.''

"Important?"

"Important. To the mill workers who have been disabled by cotton dust. They need help, and no one knows it better than you. I need to discuss a couple of matters with you. Now how about it?''

"Since you put it that way, how can I refuse?" She smiled into the phone, picturing Doug's warm hazel eyes. She'd like to see him.

"I'll pick you up, say, at seven?"

"Could we go earlier? Since I've been pregnant, I don't like to eat that late. I mean, would you mind?"

Doug's voice was warm, caring. "Have I ever minded adjusting my plans for you? Remember the time I gave up a junior high school track meet to stay home and help you nurse a sick hamster? I was a sure bet to win the hurdles in that particular meet, too."

"I remember, all right! The hamster gave birth to a fine, healthy litter." Doug had been so gentle, so genuinely interested, that day. He hadn't changed a bit. That was the way he was now. Those qualities were what made him a good lawyer as well as a good friend.

"So after I gave up a track meet, picking you up at six o'clock instead of seven seems minor. I'll see you then, Eve."

"Okay," she said before replacing the phone carefully, thoughtfully.

"How's this for a casual weekend at home?"

Eve looked backward up the staircase to see Derek descending with a sheepish grin on his face. He wore a silver-gray pullover sweater with a white shirt under it.

"Very nice," she murmured approvingly. "Are you wearing that to work?"

Derek noticed that Eve, perched on the bottom step, looked strangely reflective. As usual, not one hair on her head was ruffled or out of place, and he was impressed all over again with the precision of her. Something leaped inside his chest, and for a moment it threatened to distract him. But he recovered when he recognized the warm interest in Eve's eyes.

"I," he announced, parading in front of her and giving his reflection in the hall mirror a thorough once-over, "am not going to work today."

"You always work on Saturdays," she pointed out, trying in vain to lurch off the bottom stair to a standing position.

"Yes, but not today. It's my favorite month of the year. And it's time for Oktoberfest. You and Aunt May are going with me. Aren't you, Aunt May?"

"What's that?" Aunt May said, wandering in from the kitchen. Eve thought it doubtful that Aunt May was wearing her hearing aid. Her expression was too dreamy.

"The Oktoberfest," Derek said loudly. "I've invited you and Eve to go with me."

Aunt May made a face. "That big German festival in the park? Where they have this big band with tubas blaring away so that I have to turn my hearing aid off and where everyone drinks beer? Derek, you should know by now that beer isn't my cup of tea." She fluttered her fingers in distaste and tottered through the living room toward the sun room.

Eve wrinkled her brow, trying not to laugh at Aunt May's mixed metaphor.

"Eve? How about you? Oktoberfest is really not as bad as Aunt May says it is. Instead of walking around the block again, why not come with me and do your walk-

HIT THE JACKPOT WITH HARLEQUIN

Scratch off the 3 windows to see if you've HIT THE JACKPOT

If 3 hearts appear—you get an exciting Mystery Gift in addition to our fabulous introductory offer of

4 Free Books Plus an Exquisite Pen & Watch Set

IT'S A JACKPOT OF A GREAT OFFER!

- 4 exciting Harlequin novels—Free!
- an LCD digital quartz watch with leather strap—Free!
- a stylish ballpoint pen—Free!
- a surprise mystery bonus that will delight you

But wait...there's even more!

Special Extras—Free!

You'll also get our monthly newsletter, packed with news on your favorite writers, upcoming books, and more. Four times a year, you'll receive our members' magazine, *Romance Digest.* Best of all, you'll receive periodically our special-edition *Harlequin Bestsellers* to preview for ten days without charge.

Money-saving home delivery!

Join Harlequin Reader Service and enjoy the convenience of previewing new, hot-off-the-press books every month, delivered right to your home. Each book is yours for only $2.25—25¢ less per book than what you pay in stores! Great Savings plus total convenience add up to a winning combination for you!

YOUR NO-RISK GUARANTEE

- There's no obligation to buy—and the free books and gifts are yours to keep forever.
- You pay the lowest price possible and receive books before they are to appear in stores.
- You may end your subscription anytime—just write and let us know.

TAKE A CHANCE ON ROMANCE–THEN COMPLETE AND MAIL YOUR SCORECARD TO CLAIM YOUR 7 HEARTWARMING GIFTS.

PLAYER'S SCORECARD

MAIL TODAY

FREE BOOKS
Free Pen & Watch Set

Did you win a mystery gift?

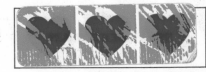

☐ YES! I hit the jackpot. I have affixed my 3 hearts. Please send me my 4 Harlequin American Romance novels free, plus my free watch, free pen and free mystery gift. Then send me four books every month as they come off the press, and bill me at just $2.25 per book (25¢ less than retail), with no extra charges for shipping and handling. If I am not completely satisfied, I may return a shipment and cancel at any time. The 7 gifts remain mine to keep.

NAME

ADDRESS   APT.

CITY

PROV./STATE   POSTAL CODE/ZIP

ing in the park? You must be ready for a change of scene.'' His smile was engaging.

"They really should go," Aunt May quavered loudly from the sun room as though she were talking into a void. "Derek so seldom gets away from work. Eve ought to go with him." Louise was humming to herself in the kitchen, so Eve knew Aunt May was talking to herself. It was hard to get used to hearing herself be talked about to no one. This habit of Aunt May's annoyed her this morning more than usual. And not being able to get herself up from the bottom step annoyed her even more.

"If I can't get up from this step, how am I going to manage Oktoberfest?" Eve said irritably. "Derek, could you lend me a hand?"

Derek knit his brows at her. He hadn't noticed that she'd been trying to get up. "Why didn't you say something?" he demanded, hauling her to her feet.

"Well, it's embarrassing not to be able to do things for myself," she answered scowling.

He'd never seen her disgruntled. For a moment, this new demeanor startled him. Then he grinned. Of course. All pregnant women got this way. Isn't that what the popular literature said? He was lucky she hadn't asked him to go out in the middle of the night to buy pickles and ice cream. But that was silly. Eve would never do that, although it was something wives asked of their husbands. But their situation was not that of husband and wife.

He cleared his throat. "If you get stuck somewhere at Oktoberfest, I'll help you up. Promise," he said, sketching an absurd "cross my heart and hope to die" across the chest of his new gray sweater.

And so, cajoled by Aunt May, urged by Derek, Eve went upstairs and dressed in a pair of rust-colored ma-

ternity slacks and an amber-colored mohair sweater with
a big cowl neck that almost covered the lobes of her ears.
It was the shoes that were a problem. None of her shoes
fit, her feet had swollen so. She finally settled on a pair
of black corduroy bedroom slippers that looked exactly
like black corduroy bedroom slippers and would fool no
one. She, who always wanted colors to match or at least
complement each other, who winced when people wore
sandals with tailored suits or white shoes with a black
dress, didn't really care about this today.

When she was ready, she found Derek waiting outside
in the driveway, noisily warming up the Corvette's engine.

"You look marvelous," he said as she opened the car
door, and then his eyes fell to her feet as she folded herself downward into the low-slung sports car and tucked
her feet in after her.

"It's probably out of line for me to mention this," he
said, "but haven't you forgotten to put on your shoes?"

"Unfortunately, these *are* my shoes," she said.
"They're all that fits anymore." She regarded her ill-clad
feet as though they belonged to someone else.

"Your feet are *that* swollen?" Derek looked aghast.

"I'm afraid so. It's all right. These are comfortable."

"But Eve, you have to have shoes," he said, trying to
reason with her.

"I do," she insisted. "These." She grinned at him just
to show him that she didn't think her swollen feet were a
serious matter, at least not as serious as he seemed to
consider them.

"Mmm—" was all he said, and his mouth was set in a
grim line as he rammed the car into gear and backed out
of the driveway.

Minutes later they rolled to a stop in front of a porti-coed shoe store, one in which Eve had never dared even to browse because the prices were so high.

"Derek?" she ventured as he slammed his car door and came around to her side, yanking the door open.

"Come on," he said, and then his eyes softened as he looked down at her. His voice was gentle when he spoke again. "We're going to buy you some shoes."

"I don't need—"

"Yes, you do." He leaned down and lifted her hand off the edge of the seat. "Need some help getting up?"

A gentle tug, and Eve found herself rising out of the seat, found herself being hastened inside the store, found herself sitting in a blue velvet chair, being fitted with butter-soft leather shoes, pair after pair, by a sales-woman with a well-modulated voice.

"I don't need all these," Eve stage-whispered franti-cally when the saleswoman disappeared to look for an-other size in one of the styles. Derek still held her hand, she realized belatedly.

"I'll decide what you need," he said firmly.

The saleswoman returned.

"She'd like to try another pair like those suede ones. No, not those, the others. In brown. Or rust, if you have it."

"Certainly," the saleswoman said, sliding a shoe on Eve's foot. It didn't fit. The saleswoman disappeared again.

"Derek!" Eve's eyes were round, her expression one of amazement. The saleswoman came back and inserted Eve's foot into another pair.

"Walk in those," Derek commanded. Finally, he re-leased her hand, as if he'd just noticed that he held it. He dropped it as though it burned him.

Eve stood up and trod gingerly across the well-padded blue carpet to the mirror. They were beautifully made shoes of Italian workmanship with hand stitching. She could never afford them in a million years.

"I can't buy these," she hissed at him.

He pulled his eyes away from her feet and lifted them slowly to her face. Then he lowered them to take in her legs, slim beneath the rust-colored slacks, and the way her sweater fell loosely over her wide hips, and the contour of it so gently cupping her breasts.

"I'm buying them for you," he said, but the words wanted to expand in his throat, choking off air, hurting him.

Before she could object, he handed over a credit card and signed a sales ticket.

"She'll wear those," he said, pointing to a pair of rust-colored gillies, and then the shoes were being laced on her feet, and she was still speechless.

"You shouldn't have done that," she said when they were back in the Corvette, speeding through streets where defrocked trees raised spindly branches to a piercingly blue windswept sky. "My slippers were all right."

"Not if we're going to dance the polka at Oktoberfest," he said, slanting a look at her out of the corners of his eyes.

"Polka! Dance the polka! Derek Lang, you must be joking!"

"It's part of the festival. A tradition," he said as though that explained everything. He slid the Corvette neatly into a parking space between a Ford and a Chrysler.

"Wow, that's a nice car, mister," said an admiring kid whose eyes were round as saucers in his coffee-colored face.

"Thanks," Derek said, slamming his door and hurrying around to Eve's side. He handed Eve carefully out of the Corvette before he knelt to address the child.

"Do you live around here?" Derek asked in a conspiratorial whisper.

The boy nodded shyly, pointing at a neat red-brick house across the street.

"Well, do you think you could keep an eye on my car for an hour or two?"

"Sure!" the boy exclaimed, overwhelmed.

"Then here's a couple of dollars. Maybe you could buy a Matchbox car with it—a Corvette model."

"Sure!" The boy's whole face lit up.

"Good." Derek stood and slapped the boy on the back—good buddies now.

"Why did you do that?" Eve asked curiously as they wound their way through the crowd. "Your car doesn't need watching. Not here. It's a safe neighborhood."

"He was cute," Derek said, dismissing the subject.

You were so good with that little boy, she wanted to say. But she didn't. Only it was hard to understand why Derek wouldn't want his own child, who would perhaps be a little boy who loved Corvettes and liked being slapped on the back by a father like Derek Lang.

The brass band blared out German tunes, bravely rather than skillfully, but no one cared about the musicians' lack of skill. The colorful milling throng surged around the park bandstand, two thousand barrels of specially imported German beer flowed freely, and young men in lederhosen abounded.

"You didn't wear your short pants," Eve murmured, looking down at Derek's legs.

"Short pants? Ha! You just got me out of a three-piece suit, Eve. Don't expect short pants until next year!" He laughed down at her, looking genuinely happy for the first time in a long time.

Without asking her if she wanted it, he bought Eve a plate of apple strudel.

"I shouldn't eat this." She sighed before digging into it, and her gusto in eating pleased him.

For himself, Derek bought a bowl of sauerkraut from a vendor, trying to eat it neatly but unable to stop the strings of it from dripping down his chin, and Eve laughed so hard at the sight that she had to clutch her abdomen.

"You're all right, aren't you?" he asked anxiously, and she nodded, wiping tears from her eyes. The ever-meticulous, ever-proper Derek Lang, wearing a sweater and allowing sauerkraut to drip down his chin!

A fat lady yodeled. A dance club climbed up on a wooden platform and performed a German folk dance with lots of hollering and knee slapping. Afterward couples drifted onto the platform and began to dance. This festival, so ethnic, reminded her of Greek festivals attended in long-ago years with her mother and father and assorted aunts, uncles and cousins.

"Are you watching them dance? Getting some pointers?" Derek asked her, taking in the sparkle of her eyes, the tapping of her foot in time to the music. The cool, crisp air had brought a bloom to her cheeks, and she looked as though she fairly itched to dance. Was she a good dancer? He would find out.

"Yes, I'm watching, but don't expect me to get up there and make a fool of myself," she told him tartly.

"How about a waltz?" he said when the band began a new piece, a swirling Viennese number.

"A waltz?" she said doubtfully.

"Come on; let's try it," he said, pulling her to her feet. "We might as well test-drive those new shoes of yours."

Against her better judgment, she let him propel her toward the dance floor. It was with misgivings that she let him surround what was left of her waist with his arm and hold her hand high with his other hand, moving her to meet the music surely and smoothly.

And it was amazing how her new bulk flowed along with him, how easily he guided her around the floor, gently, soothingly, making her feel dainty and feminine and, well, like a young girl again.

"You dance nicely," he said in his best dancing-school voice. Of course he had gone to dancing school. It was what young gentlemen of his social stature did.

"I have a good partner," she replied easily. He held her far away, not close, which was the correct position for the proper execution of the waltz. As far as her stomach protruded, it did not touch him. She would have been embarrassed if it had.

"Let me know if you get tired. We can sit down any time you like."

She smiled up at him, the tree branches above them reflecting in the starry irises of her eyes as they whirled around the dance floor. "I wish Aunt May had come," she said.

"I'm glad she didn't" was his reply, and it was uttered with an intensity that surprised her. But there was no time to answer, because the band jumped without pause into an ear-splitting, foot-stamping polka. And before she knew it, she was doing the polka, too, slightly out of breath, her face flushed, hanging on to Derek for dear life and loving every minute of it.

"Are you okay?" he shouted at one point, and she was; she was light on her feet, buoyant in his arms, laughing back at him with an energy imparted by crisp air, good food and energetic music. When the dance was over, Eve, caught up in the spirit of the moment, dropped Derek a ridiculous little curtsy.

Someone shouted, and a little girl standing at the edge of the dance floor, waiting for her parents, let go of her helium balloon and began to wail over her loss. Derek, seeing what had happened, stopped the balloon man and bought the child a shiny new silver one. And Eve thought, *He's sensitive to children. He likes them.* And she wondered why he didn't want his own child, the child who even now floated free in her womb, dancing to the music that was her heart.

They ate big, soft, hot pretzels with mustard on them, and Derek drank a beer. Eve listened happily to the oompah-pah music, and she, who had been burdened with problem after problem for longer than she cared to remember, realized that she had never had such a good time in her life.

Then, when the sun dropped behind the lacy branches of the trees and the air cooled accordingly, Derek said, "Let's go," and he held her hand as he led her through the crowd to the car. She knew he held her hand so that she wouldn't get lost, so that he could blaze a trail through the crush of people for her, but she liked the connectedness of it, and when he let go of her hand, she missed its warmth.

The little boy they had seen earlier was perched on a tree stump, steadfastly watching the Corvette.

"Hi, sport," Derek said, tousling the boy's fuzzy hair. The boy regarded Derek as though he were nothing less than a god.

"Do you know what I want you to do?" Derek asked him.

"Uh-uh."

"Go over there—" he pointed to a balloon seller on the edge of the crowd "—and tell that man to give you the biggest, reddest balloon he's got." He slipped a five-dollar bill into the boy's pocket.

The boy clutched his pocket and broke into a wide grin. "Gee, thanks, mister. Gee, thanks." He scampered away across the dun-colored grass.

The Corvette hummed toward Myers Park, and Derek slipped a cassette into the tape deck. "It's not oompah-pah music," he apologized, "but it's not bad."

"Not bad," she agreed, leaning her head back against the headrest. "Thanks for taking me, Derek. I had a wonderful time."

"It's not over, you know. I'm treating you to dinner."

She didn't speak for so long that he knew something was wrong.

"I—I can't, Derek. I have other plans."

It hadn't occurred to him that Eve might have something else to do. She was such a homebody; she never went out.

"I'm sorry," he said. "I didn't think you'd be busy."

"Well, usually I'm not. But an old friend asked me to go out, and I said I would."

"That's all right. We can make it another time." But he knew it wasn't all right, and another time wouldn't be this time, with their euphoria coasting them along on a natural high for the rest of the evening.

"I wish we could," she said lamely.

"It's all right," he repeated a little too sharply. If he couldn't be with Eve, he'd have to stay home alone with Aunt May. The prospect did nothing to cheer him.

Eve remained silent, staring out the window, her shoulders hunched down in the seat. The joy in being together had evaporated, and the atmosphere seemed depressingly flat. Well, he could call up someone, go out, anyway. The Kleinsts—but they'd only try to push Debby Kleinst's sister off on him. Jay Stanley—although Jay would have a date, no doubt, on a Saturday night.

They barely spoke, and at the house Eve hurried directly upstairs—to dress for her evening out, he supposed. Derek mixed himself a drink and sat in the darkening living room, staring gloomily at Kelly's picture over the mantel, waiting for the ring of the doorbell, suspecting that Eve's "friend" would be a man. Why was he so sure of this? Why didn't he think she'd be going out with a girlfriend?

In due time the doorbell rang, and Louise answered it. The male voice that greeted her, that sounded pleased when Eve came down the stairs, was no surprise. Derek knew that he should go out to greet Eve's visitor, but he remained rooted to his chair. When the door closed after the two of them, he listened for Eve's clear laughter floating back on the wind, but he didn't hear it.

When the sound of the car was gone, he got up and poured himself a healthy splash of bourbon. Then he slumped in his chair again and lifted it to his lips.

"She's a good dancer," he told the gold-rimmed picture of Kelly, and then he realized he was doing what Aunt May was always doing—talking to thin air. He hoped Louise hadn't heard him, sitting here in the dark, talking to a picture of his wife. She'd think he was loony for sure.

Why should he find it so depressing that Eve had gone out to dinner with another man?

And he wondered if she'd worn the shoes he'd bought her.

As THEY WAITED for their dinner to be served at Hearthside, a steak house on Albemarle Road, Doug said, "It's like this, Eve. If we don't do something for brown-lung victims, who will?"

"Not the companies, evidently." Eve's tone was bitter.

"Not the companies. They're dragging their feet even though they've been told by the federal government to clean up the cotton dust. In the meantime, we need to educate the workers. There are people in Wrayville who have valid claims. Our job is to find them."

"And once we find them?"

"Many of these workers don't know how to go about filing a claim. Some of them are too sick to care. But they can be helped, Eve. We can help them, you and I."

"How?"

"When we locate people who have valid claims, we'll get all the claims together and file them with the state industrial commission instead of Wray Mills. It's a viable option, you know. If a company disputes a claim and refuses to reach a settlement, we're entitled to seek an award from the commission. Wray Mills has been uncooperative, to say the least, so why not go to the industrial commission? It'll be hard for the commission to ignore so many claims filed in a bloc, especially if I threaten legal action."

"I can come to Wrayville one day a week. Would that help?"

"Sure. I've had a special phone line installed in my office, a sort of brown-lung hotline. Your father and Nell Baker take turns coming in to answer it and to field questions workers have about the disease. I need someone who is good at working with people to help workers fill out forms, to help decide if they have a case. That's you, Eve, if you'll do it." His eyes burned into her with the fervor of one committed to a cause.

"You know I will." She smiled at him warmly. This was something she wanted to do. It would ease her feeling that she had given up on the problem of byssinosis when she undertook this pregnancy, and that wasn't what she had meant to do at all.

"Thanks," Doug said. "Can you come to work Monday?"

"I don't see why not. I could come every Monday, I suppose."

"Of course, if you have something else planned—"

"No. My days are free."

Doug considered her for a long interval, carefully keeping his eyes far removed from the rising mound beneath her loose smock. For a moment she felt a twinge of sadness over what might have been between her and Doug if things had been different. Her pregnancy—and its effect on her life—had changed the way she responded to Doug. Now she couldn't imagine his being anything more to her than he was at this moment—a very close and very dear friend.

"Do you mind if I ask you something, Eve?"

She was surprised. "Of course not."

"Are you happy there? Do they treat you well?"

"Doug! You make it sound as though I was kidnapped, as though Derek and Aunt May treat me like a—well, like a servant!"

"Do they?"

"Oh, Doug. Of course not. Derek is—pleasant," she said lamely, wondering how else she would describe him. Pleasant? He had been more than that today, for instance. But she had no reason to go into that now with

Doug. She plunged on, mindful of the way Doug's eyes assessed her. "And Aunt May is a dear."

"There's been no more talk about an abortion?"

"No," she said, and drew a breath to say more, but then she stopped.

"What is it, Eve?" Doug knew her too well; he sensed that there was more to this story than he'd been told.

"Derek still hasn't said he'll keep the baby." Her eyes, sad and anxious, met his over the expanse of blue tablecloth.

"So what happens to the baby when it's born?"

"I don't know. I don't know." Eve bit her bottom lip.

"If he doesn't want the baby, do you still intend to raise it yourself?"

"Yes," she whispered. She let her shoulders rise, then fall helplessly. "I don't know what else I could do."

"Put it up for adoption," he said gently. "That's one alternative you should consider."

She shook her head slowly. "I couldn't. Not now. Not after it's been a part of me. I can feel this baby, Doug. It turns somersaults inside me. Its tiny knees poke me in the ribs at night. It hears my voice, is lulled to sleep by the music I play on my radio. Oh, Doug, the only person I could give this baby up to is its natural father."

"And he's said nothing about keeping it?"

"Nothing. And he's good with children, Doug. You should have seen him today with the children at the park. He was—"

"You went to the park with him?"

"To Oktoberfest. He had to practically drag me, but Aunt May insisted, and I—" How could she explain what a wonderful time she'd had with Derek? "He's—he's a good man, Doug. I don't want you to think he isn't."

"If he is as good as you say he is, he won't let you undertake the raising of this child by yourself." He spoke softly; he truly cared about Eve. He couldn't stand for anyone to take advantage of her.

"Somehow I'll make him see that he wants this baby. Somehow I will." The fierceness of her words startled Eve herself.

"How?" Doug wondered out loud.

"I'm not sure," she said carefully, but she remembered the close feeling she had shared with Derek that afternoon. As they grew to know each other better, perhaps he would listen to her, would begin to see reason. They couldn't go on avoiding the topic indefinitely, after all.

A discussion was inevitable. But apparently it was going to be up to Eve to bring it about.

"Good luck," Doug said softly.

"I'm going to need it," she replied, not knowing at the time how true her statement was.

Chapter Eight

Derek cast about in his mind for the thing to do next, but for the life of him it wouldn't come to him. There was no plan.

God knows he had tried to make one, but every time he thought he had it figured out, something happened to distract him. Like stumbling upon Eve in the L & D Cafe. Like her dazzling smile when she danced the polka with him. Such events made all plans irrelevant.

This baby. There it was, like it or not. It was amazing, really, to think that the impersonal globe of fullness under Eve's clothing was a living, growing child.

Aunt May made such a fuss over Eve's pregnancy. She was always worrying about whether Eve napped every day or wore her boots with the nonskid soles when she went out on damp days. "I wish she'd eat more," he heard Aunt May say to no one in particular when she was out poking around in the pansy bed one day. "I wish he'd *talk* about the baby."

Derek, on this occasion, had ducked guiltily beneath the grape arbor, bare of leaves now and affording little concealment, before Aunt May detected his presence. He had little doubt that she was speaking of him and his refusal to even mention the child.

Well, what was he supposed to do? He didn't want the baby now; that was all. He felt responsible for it, and for Eve. He'd sheltered her under his roof, hadn't he? And here she was, a small, bright presence to whom he had become ridiculously attached in so short a time.

Those children at the festival in the park—the little girl who lost her balloon and the kid who'd watched the Corvette for him. Cute. He liked kids. But the responsibility! Their illnesses! Their education, their clothing needs, their table manners, for goodness' sake! PTA meetings. Sewing pink satin ribbons on a girl's toe shoes. Making a pinewood derby race car for Cub Scouts. How could he take all that on by himself? With Kelly it would have been fine. Kelly managed things so well. But a child needed two whole parents, deserved to be brought up by two parents rather than a busy textile executive and an eccentric great-aunt. And Kelly was gone.

Instead, there was Eve, who stared at him with her big brown gazelle eyes and left so much unsaid. He thought about the things she might have said at times when he was away from her, for instance at work, when he should have been concentrating on working up his presentation before the governor's task force on textiles.

Eve—she'd stayed out late with that fellow, that friend she went out to dinner with. And at a time when she needed her sleep, too. It angered him when she'd wandered in after midnight. Where had she been all that time? At the guy's apartment? In a bar? Both of those seemed unlikely places for Eve to be.

He'd started working straight through lunch in the days after Kelly died so he wouldn't have to go home, as he always had before at lunchtime. But on the Monday after Oktoberfest, he'd careened home in his Corvette, only to be disappointed that Eve wasn't there.

Aunt May found him in the kitchen, staring out the window at the driveway where Eve's Volkswagen should have been parked. Aunt May brightened immediately.

"Why, what are you doing home, Derek?"

"Looking for Eve," he said moodily.

"Well, you can't *leave*," she said in annoyance. "You just got here."

"Not leave. *Eve*."

"Oh, Eve. She's not here."

"Ye gods," he muttered under his breath before freeing himself of Aunt May and rushing off to a drug store lunch counter where he disconsolately made do with a soggy cheeseburger.

What was this private life of Eve's about which he knew so little? Where did she go? Whom did she see?

"I don't think you should be driving yourself places," he told her seriously that night after dinner. They had been watching television, with Eve in charge of the remote control. He spoke during a commercial featuring a bald man whose shiny head was being sectioned off with Magic Markers. To his relief, Eve clicked the TV set off just as the man turned around with a whole new head of hair.

The silence was deafening.

"Dr. Perry says I can drive right up until the last minute unless something goes wrong," she said at last and with a cheery smile.

"But I worry about you," he said, as though that should be enough to make Eve hang up her car keys for the duration.

"Do you, Derek?" She regarded him calmly with a level gaze.

"Well, of course," he said, wishing suddenly that he hadn't begun this.

"I'm glad to hear it. Because that must mean you're concerned about the baby, too."

"I suppose so," he allowed cautiously. He didn't like the glint in her eyes.

"I'm concerned, too, Derek. About what's going to happen to the baby after it's born."

"I think it should be put up for adoption. There's a shortage of babies, and somebody out there is looking for a healthy infant."

"You would put Kelly's baby up for adoption?" Her voice was softly incredulous.

"Do we have to talk about this?" Impatiently, he stood and walked to the window. Outside, cars whooshed silently by the house. The air hung heavy with the smoke from neighborhood fireplaces. He'd have to lay a fire in the fireplace soon himself. He felt a definite chill in here.

"Derek, how long are you going to avoid this issue?"

"Eve, I—"

"This baby was a wanted child once," she reminded him in a troubled tone. "Your and Kelly's child. Your firstborn, Derek."

She almost didn't catch the murmured words he spoke. "Not my firstborn," he said.

"What?"

"Not my firstborn. Kelly was pregnant once. Didn't she tell you?"

"N-no," Eve breathed, sinking down on the couch. "No."

He turned to face her, his eyes dark. "She was pregnant. Oh, it was before her hysterectomy. She lost the baby in her seventh month."

"I'm so sorry. I didn't know." She sat perfectly still on the couch while Derek paced the floor, agitated now.

"She was so happy to be having a baby. *We* were so happy. And I went to the Far East on a trade mission for the textile board, and Kelly was here with Aunt May, and she tried to lift a heavy chair to move it, and she felt pains and was rushed by ambulance to the hospital. If I had been here, I would have done that lifting for her, but no, she couldn't wait. I could have come home a week early. I wanted to, in fact, but at the last minute the coordinator of the mission had to put a report together and I stayed to help him. I knew Kelly was all right at home; I mean I *thought* I knew it, and she wasn't. And she had the miscarriage all alone, with no one but Aunt May, and I wasn't even in the country. Didn't get home until days afterward." He lifted his hands helplessly, and there was no mistaking the anguish in his eyes.

"Derek, chances are you could have done nothing to prevent it," she said comfortingly.

"That's what they all said. But I still felt responsible. Because I had the chance to come home, you see, and I didn't take it. Because I wanted to be the boy wonder, not just a tagalong on the trade mission. I wanted to show my stuff and prove that I could wheel and deal as well as the rest of them, even though I got my position and my power by inheritance, not because of anything I did to earn it." His mouth curled downward at the edges in self-disdain.

"Oh, Derek" was all she could say. He sank down on the footstool and stared up at her, his voice hollow.

"And afterward she had the hysterectomy because of complications; she was never all right again after that miscarriage. Poor Kelly. It was very hard on her. But she never changed; she was always cheerful and happy, and I tried to forget by burying myself in work, and I neglected her. Work was a convenient excuse—I was never there for her.''

Eve's hand moved slowly of its own volition to touch his bowed head ever so gently. "It's all right, Derek," she said soothingly, softly. "It's all right. You can't go on blaming yourself." She couldn't comprehend the weight of guilt under which Derek Lang had lived for so long. But maybe she could alleviate it.

"It's not all right," he whispered as her thumb began to caress his jawline. He closed his eyes under the comfort of it. It had been so long since anyone had touched him in tenderness. He lifted his own hand and held hers where it rested against the lean, hard planes of his face, and the inside of his arms ached with the yearning of wanting more of her comfort, more of her touch.

He had loved Kelly so much that he didn't think he could love another woman that way again, but suddenly he wanted to. It was more than an awakening of desire. It was a longing for all the other things love meant to him, for companionship, for parallel thoughts, for caring and nurturing. But he didn't want to mix these longings up with Eve, with the way he felt about her, with his wistful wish for her gentle, abiding warmth.

Still, his arms reached out to her, went around her slim, fragile shoulders, and his head came to rest on her broad, curving breast. The scent of her was fragrant and sweet, filling his nostrils and lingering at the back of his throat. The skin of her cheek was as soft as a butterfly wing upon his, and a swinging arc of silky hair, black as midnight, feathered across his temple. His heart was eased by her.

She murmured something, lots of things, but the words were only shapes and not real. The comfort was real, the comfort of Eve, and she herself was real. Without thinking, he sought her lips. They were pliable beneath his, sensitive, responsive. He could have gone on kissing her—it would have been easy—but as he drew even closer to her, the hard, round knob of her pregnancy pressed against him. Startled, he pulled away. He hadn't expected the child to feel so hard. He thought it would be soft, like Eve herself. But there it was, between the two of them, implacable in its presence.

"I'm sorry," he said with dignity. "I shouldn't have done that."

Eve's eyes were round and soft and vulnerable. "Derek, it's—"

"No," he said harshly. "No." He whirled away from her and walked swiftly from the room.

It was only afterward that he wondered what she had been about to say.

"EVIE, EVIE, you look like a million bucks!" Her father held her away from him, his eyes sparkling.

"Thanks, Dad," she said, laughing. It was so good to see him again, and he wasn't wheezing as much as he had been; she was sure of it.

"Look, this is where you'll work," he said, showing her a scuffed gray metal desk that had somehow been wedged in between the door and the table in the waiting room of Doug's office where her father and Nell took phone calls on the brown-lung hotline.

"Where'd you get the desk?" she wanted to know.

"Oh, Nell dragged me to a garage sale Saturday," he said sheepishly. "We paid ten dollars for it."

"It's a bargain," she told him, sitting down in the swivel chair and opening and closing the metal drawers.

"Claim forms, pencils, pens; everything you'll need is right there," Al said proudly. "I've got two people coming in this afternoon just to talk to you. I told them, 'My daughter will know if you've got a claim or not.'"

"And if she doesn't, I will," Doug added, ambling in from the inner office and perching on the side of Eve's desk.

The outside door swung open with a blast of chill November air. "Excuse me, is this the place to go if you know about a case of brown lung?" The woman who stepped inside rubbed raw red hands together; she wore a defeated look.

"Yes," Eve said, smiling encouragingly. "We can help you."

"It's about my brother," she said worriedly. "I keep telling him, 'Sam, you've got some of that brown-lung disease.' But he ain't so sure. Says its a cold that hangs on and on. But a cold shouldn't last over a year, should it?"

Doug and her father discreetly withdrew. "How long has your brother worked in the mill?" Eve asked briskly, poising her pencil over a yellow legal pad.

"All his life. Since he was fifteen. Like all the rest of us."

And so Eve jotted down the details of a life story that was to become depressingly familiar in the next few weeks. A job in the mill, entered into in good faith when the employee was young. A surfeit of cotton dust, dust everywhere, dust that clung to clothes and nostrils, eyebrows and eyelashes, ingested and inhaled until the body rebelled.

Byssinosis. Brown-lung disease. A malady that many textile manufacturers claimed did not exist. A disease for which even some of the biggest, best-known textile companies refused to acknowledge responsibility.

"It's depressing," Doug said later over a cup of coffee in the nearby Wray Cafe. "I wonder how long the mill management can go on ignoring it?"

"A long time," Eve said. "No one makes them comply with government regulations. The textile industry wields so much clout that government officials are discouraged from insisting on safeguards in every mill, everywhere. In the meantime, many workers get sick and die without ever getting around to filing a claim. It's sad."

"We're making progress, though," he said, looking optimistic. "Thanks for helping, Eve."

"I couldn't *not* help," she confessed. "Not the way Al is. Whatever we do, whatever progress we make, it's bound to benefit Al. He looks so much better, Doug. I think it's because he has something important to do, answering that hotline."

Doug laughed. "I'm not so sure it's the hotline as much as it's the widow Baker. You should hear them in there when she arrives to take over his phone shift. She always shows up early, and they sit in my waiting room and laugh and talk like two kids."

"Really? That's amazing!"

"Yeah, I know. Nell and Al have known each other for years, but I don't think they ever *really* knew each other until Al moved in with her."

Eve grew suddenly quiet. It was much like her situation with Derek, she thought. She was getting to know him so well, now that they lived in the same household.

Getting to know him well but not yet well enough. Not well enough to convince him to do the right thing by this baby.

"WHERE IS SHE?" Derek fumed, pacing up and down the foyer. It was Monday, and Eve wasn't home yet. She was never home when he got in from work on Mondays.

"He wants to know where she is," Aunt May explained to the air.

"She should have been home before this storm started. The roads are icing up."

"What did you say?"

"The roads are icing up," Derek said, peering out one of the sidelights.

"Rising up?"

"*Icing* up," he repeated, none too patiently. Then, more kindly, he said, "Why don't you help Louise get dinner on the table, Aunt May?"

Aunt May teetered off obediently, and Derek resumed his vigil. He supposed he wouldn't worry so much if it weren't for what happened to Kelly. Now he distrusted damp pavements.

He interrupted his pacing to switch on the TV in the den. The program was interrupted by a weather bulletin.

"Motorists are warned to drive carefully," the patent-haired announcer intoned. "With temperatures below the freezing point and a light drizzle falling on Charlotte tonight, ice will be a hazard on area roads."

Morosely, Derek opened the front door and stood framed in the doorway for a moment, as if such action would conjure up Eve's VW at the end of the street. When it didn't, he went back inside and slammed the door, hard.

"Is that Eve?" Aunt May called from the kitchen.

"No," he replied.

He considered phoning the police to see if any accidents had been reported in the area. Which was ridiculous. She wasn't late, not in the strictest sense of the word. How could she be late when he never knew what time to expect her home? Well, he could hardly impose a curfew on her. But didn't he have a right to know, when she wasn't there, where she was and whom she was with?

He supposed not. Still. The very fact that she lived in this household gave him some right to know that she was safe. Didn't it?

He dug in the bow-front chest on which the hall telephone sat and surfaced with a dog-eared phone book. He looked up Hospitals in the Yellow Pages. He considered calling an emergency room. Which one, though?

Not a very good idea, so he shelved it and the phone book, as well. He could just imagine calling an emergency room and telling the answering nurse, "I'm looking for Eve Triopolous," and the nurse would say with annoyance, "What relationship, please," and he'd answer blankly, "What do you mean?" and the nurse would say impatiently "What relationship—sister, wife, mother, niece, grandmother?" and he would hang up. Because she was no relation.

Mother of my child. The words came out of nowhere, focused on the deepest recesses of his mind and branded themselves there. For the first time, he confronted the fact that his tender feelings for her were more than that.

Eve was the mother of his child, and he panicked with the fear of one who had already lost the most important person in the world to the whims of the weather. The weather had been responsible for the accident that had taken Kelly's life, and he could not bear the thought that Eve was endangered in any way by the capricious weather.

"I'm going to go out and find her," he said, reason eroded by his terror.

"I'm not sure that's such a—" Aunt May ventured with startled blue eyes. "Why don't you just—"

But he'd already yanked on his Burberry raincoat. He raced out the back door through the garage to where his Corvette was parked in the driveway.

He'd forgotten the key, so he had to run back inside, all the way upstairs, where his car keys reposed in blessed unknowing innocence on his dresser. He grabbed them and took off down the stairs, taking them two at a time all the way down.

Out the door again, then fumbling with the lock on the Corvette. It was iced over, and he cursed. Dropping his keys, scooping them up off the slick pavement of the driveway, his fingers shook.

And then the distinctive metallic chatter of the VW's engine. He looked up through the misty drizzle illuminated by the headlights. A rainbow surrounded the car for a brief moment until Eve shut the lights and engine off and stepped blithely out into the rain.

She was surprised to see Derek there.

"Oh," she said, and he could have sworn that the simple one-syllable word wore shades of disappointment it had never worn before. "You're going out."

"No. Not now. I was going to go looking for you." Mist beaded on her eyelashes. It glittered in the overhead outside light.

"Looking for me? What on earth for?" She stared at him through the mist.

His eyes dropped to the gourdlike shape beneath her raincoat.

"I was worried," he said.

"Oh, Derek. You shouldn't have been." She gestured at the bag of groceries in the back of the Volkswagen. "I stopped off at the store. I've taken over the grocery shopping. You'll be pleased to know that I've bought a beef roast for Sunday dinner. No more pickled sausages, I'm afraid. And guess what—I bought you a package of cheese doodles.'' She smiled, then laughed. "And here we stand out here in the rain like two people who don't have enough sense to come in out of it." She whirled, light on her feet, and his heart flew to his throat.

"Careful," he said tightly, grasping her arm above the elbow. "Don't prance like that! You could fall. Do you have on your boots with the nonskid soles?"

"Prance! Derek, my prancing days are over. And yes, these are the proper boots for the weather. Honestly, you're getting as bad as Aunt May! Look, why don't you carry in that bag of groceries?"

But thinking about what might have happened to her, about how worried he had been, Derek remained serious all through dinner, all through the evening, when he barely left Eve's side while she watched television and then dozed.

Eve couldn't help dozing, but she wasn't really asleep. She was only resting. It had been a difficult day for her in Doug's office. Two people had showed up who clearly had no brown-lung claim but were obviously trying to take advantage of what they perceived as a possible cash handout. It turned out that one had had asthma ever since she'd been a small child and the other one was faking entirely. It had taken more than an hour in each case to wheedle the real information out of them, and then she'd been angry. Because, as she told Doug afterward, such people were harming the chances of workers who really had contracted brown-lung disease. Plus, advocates of help for brown-lung victims didn't need any fakers. There were enough residents of Wrayville who were sick with the real thing.

"Anybody want to play Trivial Pursuit?"

Eve jerked awake to see Aunt May standing in front of her, holding the two blue Trivial Pursuit boxes and playing board in her hands.

"Not now, Aunt May," Derek said peremptorily. "Eve's tired."

"Oh, but Derek," Eve said gently as a look of disappointment slid over Aunt May's pudgy features. "I think I'd like to play Trivial Pursuit. Yes, I really think I would." She gazed mutely at Derek, and he knew she was tired but was thinking of Aunt May's feelings.

His heart softened. "Just a short game, then," he said, and warmth crept into his voice in spite of himself.

They set up the board on the card table that Kelly had prized so much, a cherry-wood antique with inlaid ivory marquetry. Aunt May hummed as she distributed the markers and the single die with which the game was played.

Derek studied Eve covertly as they took their places around the table. Her dark hair shone blue-black under the light from the lamp, and her fingers, with their fine white skin, were so smooth as to look disjointed, like the fingers of a porcelain doll, until she moved her marker along the playing board and proved that her fingers had joints, after all. Derek sat close enough to her to sense a scent reminiscent of white violets. Surely white violets had a scent? Or if they didn't, this is what they would smell like, this heady sweetness that permeated her hair and filled his nostrils and tasted so good when he kissed her.

Kissed her. He had actually kissed her. It had been crazy to do that, crazy. *He* had been crazy. It never should have happened.

Her low laugh at something Aunt May had said, something that wasn't all that funny, chimed with the mellow timbre of English church bells.

It was his turn, and he tossed the die. And she asked him the next question, her voice cool and flowing, draping syllables over the air rather than stabbing through it like Kelly's.

"What?" he had to say, pulling himself with great effort out of his reverie.

"Your question is 'What baseball player advised, "Avoid running at all times"?'"

He had to stop and think. He wasn't with this game, not at all.

"Well," he said, because he had heard the quotation before. But now all he could do was listen to the echoes of Eve's soothing voice asking the question, and he couldn't for the life of him think of the appropriate answer.

"Do you give up, Derek?" Aunt May asked eagerly.

"I give up," he said.

"Satchel Paige," Eve said triumphantly, dropping the question-and-answer card in the back of the box. "Your turn, Aunt May."

Satchel Paige. Of course. Satchel Paige had been one of Derek's favorite philosophers, and a great pitcher to boot.

What else had Satchel Paige said? Something like "Don't look back. Something may be gaining on you."

Yeah. The old fellow was right, and he hadn't been talking only about baseball.

Something was gaining on Derek, all right. Contentment, sitting here with Eve and Aunt May so cozy in the haven of his home, with the weather surging against the window in sheets of rain and rattles of wind, a chill November night pressing in upon them in all its fury. Contentment had settled on this house, and peace, and, yes, more than that. And it had come in the person of Eve Triopolous.

Was it disloyal to Kelly to feel contentment in Eve's presence? His mind grappled with the thought, but as generous as Kelly had been, as loving, he knew she would have approved. She had loved Eve, Kelly had. She had chosen Eve, after all, to be the mother of their child until it could be safely born.

Whatever it was that was gaining on him, Derek thought in a flash of perception, it was something good.

"Your turn, Derek," Aunt May said again.

"Yes," he said, but he wasn't talking about Trivial Pursuit. He was talking about a pursuit that was, to him, anything at all but trivial.

At long last, a plan began to take shape in his mind.

Chapter Nine

If the early December weather was any indication, Charlotte was in for a severe winter.

Snow seldom intruded into the mild climate of that Southern city; when it did, it usually made its brief appearance in January or February. But by mid-December of this year, a few random flakes had already fluttered halfheartedly down from gray windswept skies.

Eve spent a Christmas divided between Wrayville and Myers Park, between Aunt May's dainty Christmas cookies and Nell Baker's more robust homemade fruitcake, between the elegant beef Wellington Louise served on Kelly's graceful Rosenthal china and the baked ham offered by Nell on her new ironstone dishes from K mart. The contrast of Christmas celebrated in the two households was striking in the extreme, but oddly enough, this Christmas satisfied Eve as no other had.

In Wrayville she did not feel the weight of home and its responsibilities settling slowly on her narrow shoulders. The burden was lifted now that she perceived Al's well-being as held firmly in the capable hands of Nell Baker. Somewhat to Eve's surprise, she found herself feeling enfolded and protected by each of her two separate families. By this time, living in such close proximity, bound by their shared memories of Kelly, she had definitely grown to think of Derek and Aunt May as family.

"Maybe it will snow for Christmas," Derek remarked hopefully on Christmas morning after he had exclaimed over the soft blue sweater Eve had knitted for him and after Eve had thanked him for the neat cosmetic case he had given her.

"Snow?" Aunt May snorted gently. "It's never snowed on Christmas, at least in my memory."

And it didn't snow on Christmas. But it did snow the next day, the snowflakes stealing softly down upon them in the night when the weather forecasters had assured them that there was no chance of it.

Eve awakened early the morning after Christmas and blinked her eyes against unaccustomed glare beaming onto her drawn draperies. When she parted the fabric at the window, the mantle of just-fallen snow glistened from garden and garage, from branch and fence post. The world was quiet and new, the sere buffs and browns of winter gracefully hidden by the sparkling white blanket that covered everything in sight.

"I'm going out," Eve declared after a hurried breakfast with Derek and Aunt May.

"But it's *not* snowing out," Aunt May insisted loudly. "That was last night, dear."

"Eve said she was *going* out, Aunt May," Derek said, drawing his eyebrows together at the sight of Eve arranging her down jacket over her bulky form. "And Eve, I don't think you should."

"Nonsense," she said briskly. "I love the snow. And we've seen precious little of it the last couple of years. Just a walk in the snow and I'll be back in, safe and sound." She smiled at Derek reassuringly.

"Well, if you insist," Aunt May said doubtfully. "I'll ask Louise to put on a pot of hot cocoa for you for afterward. Nothing like hot cocoa to warm a person, I always say." She wobbled toward the kitchen on impossibly high red heels, a holdover from Christmas Day.

"No one's shoveled the walks. They may be icy. I don't even know where our snow shovel is. Be sensible." Derek stood up the way he always did when he wanted to exert his authority in this household of women.

He'd been so thoughtful of her lately that Eve hated to deny him anything. But she would find the outside so invigorating; it would feel so healthful. Aunt May kept secretly nudging up the thermostat so that the temperature in the house was hot to the point of stuffiness.

"Why don't you come outside with me?" Eve invited Derek on the spur of the moment. "It's a mere four inches of snow. Hardly a threat for me or for anyone else. Come on, Derek; it will be fun." She fairly glowed with well-being.

Derek looked distinctly uncomfortable. He ran a finger under the collar of his shirt, a new flannel one he had bought recently and which was so casual that he still felt out of place when he wore it.

"Me? Out in the snow? Why?" He looked so puzzled that Eve almost laughed.

"To feel it. To scuff your feet in it. To throw it, for heaven's sake, Derek. Haven't you ever thrown a snowball?"

He thought for a moment. "Well, not since I was a child. Snow is for kids."

"Derek, Derek." She laughed, tugging his jacket from a nearby coat tree. She tossed it at him, and he caught it with a startled look. "Come on. You're going to throw a snowball. You're going to make a snow angel."

Reluctantly, he slid his arms into the sleeves of the jacket.

"What's a snow angel?" He looked so genuinely perplexed beneath that well-groomed thatch of butternut-brown hair that Eve laughed again.

"I know you're a Southern boy, Derek, but you must know what a snow angel is. I grew up around here, too, and I've made whole flocks of snow angels."

"The process sounds fairly vigorous," he remonstrated, throwing her a look of pure concern as she pulled him out the back door and down the wide steps. He held her hand tightly in case she slipped on the icy bricks. "Are you sure you're able to make snow angels?"

This time her laughter echoed off the rooftop, tinkled like bells in the crystalline air. She took a few giant steps, and snow crunched beneath her boots. She left dark footsteps in her wake, and dead sprigs of grass popped up in the middle of them. She inhaled the freshness of the crisp, sweet air and flung her arms out wide, spinning in place with the glory of this beautiful winter morning.

She bent, graceful in spite of her clumsy contours, and scooped up a handful of powdery snow. She tossed it at Derek.

And he, because she looked so young and so carefree and so beautiful that he could hardly stand to look at her, hid his feelings by tossing a handful of snow at her. And then they were yelling and laughing and chortling into a veritable blizzard that they stirred up themselves, until Derek yelled, "Uncle, or whatever it is I'm supposed to holler when I give up!"

"Oh, Derek," Eve gasped. "If you only knew how you look. Like a little boy all lit up with happiness." And he did, too. His hair fell boyishly over his forehead, and he seemed to have shed a weight or a burden so that his expression reflected a lightheartedness she had never noticed about him before.

"I've suddenly remembered how to build a snowman," he announced to Eve's delight. His smile spread wider and shone bright as the sun.

"Let's!" Eve said. "We'll build one where Aunt May can watch us from the bow window in the breakfast room!"

But Derek's idea of a snowman was not simply ordinary balls of snow rolled to graduated sizes and stacked one on top of the other. Derek's version of a snowman was an elaborate snow sculpture.

They worked together to stack the snow as high as a man, and then Eve stood back and offered sprightly commentary while Derek molded it with his hands so that it had legs, feet and gently curved arms bowed gracefully over its stomach.

"That's not a snowman," Eve said, puckering her forehead in consternation. "It's a snow woman! And a pregnant one at that!"

Derek stepped back and judiciously regarded his creation. He clapped a hand to his forehead. "You're right! But it was a subconscious creation."

He patted the belly of the figure into a more rounded form. Eve watched his gloved fingers, so strong and sure as they lingered upon the shape of the woman, and suddenly she felt so embarrassed that she had to turn away.

But Derek seemed pleased with what he had wrought.

"Be back in a minute," he tossed back over his shoulder as he galloped toward the house, and true to his word, he appeared a short time later with a fluffy organdy-draped hat in his hands. He tilted it to the side of the figure's head, stepped back and squinted his eyes critically, then produced a black lace scarf from his pocket and wound it around the snow woman's neck, leaving the ends to flutter in the slight breeze.

"And she needs a nose," he said, embellishing the face with a red radish. With a flourish, he produced two chocolate bonbons. "Eyes, donated to the cause by Aunt May."

From the window, Aunt May waved her smiling approval.

"Isn't our snow woman gorgeous?" he asked Eve with a twinkle.

"Lovely, Derek. You've outdone yourself."

"You're right. And I'm more than ready for Louise's hot cocoa. But first you're going to teach me how to make snow angels!" Derek grinned at her, more carefree than she'd ever seen him. He seemed to have shed completely the veneer of sophistication and perfection, seemed to have relaxed in her presence, seemed to be having fun.

"We have to find the right patch of snow," she said, unthinkingly grasping his hand in hers. She led him to a likely spot. "And then lie down in it." Which Eve awkwardly proceeded to do, flat on her back, much to Derek's consternation. Inside her, the baby battled for a position at this new angle, jolting her, but pleasantly.

"Do I have to lie down, too?" Derek looked as if it would hurt to shed his last invisible shred of dignity.

But Eve didn't laugh, although she wanted to. "Sure," she told him. "Right next to me."

He did, albeit reluctantly.

"And then," she said, demonstrating vigorously, "you move your arms up and down."

He sat up straight, frowning down at her. "Good heavens," he muttered. "How ridiculous."

"Well, maybe," Eve admitted, pumping her arms harder than ever. "But this makes the angel's wings." With one last dubious look at Eve's face, framed so cunningly against the snow by the red knit cap she wore, Derek lay down again.

Derek waved his arms up and down in the snow.

"Like this? Am I getting the technique right?"

"Well, you don't have to do it so hard. You're throwing snow clear over to that dogwood tree."

Derek slowed down.

"Now what?" he asked, stopping and turning his head to look at her. Locks of short curved hair had escaped her cap, enclosing her face in parentheses.

"We do the same thing with our legs." Eve concentrated on moving her legs. That was a little harder, especially since her abdominal muscles seemed to have migrated northward.

But Derek managed all right.

"When are we finished?" he asked, as though begging for mercy.

"Now. We can stand up—carefully now; you don't want to mess it up—and look at them."

Derek loomed over her, hands on hips, looking askance at the angel he had made.

"It's not bad for the first snow angel I ever accomplished."

Eve lay on her back, admiring the shape of his head against the brilliant blue sky. He was a handsome man, was Derek.

"You mean you'll make more sometime?"

"Every time it snows," he said soberly. "Now that you've taught me what to do with it."

Eve snickered. "You've openly cavorted, Derek. Do you realize that?"

Derek pretended to look horrified. "I'll never live it down if they find out at the office."

"Your employees probably think you were born wearing a three-piece suit."

"Yup. And a pair of wing tips."

They laughed together. Their laughter swooped upward and out, startling a blackbird on the telephone wire. The bird winged across the sky, air bound. Eve lay in the snow, earthbound.

"I hate to have to ask you, Derek, but I can't get up. Help me, please."

"What's wrong? Is anything wrong?"

His anxiety was touching, almost comical.

"No, what I mean is, I can't get up without rolling over onto my side, because I can't sit up from this position, and if I rolled over on my side, I'd mess up a perfect angel. Just give me your hand, please."

Derek reached down for her, she placed both mittened hands inside his gloved ones, and he lifted her neatly to her feet. He stood so close that there was scarcely any space between them, so close that she smelled the clean, fresh evergreen scent of him. She was enfolded in his misty breath.

"I'm sorry," she said by way of unnecessary explanation. "I just couldn't get up." His lips were full and slightly parted, and they slowly drifted down toward hers.

"Don't apologize to me for your condition," he said fiercely, an unnamed emotion gleaming behind his eyes. "Ever."

If she hadn't broken away in confusion, they would have gone on standing there, and he might have kissed her. But she said, with an attempt at gaiety, "I'm ready to go in and see what Aunt May has to say about our handiwork," and she walked rapidly away over the snow.

Oh, what if he had kissed her again? She remembered very well that time in the living room—how soft his lips had felt against hers, how warm. How delicious they had tasted....

"Hang Aunt May," Derek mumbled under his breath, but she couldn't hear him, and after he said it, he was ashamed of himself and glad Eve hadn't heard.

Eve had reached the middle of the steps by the time he thought of it, and unwilling for this time with her to end, he said suddenly, "My mother used to make snow ice cream."

Eve half turned, a gently curving smile upon her lips. "Oh, my mother did, too."

"Could you remember how to make it?"

"Maybe. I think so."

He smiled, pleased that he had thought of this one more thing they could do together. "I'll bring in the snow," he said, heading for the garage and a space of snow that was unsullied by their antics.

"I'll help—" Eve said eagerly, swiveling around, and then it happened.

Her feet flew out from under her on a patch of snow-covered ice, she grabbed wildly for the handrail and missed, and she thumped down all five steps before landing in a wildly skewed position at the bottom of the stairs.

Derek watched, unable to reach her in time to do anything. His heart flew to his throat. Suddenly the blue sky, the glistening snow, the joy in his heart—all were gone, and in all of his consciousness only Eve was left. Eve, sprawling in the snow and lying so still that he dared not breathe.

It took less than two seconds for him to reach her. He fell to his knees, his arms enfolding her without thought, his eyes wildly searching the pale face beneath the red knit cap.

"Eve— Oh, my God!" He brushed snow from her cheek; it melted and left a wet trail down her cheek, a trail that might have been traced by tears.

"Is she all right?" cried Aunt May, who had come running awkwardly outside on her high heels. "Is she hurt?" Aunt May hugged herself against the cold.

Eve's eyes fluttered open beneath those remarkable winged brows. "I'm fine," she said breathlessly, aware only of Derek's panicked face in her field of vision. "Just a little shaken up."

"I thought you were unconscious," Derek said unsteadily.

"No, just had the wind knocked out of me. Whew!" she said, pushing him away. "Let me up."

He held her gingerly by the elbows once she was safely on her feet. "I should never have left you on those stairs alone. I knew they might be icy."

"It's okay," she insisted. "It could have happened whether you were with me or not."

"I should never have left you," he repeated. "Never."

Eve took the stairs one step at a time, pausing for a moment on each, with Derek holding on to her the whole time as though she would break if he let go.

"I won't have you feeling guilty," she murmured softly, with a meaningful look that was not meant for Aunt May to see.

But Derek did feel guilty, overwhelmingly so, and even though he relinquished Eve to Aunt May's fussing ministrations and Louise's anxious queries, he continued to watch her as they unwrapped her from her coat and brought her a towel to dry her face, waiting for a sign of trouble. Pregnant women weren't supposed to fall down flights of stairs, and she'd had a pretty hard fall.

"Are you sure you feel all right? Do you want me to call Dr. Perry?" he kept asking even when Eve was ensconced on the couch with a heating pad for her feet and a mug of cocoa steaming color into her cheeks. "Are you sure you don't feel any pains?"

"I'm as strong as a horse," she reassured him. "And after all, I landed on a pretty well padded portion of my anatomy. Except for a few black-and-blue marks, I'm going to be fine. Really."

"I'm calling the doctor," he said, "just to be on the safe side."

When Derek had Dr. Perry on the line, he asked to speak with Eve, who answered the doctor's questions briefly and then hung up.

"What did he say?" Derek demanded.

"He said not to fall down stairs again," Eve told him demurely.

"Eve—"

"No, honestly. He told me to watch for warning signs, but I feel okay. I'll stop by his office tomorrow and have him make sure everything is all right."

"Eve, can I get you anything?" Aunt May hovered so close that she gave Eve claustrophobia.

"No, and I believe it's time for *Love of Hope*. You don't want to miss it. Today's the day the hockey player's dachshund digs Susan out of the cave she's been hiding in since October."

"It is? Oh, indeed it is! And the hockey player's ex-fiancée is going to decide whether to marry the lead singer of Purple Madness, who's been in the hospital waiting for a kidney transplant! Well, if you don't mind..." And Aunt May wobbled away in her red shoes.

They heard her in the sun room, ruffling through the wrappers in her almost-empty box of chocolates and muttering to herself, "I wonder why they named the hockey player's dog Albert. That's such a funny name for a dog, and I wonder what the baby's name will be; Eve hasn't mentioned anything . . ." And then the rest of her solitary conversation was lost in a loud torrent of words from Aunt May's currently favorite soap opera.

Alone with Derek, sure of his undivided attention and grateful to Aunt May for unwittingly supplying an opening, Eve said meaningfully, "That is a good question, you know—what to name the baby." Kelly had told Eve what names she had chosen; did Derek know what they were?

Derek felt distinctly uncomfortable and somehow betrayed. He was so worried about her that he could hardly sit still, and *she* wanted to talk about a topic that he'd been deliberately avoiding. He'd gone so far as to make a plan, sure, but the plan Derek had made did not include discussions of the baby. It would have to, eventually, he supposed, but Eve's remark left him at a loss for words.

Nevertheless, he figured there was nothing to do but answer her somehow. "I guess it depends on if the baby is a boy or girl," he said carefully after a long time.

"I guess it does." And Eve watched him over the rim of her mug as the melodramatic theme music from *Love of Hope* enveloped them in its crashing refrain. She was ready to tell him Kelly's choice of names, but as usual he seemed unwilling to talk about anything concerning the child she was to bear.

Oh, why won't he confront the problem of the baby, Eve thought impatiently. She hadn't pushed him for any answers; she had waited as quietly and as patiently as she knew how. But soon—the baby's birth was little more than a month and a half away—she would have to know if Derek planned to keep this baby.

He was softening. She knew he was. As they became better friends, she saw the kind, thoughtful man that Derek Lang really was, and she didn't think he had the heart to give away his own flesh and blood. But the way his mind worked, with the guilt about Kelly's miscarriage all mixed up in his feelings about this baby, she knew he felt unworthy of being a father. And if his own unworthiness was all that was preventing him from accepting this baby, she'd have to make him see that he was wrong.

"Derek, you'd make a wonderful father," she said softly.

His head, which had been bent low over his folded hands, shot up sharply.

"That's what Kelly said," he told her.

"Kelly was right."

"Kelly was right about a lot of things." His eyes were clear now, not troubled. "She was right that you were the proper person to carry our baby to term. But today I feared for you, Eve. Seeing you like that, in a heap at the bottom of the stairs—" He gestured helplessly with his hands, then folded them beneath his chin and leaned forward, elbows on his knees.

"But everything is all right." Her eyes regarded him seriously. He could scarcely look into their depths, because to do so would reveal too much too soon. Why this reluctance for her to know what he felt? Was it because he was afraid of rejection? Or was it because of their business agreement, that he felt constrained because the baby was between them?

It wasn't the baby he was thinking of; he didn't care about the baby. He simply couldn't think of the baby, because it was so seldom real to him. But Eve was real, Eve was here, Eve was Eve, and ever since Eve had moved back into this house, he'd felt like a new person. Eve filled him up, leaving no room for anything else.

"It was not the baby I feared for, Eve. It was you." He said this firmly.

What an inappropriate time for the phone to ring! It was like a scene from one of Aunt May's soap operas, the phone barging in at exactly the wrong time in order to keep the man and the woman apart. Exhaling sharply when Louise brought the telephone and plugged it in so Eve could speak without having to get up from her warm spot on the couch, Derek stuffed his hands deep in his pockets and walked to the window overlooking the snow woman they had built.

Funny how he had sculptured a pregnant woman, all the while unaware that he was doing so. Funny and Freudian, as though he were aware of the baby on some deep psychological level even though he could scarcely stand to acknowledge its existence most of the time. He didn't want to think about it, didn't want to talk about it. He only wanted to think about Eve, of her sweet laughter, of her gentle touch, a touch he wanted to know more of and didn't know how to get.

Behind him, Eve laughed and said, "I'll meet you at two o'clock, Doug, on Friday as planned. Don't worry. No, I'm fine. Stop worrying, I said! Give Al and Nell my love."

That man—it was that other man that Eve went out with. A surge of jealousy washed over Derek in a giant wave, jealousy such as he had never known. Who was the guy? What was his role in Eve's life? How often did he phone her? Where did she meet him? Was he some fellow she'd known before to whom she'd return once the baby was born? And Eve would be twelve thousand dollars richer, he thought cynically. Let's not forget that.

The television noise from the sunroom ceased abruptly, and Aunt May wandered through the breakfast room, yawning. She popped a malted milk ball into her mouth and said through it, "Why don't you offer Eve some more cocoa, Derek?"

"You do it," he growled in as sour a mood as he'd ever known, and while Aunt May clamped her mouth abruptly shut at his surliness, he stomped away upstairs and slammed his bedroom door hard.

He stared at his image in the mirror over the dresser. His chest heaved beneath the flannel shirt—a flannel shirt, for Pete's sake! If it weren't for Eve, he wouldn't be wearing a flannel shirt, even though it *was* specially ordered from L. L. Bean. She'd probably have him wearing gold chains around his neck next.

He had rearranged his life, changed his mode of dress, the way he spent his time. All for Eve, and why? Abruptly, he realized that she had a whole life apart from his, had always had a life apart from his, and he knew nothing about that life.

He furrowed trembling fingers through his hair, leaving it uncharacteristically rumpled.

Once the baby was born, Eve would go back to the life she had left, although it appeared that she hadn't ever left it. Her previous life trailed along after her, humming along on phone lines, luring her somewhere on Mondays, a persistent but apparently welcome force.

So what should he do? Ignore it? How could he? She had a past, and well he knew the influence of the past on the present and the future. Okay, so he'd have to learn about her previous life. Should he hire a detective? No, that smacked of invasion of privacy.

He'd get her to talk about it, then. Find out what kind of home she came from. Who her friends were. What kind of job she'd had before she had decided to become a surrogate mother.

He couldn't believe he'd ignored all these things for so long. But of course there'd been no reason *not* to ignore them. Because you always ignored things that were not relevant, and Eve had not been relevant. Until he had grown to care for her.

"I DON'T KNOW, Eve. I want to buy Nell something nice for her birthday, but I'm not much good at choosing presents for women. That's why I wanted you to help me." Doug poked through a rack of women's sweaters in the small specialty shop. He held up a pink angora pullover and studied it. "Does this look like something Nell would wear."

Eve shook her head at the idea of Nell's rotund figure encased in pink angora. "Not really. How about a nice cap and matching scarf?" She shook them out for his inspection.

"No, she has something like that already. Come on; let's walk over to Belk's."

He offered Eve his arm, and she took it companionably. Crowds had thinned out; the after-Christmas sales at Eastland Mall were almost over, but several days after Christmas there were still bargains to be had.

"I can't imagine having a birthday so close to Christmas," Doug said. "Poor Nell. At least mine's in July. That means I get presents at two different times during the year."

"The baby's birthday will be in February," Eve told him. "Kelly and I planned that well, didn't we?"

"Mmm, you certainly did. Say, let me know if I'm walking too fast. I'm still worried over that fall you took."

"It caused no permanent damage, although I've got a bruise you wouldn't believe. Anyway, I visited Dr. Perry to reassure myself and everyone else, and everything is okay."

"I'm glad." They walked on, stopping to look in windows, pausing once to watch workmen removing a giant Rudolph the Rednosed Reindeer display.

"I keep thinking of the baby," said Eve as they watched Rudolph being carted down the mall concourse. "Next year it will be having its picture taken with Santa. Somehow it's hard to imagine."

"It is, isn't it?" They walked on a few paces. "Has Derek decided to keep the baby, or don't you know?"

"I think he's working around to it. He seems to find it difficult to discuss. I was going to ask him if he would go to Lamaze childbirth classes with me. I want to do prepared childbirth, but I don't think Derek's ready for that. Oh, Doug, I don't know."

Doug gazed down at her and gently patted her hand where it rested on his arm. "If you ever need me for anything, Eve, I'm here. To drive you someplace, to take you to the doctor, even to go to Lamaze classes with you. You're not alone, Eve. I want you to know that."

"Oh, Doug, that means a lot. You've been the most supportive friend." She swallowed the lump in her throat, touched by what he was offering.

In Belk's, Doug bought Nell a warm cardigan. "It's for her to wear in my office when she's on duty answering the hotline,'' he said. ''It gets chilly out in the waiting room sometimes.''

''How are things going with the filing of the new brown-lung claims?'' Eve asked Doug as they left the store.

''That's one of the things I wanted to talk with you about today. Wray Mills's management found out what I'm doing, and they've asked me not to file claims with the industrial commission until after the takeover by the conglomerate is complete.''

''You mean they've finally admitted that another textile firm is buying Wray?''

Doug nodded. ''Yeah. But they're not saying who it is. Apparently the deal is so far along that the Wray Mills's management doesn't want the conglomerate to know that it's acquiring workmen's comp problems along with the mill. Until money actually changes hands, management wants to soft-pedal any claims, and they're very nervous that we're signing up brown-lung claimants. They don't know how lucky they are that we're not suing anyone—yet.''

''Well, who's taking over the mill? Have they told you the name of the firm?''

''No. Nobody's talking. It's hush-hush, like a lot of these big takeovers often are. Everybody's keeping quiet so as not to get the employees upset. You know as well as I do that a takeover by a conglomerate often means a layoff. And Wrayville's economy can't take massive unemployment right now. Local people look at Lincolnton, at Greenville and at Roanoke Rapids where workers are unemployed due to plant cutbacks and closings, and it doesn't look good.''

Eve shot him an exasperated look. ''So what are we going to do? Stop signing up brown-lung claimants?''

Doug's lips drew into an uncompromising line. "No. I've got at least twelve good solid claims, claims you helped me get, and I may have more."

"Those people worked hard for the mill, and the mill owes them something," Eve said.

"I've been thinking about sitting on these claims until I find out who's buying Wray Mills. I'd much rather deal directly with the company than with the commission, because the commission is notoriously slow in settling. When new management takes over Wray Mills, maybe they'll have a heart. Not all mill owners fight workmen's comp claims or government regulations. There's a mill owner in Loomsdale who has spent at least three million dollars on new equipment to cut down on the amount of cotton dust in the air at his plant." Doug opened the outside mall door for Eve, and she walked ahead of him into the cold air toward the parking lot.

"If only—" she said, and then gasped. At first she thought the pain was due to the frigid blast of December wind she inhaled into her lungs, but when it happened again, she knew it was more than that.

She clutched at Doug. "Doug," she managed to breathe.

And she knew at that moment with agonized certainty that something was wrong, something was terribly, terribly wrong.

Chapter Ten

What is happening? What? Am I having a miscarriage? Why does it hurt so much? Derek! Derek!

Had she called Derek's name out loud? She didn't know, didn't know anything except that it was cold and it hurt, and she knew that the ambulance attendants didn't mean to be rough, but there was this spasmodic knifing pain in the small of her back. She was absolutely terrified.

"Eve, don't worry; we're rushing straight to the hospital," Doug said with unflappable calm, holding her hand tightly once they were inside the small confines of the ambulance.

The hospital! She tried to block out the wail of the ambulance siren, but it was impossible not to hear it, impossible. She clenched Doug's hand hard and fought the worst panic she had ever known. The pain wouldn't let her think about much else; her whole being was focused on the pain streaking through her body. Was it going to get worse? What was happening to her body? It always functioned at optimum efficiency, doing what it was supposed to do, walking, breathing, getting pregnant, everything, but her body seemed alien to her now, a thing apart. *She* could not be in such pain— The worst pain she'd ever felt in her life before this was from a broken collarbone, but this was terrible!

She heard the ragged sound of someone sobbing and realized it was she who cried; out of sheer terror or pain, she didn't know which. Doug's familiar face, so worried, swam woozily in front of her, but it shouldn't be Doug; it should be Derek. Where was he?

She didn't know if she asked for Derek, but she must have, because Doug said gravely, "I'll call Derek as soon as we get to the hospital. I promise," and she sank back on the pillow and somehow found her other hand and pressed it instinctively against the baby, trying to comfort the child she had carried within her all these long months, worrying that their journey together was ended, was over, and if that was true, it was not good.

The hospital—noise and white uniforms blurring in front of her, the pervasive hospital smells and sounds, the strange vocabulary—"Ritodrine? You want ritodrine?"—and then someone yelling "Stat!" too close to her ear, and a sexless being looming over her in a mask, and Doug letting go of her hand, which felt like a lifeline being snatched away.

It wasn't what she had wanted, this chaotic way of entering the hospital. She had wanted peace and serenity for this baby, but this scene was neither peaceful nor serene, and the unfamiliar faces around her made her feel lost and misplaced.

"What week of your pregnancy is this?" a rasping voice behind her demanded. Without ever seeing who it was, Eve replied automatically, "Thirty-fourth week." The voice said crisply, "She's thirty-four weeks, six weeks from her due date. Has anyone palpated the fetus for size?" and then she heard, blessedly, Dr. Perry's familiar deep voice asking questions, and she fought the tears of pain and panic, wanting to keep her wits about her so that she could help him with whatever he had to do.

He examined her quickly but thoroughly.

"The baby's head is in position, and your cervix is dilating, Eve," he said somberly when he had finished. "The ritodrine doesn't seem to be stopping your labor. It looks like you're going to have this baby."

"But it's too soon!" she cried.

"We have a wonderful neonatal intensive-care unit at this hospital," he soothed. "Your baby is premature, and it's small, but it will have a good chance at survival."

A good chance! Only a chance? But this baby was important, damn it, important for Kelly's sake, and because she had sheltered it under her heart, *in* her heart, this baby *had* to live!

She had a sudden mental picture of the baby the way she had envisioned it, a roly-poly cherub with fat rosy cheeks, an upstanding tuft of blond fuzzy hair like Kelly's, with eyes that would not change from the new-baby gray color but would remain gray, the color of the irises lightening until they were small replicas of Derek's eyes. And then the vision dissolved in a racking pain that was much worse than any of the previous ones.

Oh, Derek, why weren't you with me? she cried inwardly when the pain had passed, and as they wheeled her through the wide swinging doors to the delivery room, she thought with a jolt, *What if Doug forgot to call him?*

DEREK WHEELED recklessly into the parking lot of the hospital in his Corvette, damning the lack of parking spaces, damning the elderly flower-laden ladies who blocked his way, damning hospitals and life in general.

The phone call had interrupted an important meeting about the acquisition of Wray Mills, a meeting in which they were tying up all the loose ends, but none of that mattered to Derek. He'd startled all the managers and lawyers by leaping out of his chair in the conference room as soon as he scanned the note Maisie slipped to him, by letting Maisie to provide inadequate explanations, by running from the building as though the Furies were after him. Which perhaps they were; he recalled from his study of Greek mythology that the Furies punished the perpetrators of unavenged crimes, and in his own eyes Derek was guilty.

It was as though this crisis with Eve were Kelly's situation all over again, with Eve being rushed to the hospital too early. Only this time, he, Derek, was going to be there, no matter if work had to wait, even if his rushing to be with Eve in her hour of need scotched the new mill deal. This was his chance to make reparations for his absence when Kelly had miscarried; at least that's how it shaped up in his own mind. Silly, maybe, because he knew it was too late to ever make anything up to Kelly. But it wasn't too late to do something for Eve. And he was convinced deep in his heart that he had a lot to make up to her.

"Eve Triopolous?" he said briskly to the pink lady, or whatever they called the volunteer workers, and she looked Eve's name up on a list, slowly running her manicured finger down the column of names until Derek wanted to scream with anguish at her uncaring, lackadaisical attitude.

"Third floor," she said sweetly and with a smile. "Room—"

But he didn't hear her. He was running down the aisle to the elevator, was staring at his distraught reflection in the stainless-steel walls of it as it slowly climbed, stopping interminably on the second floor for a group of orderlies and student nurses who giggled over something stupid one of the orderlies said, and then he was out and running again, but was stopped by a guy in a white coat with a stethoscope around his neck.

"Where do you think you're going?" the doctor demanded.

"Third floor, Eve Triopolous—she's pregnant," he blurted out.

"Well, if she's pregnant, you're on the right floor, the maternity wing. Don't recognize the name, though. If you'll—"

And then Derek spied the wiry fellow in blue jeans glowering at him from the waiting area, and he knew somehow that this was the fellow Eve sometimes met, Eve's friend, the guy who took her out.

"Derek Lang?" the fellow said.

"Yes," he said, pulling himself up to his full height and appraising the other man.

The guy stuck out his hand. "Doug Ender. I'm the one who called your office."

"Where is Eve?" he demanded. "What's going on?"

"Actually, I suppose her doctor could tell you more about it, but he's with her in the delivery room now."

"The delivery room!" Derek rocked back on his heels, stunned.

Doug Ender regarded him coolly and without liking. "She's giving birth prematurely, Lang."

"Oh, God," Derek said, and sank down on the nearest chair.

Silence engulfed them, and surprisingly, Doug felt sorry for the man. He had expected to feel antagonism, anger, anything but sympathy. But it was clear that Derek Lang was deeply stricken by this news.

Doug cleared his throat. "I was with Eve when she felt the first pain," he began.

"She was in pain? How much pain?" Derek's words sliced jaggedly through the air, and his eyes were red and filled with a silent pain of his own.

Doug straddled the straight chair beside him. "I rode with her in the ambulance, and they did everything they could for her. They tried to stop the contractions, but they couldn't, so they wheeled her into Delivery half an hour ago."

"The—baby?" Derek whispered hoarsely. "They can save the baby?"

"I don't know," Doug said slowly. "The doctor didn't have time to talk to me, and I'm not directly involved, so I don't know if he'd tell me, anyway."

Derek closed his eyes, tight. If anything happened to this baby, Eve would be shattered. If anything happened to this baby—well, it was unthinkable, but he *was* thinking about it, and he wondered how he could ever have wished this baby dead.

"How could I have been so stupid?" he mumbled as if to himself. "How could I have been so blind?"

"I beg your pardon?" Doug looked genuinely confused.

"I didn't want her to have this baby," he said slowly, his desperation making him uncharacteristically talkative. "I wanted her to have an abortion."

Doug didn't speak for a long time, but finally he thought that he had been mistaken about Derek Lang. If he, Doug, was any kind of friend to Eve, he would also be a friend to this man, whom Eve liked and admired. It was clear that Derek Lang had suffered, was still suffering.

"She told me about it," he said to Derek reluctantly. "We've been friends since we were kids; we grew up together, and I'm an attorney. It was natural for her to talk to me about her situation." He shrugged. "I didn't have such a high opinion of you, to tell you the truth." His clear eyes assessed Derek. "But now—"

"Now?"

Doug shrugged. "I see what Eve meant. You don't mean her any harm."

"No, I never did. I wish she'd never been dragged into this mess, had never become—" He stopped abruptly. He had been about to say that he wished Eve had never become pregnant, but was that true? Eve herself had said that she was glad she was pregnant in spite of everything. Derek searched his mind, searched his heart, and in them he found gratitude.

This baby that was being born now, this very second, was his flesh and blood. Eve could so easily have gotten rid of the baby when he pressured her, but she hadn't. She had gallantly and valiantly refused to have the abortion, and she had taken care of herself and the baby, as well as her dependent father, before Derek had found her again. How could he, Derek, have been so stupid, so foolish, so confused? It must have been his grief over Kelly that had kept him from thinking straight. For now, with the impact of a blow to his solar plexus, he saw that the baby was worth her protection, was worth something in his eyes. It would be more grief for him if it didn't survive, because the child was his own—and Kelly's.

"She insisted on saving the baby," he said softly. "She was right." A fierceness came upon him when he thought of the defenselessness of the child, and adrenaline surged through him. He would protect the baby now, if only he could. He couldn't bear the thought of anything happening to it. But how like him, he thought bitterly, always too little too late.

"I should have helped her up the stairs; then she wouldn't have fallen," he said helplessly. He stared into space, seeing Eve's crumpled body lying so forlornly in the snow only a couple of days ago, when they had built the snow woman.

A nurse in a stiff white cap arrived silently on crepe soles and looked from one of them to the other. "Which one of you is Mr. Lang?" she asked.

Derek sat up straight. "I am," he said.

"Dr. Perry will speak with you now. Follow me, please."

IT WAS DARK outside when Derek finally crept into Eve's hospital room.

Her body scarcely mounded the white bed coverings; the bed seemed so large it almost swallowed her up. The covers rose and fell with the steady rhythm of her breathing, and Derek paused in the doorway to collect himself, to steady himself after the events of the day. He sagged with the burden of his weariness; his gray eyes were smudged shadows beneath his brows. Nervously, he twisted the bright bow attached to the vase of flowers he had bought in the hospital gift shop; they were carnations, which he would have preferred not to buy for Eve. She wasn't a carnation type, but carnations were all they had, and so carnations they were. He would have to find out what her favorite flower was.

"Derek?" she said fuzzily, turning her face toward the door. His heart turned over in his chest at the sight of her familiar winged eyebrows, the generous mouth, her dark hair cupped so perfectly to her head. She looked pale and wan after her ordeal; one hand was attached to tubing running to an IV hanging from a chrome stand.

"Yes," he replied, shutting the door silently behind him and not knowing where to go.

"You can sit down," she said, lifting her free hand as though with great effort. "Over here." He saw an orange plastic chair beside the bed.

"Eve—"

"I heard the baby cry," she said softly, her eyes huge and velvety. "He cried. That's a good sign, don't you think?"

The thought of what she'd been through hung like a weight on his heart. "I hope so. I hope so, Eve." He set the vase of flowers carefully on the radiator cover in front of the window, hiked his pants legs by the creases at the knees and sat down in the chair.

"Oh, Derek," she said, looking at him, and her voice sounded sleepy like a young child's. "Your tie is perfect, and your vest is buttoned. Not even rumpled. How like you."

"Eve, I've been frantic with worry. I didn't want anything to happen to you or the baby." His eyes searched her face urgently.

"I knew. I don't know how I knew, but I did."

He swallowed. "And now, if the baby doesn't live—" he began, but he couldn't continue.

Her hand crept across the counterpane, found his and nestled into his palm. Slowly he lifted his eyes to hers, and he saw that hers glimmered with tears. But there was courage in the set of her chin.

"The baby will live, Derek," she said, because it was what she had to believe. The tears spilled over and trickled down her cheeks, dropping to the white coverlet, where they left small damp patches.

And he couldn't speak, because his mouth ached from holding it so stiffly, but he knew it was right to gather her in his arms, to hold her close to his heart, and so he did, being careful of the IV apparatus taped to her hand. And when he saw her eyes closed, the shadow of her damp feathered eyelashes dark against her cheek, his heart was full. She was so beautiful and brave and strong that he should have admitted his love for her long ago.

He had almost lost her—Dr. Perry had made it clear that he had almost lost Eve—and he couldn't have borne that loss. And if they lost the baby... But Eve did not believe the baby would die. She had been right about a lot of things, and perhaps she was right about this, too.

Derek had a son. And he wanted that son to be part of his life as he had never wanted anything, except Eve herself.

BLESS DOUG, Eve thought the next morning. He had taken it upon himself to go to her father and to break the news that the baby had been born prematurely. And Al had withstood the news well, considering his concern about Eve. His voice had sounded stronger than Eve had expected when he called Eve first thing in the morning.

"You take care of yourself, Evie," he cautioned. "Don't be up and around too quick, now."

"I'll be all right," she assured him. She was sitting up in bed this morning; she was regaining her strength.

"I'll come see you as soon as Nell can drive me," her father told her. "Probably this afternoon during visiting hours."

They hung up, and Eve lay back on her pillows, thinking. She knew how much her father had looked forward to grandchildren. She could only imagine what he must be feeling over his own daughter's risking her life for a child that was not even hers.

But the baby felt like her own; that was the thing. Intellectually she knew it was Kelly's and Derek's—but emotionally she was bound to the baby as though it belonged to her.

"Ready to go see your new baby?" caroled a nurse as she maneuvered a shiny wheelchair through the wide hospital doorway. The nurses didn't know the circumstances of this baby's conception. That secret rested solely with Dr. Perry.

"Oh, yes," Eve said eagerly. This morning she had eaten well and was feeling much less groggy. Dr. Perry had stopped by; so had Dr. Ellisor, the pediatrician. He had been serious but not unencouraging.

"The baby is very small, Ms. Triopolous," Dr. Ellisor had told her. "Only four pounds. And we can expect him to lose some of that birth weight—all babies do."

"But otherwise he's normal?" She held her breath while waiting for the answer.

"As far as we know," he had replied. "But of course," he cautioned, "he's not out of danger yet. Barring any unforeseeable circumstances, though, I'd say you have a healthy infant who will pull through this."

Eve found the pediatrician's words encouraging despite this cautionary note. And now she was to see the baby!

The helpful nurse installed her in the wheelchair with a blanket tucked around her legs for warmth and Eve's IV attached somehow to the back of the chair; then she wheeled her cheerfully down the hall and around the corner. The neonatal intensive-care nursery was separate from the regular newborn nursery, which they passed in transit.

A proud grandmother stood at the window of the newborn nursery, tapping the glass and cooing to a pink bundle being held up for her inspection on the other side. In their Isolettes lay sturdy babies with fuzzy heads, red faces howling mercilessly, tiny ears as pink as seashells and dimpled fists experimentally flailing the air. The healthy babies, born at or near term.

Eve's heart beat faster as they approached the intensive-care nursery, where the most advanced technology aided premature babies, all of whom fought for every heartbeat, every ounce of body weight, every precious breath.

But no one had prepared Eve for what she would see there—for the immense room, all intimidating stainless steel and glass, for the tiny babies cradled in something called Ohio beds with tubes and wires crisscrossing their wizened bodies and the air filled not with lusty cries but with the hums and bleeps of monitors.

The picture of a rosy-cheeked baby faded forever in Eve's mind when she first glimpsed the child she had carried inside her for the past seven and a half months.

His face was wrinkled and red, and his eyes were swollen shut. A scattering of brown fuzz was the only hair on his head. He lay naked in the position the nurses had placed him, and he did not respond to Eve's presence.

Then, completely without warning, she burst into tears. Before she had been sure that the baby would live. She had been, she thought, unshakably sure. But that certainty was gone now that she had seen him. He was so little, so helpless.

"There, there," comforted the nurse, but the words were no comfort at all.

Why hadn't anyone told her how he would look? Why hadn't she been better prepared for the neonatal intensive-care unit? Clucking like a mother hen, the nurse wheeled her swiftly back to her room, Eve sobbing into her hands all the way, eliciting concerned looks from each person they encountered in the hall.

Eve huddled in her bed afterward, refusing lunch.

And then Aunt May descended upon her, bringing Eve's toothbrush and offering chocolates and solace of a sort, and Aunt May asked her if she had seen the baby yet, whereupon Eve cried and cried. And then her father and Nell came, fast on the heels of Aunt May, and her father caressed her shoulder, and Nell maintained a chirpy one-sided conversation, and Eve cried some more.

Where was Derek? Why didn't he come? They would let Derek see the baby; they wouldn't let Aunt May or her father or Nell, but Derek, as the baby's father, would be allowed to see him. And then she would have someone who understood. And then she would not feel so utterly alone.

THE INTENSIVE-CARE NURSERY was not an encouraging place. The baby was not a beautiful baby. But nothing could describe the thrill that Derek Lang felt when he first laid eyes on the small scrap of humanity that was his son.

"My son," he said out loud as though he could not believe it.

"Yes indeed," said the nurse who had brought him there before she discreetly bustled away.

"My son," he said again humbly, knowing that the world was not a place worthy of this child, that life would be harder than a child could know, that this baby deserved the guidance and care of his father in order to make his way through it all. And he would have that care and guidance, no matter what.

"I love you, my son," he whispered over the hum of the machinery that kept his baby alive, and his eyes filled with sudden tears.

EVE WAS SLEEPING when he entered her room, and he sat for a long time beside her, feeling thankful that he and Kelly had chosen Eve and not some other surrogate mother. For Derek well knew that many another woman would have bowed to his wishes for the abortion. The thought made him shudder.

At long last, she opened her eyes, instantly awake.

"I saw the baby," he said. "He's beautiful."

"Beautiful?" was all she could say, and then her eyes clouded with tears that she could not stop.

He held her again, hugging the warmth of her body against his. "Shh, everything is going to be all right. He's going to make it."

She managed to stop crying. He handed her a tissue, and she blew her nose. "I wish I could be like the heroines in books and cry without looking awful," she said shakily.

He laughed. "You look beautiful," he told her.

A nurse's aide came in with a bouquet of flowers. Then she hurried away.

"We need to decide what to name the baby," Derek said, walking to the window and then turning to face her. "He should have a name."

Eve stared at him, the afternoon sunlight slanting through the blinds and marking his face with a pattern of light and shadow.

"But that must mean that you're—that you're going to—" She stumbled over the words as the full impact of what Derek had said hit her.

"That I'm going to keep the baby. Yes." He smiled at her, but his smile was serious and not frivolous.

"But that's—that's—" She had been going to say that it was wonderful, but the words wouldn't shape themselves. If Derek kept the baby, then she would not be able to. *If* the baby survived, that is. And she could not imagine being parted from this child, could not imagine, after all the two of them had been through together, giving him up. She would have gladly died for this baby, who had been part of her but not of her; because of her pain he was even more indelibly hers than Derek's. She began to cry, not bothering to hide her face, just letting the tears slip down her cheeks.

"Now, Eve," Derek said, hurrying to her side, and his touch was gentle upon her face, drying the tears.

"It—it's normal to have postpartum crying jags," she said when she was able to speak. "Perfectly normal."

"What should we name him, do you think?" he said, reasoning that if he could get her thinking about the name, she wouldn't feel like crying. "Naming him is an act of faith," he explained as he eased himself down on the edge of her bed. "Somehow he will know that we expect him to live if we give him a name."

Eve pleated the sheet into accordion folds, avoiding Derek's eyes. She had once tried to get Derek to talk about names. It had been fruitless then. His willingness to do so now signified his change of heart. It should have made her happy, but it didn't.

"Kelly wanted to name the baby after you if it was a boy," she told him, her memory conjuring up the night she and Kelly had stayed up to watch *The Late Show* on television because Derek was working late. They had propped the popcorn bowl on a cushion between them, and Kelly had confided that she wanted the baby to be Derek if a boy and Elizabeth if a girl. "Kelly wanted to name him Derek Robert Lang, Junior. She said he would be called Dob."

"All right," said Derek. "Derek Robert Lang, Junior, is his name. Would you like to go see him?"

How could she say no, with Derek gazing at her so expectantly? After all, she had hoped for so long that he would recognize the baby as his, and he had. Now she would have to nurture that relationship and make sure bonding between father and son took place. It was the last thing she could do for the baby, after all, before she left him. It was the last thing she could do for Kelly.

She remained silent as Derek wheeled her to the intensive-care nursery himself. As they stood together—well, actually only Derek stood; Eve sat in her wheelchair—looking at little Dob, Derek's hand rested lightly on Eve's shoulder.

"Look, Eve," he pointed out, his voice eager. "He has Kelly's mouth! Doesn't he?"

Eve nodded, nervously biting her lip in frustration that this baby didn't look like the healthy newborns. But she had to admit that Derek's son's skin looked a little pinker this afternoon and that he reacted to the noise when someone dropped a metal pan in an adjoining room.

"I think he smiled," Derek said in an awestruck voice. Eve leaned forward in her wheelchair, straining to see. And yes, even though Dr. Ellisor might have denied it, she *did* think Dob smiled.

Yet after Derek had wheeled her back to her room and kissed her elatedly on the cheek, declaring that he was going to pass cigars out in the hospital lobby, Eve sank even deeper into devastating depression. On top of her failure to accomplish the carrying of this baby to term, she had to deal with the fact that he was no longer hers in any way.

Dob was Derek's child. Irrevocably, undeniably, scientifically and for all time. Nothing in the world could alter that irrefutable fact.

Chapter Eleven

"Eve, dear, imagine my surprise when Susan turned out to be the sister of the lead singer of Purple Madness. You know, *he's* the one who's been waiting for a kidney transplant, and now they're all putting pressure on her to donate one of her kidneys to her long-lost brother so he can marry the girl who used to be engaged to the hockey player, but Susan doesn't want to donate her kidney because her brother was so rotten when he was a kid, but he's reformed, and I really think that Susan ought to be nicer to her own *brother*. I don't care if she's been living in a cave for the past three months; she still has her suntan, so she's probably very healthy and all—" Aunt May continued loudly on and on in this vein, filling Eve in on what had transpired on *Love of Hope* since Eve went into the hospital.

I suppose it's too much to wish that Aunt May came equipped with a volume knob, Eve thought wearily as Aunt May plodded through the plot of her favorite soap opera. As though she could care about the hokey problems of Susan and the hockey player or the surly lead singer of Purple Madness while Dob, poor little Dob, lay helpless in his crib.

Five days after Dob's birth, Eve had gone home from the hospital. Dob had not. He would not be allowed to leave the hospital until his weight reached four and a half pounds and he was able to take nourishment by mouth.

Nell had invited Eve to come home to Wrayville where Nell would care for her, but Eve insisted that she wanted to visit the baby three times a day, and Wrayville was too far for that. And so she went home to the Myers Park house where Aunt May and Louise cosseted her and catered to her more than she had any right to expect.

"Ready, Eve?" Derek's smiling face appeared around the arch leading into the sun room.

"Yes," she said gratefully, glad to be spared any more of Aunt May's interminable saga. Derek helped Eve with her coat, solicitously suggested that she wear her gloves, and held the door for her as they trooped out to his car.

"Aunt May driving you crazy?" he asked with an understanding sidelong look at her profile once they were headed down the street in the Corvette.

"Not exactly," she said, staring straight ahead with a distracted air about her.

In the old days she would have defended Aunt May. Derek concentrated on his driving, worrying about Eve. She wasn't the same person since the baby had been born, and he missed her cheerfulness, her optimism, and most of all, her willingness to converse with him. They had had some interesting and spirited conversations in the old days.

Derek drove to the hospital to see Dob three times a day, once in the morning, once in the afternoon and once at night. His work schedule was suspended for the time being. Whenever it was possible, he went in to the office, but when it was not, he delegated his duties to subordinates, new mill or no new mill. Acquisitions, foreign textile quotas, the governor's task force on textiles—all seemed of little importance. For now, Derek wanted nothing more than to be with Eve and his son.

"Dr. Ellisor called just before we left the house," Derek told Eve.

Eve snapped her head around, clearly surprised. She had heard the phone ring during Aunt May's recitation, but she had felt too weary to break the long monologue to go answer it. Louise would answer it, or Derek would answer it. Phones were not part of her world these days. Nothing was important to her except Dob.

"What did the doctor say?"

"Just a progress report. Dob is doing fine."

She sank back into the Corvette's bucket seat and blinked rapidly. Her forehead ached from dammed-up tears. Surely the doctor had said more than that. Maybe Derek was keeping something from her. She wished now that she had spoken to Dr. Ellisor herself, just to reassure herself that Dob was all right, really all right. In spite of all the attention and sympathy, day by day Eve sank even deeper into a morass of depression. Seeing Dob three times a day, watching him helplessly as he lay there, did not help matters.

"Don't worry," Derek said when they finally stood in the intensive-care nursery looking at Dob. He couldn't help but be concerned about Eve these days. This Eve was so passive, so quiet, so unlike the Eve he had known before the baby was born. Failing to rouse any response in her, he turned his attention to the baby.

"Hi, Dob," Derek said gently, as he always did. "Hi there, fella." Dob wriggled in response to Derek's voice.

"See that? He knows you," the nurse said, smiling in satisfaction.

Eve leaned anxiously over the baby, watching him intently. Derek thought, *If only she would talk to the baby, speak to him!* But she never did. She always left the talking to him.

Eve tried to ignore the noises coming from the monitors, the screens that told their tales of the preemies' health. She kept her arms tightly folded across her stomach, the place where she had once carried Dob close to her heart, gripping her elbows with her hands. Her arms ached to hold this baby, but she knew she never would. And she didn't know if she could stand not holding him.

A loud beeping noise startled her, scared her out of her wits, and when she realized that the warning signal emitted from Dob's monitoring equipment, a hundred raw nerve endings transmitted the shock to her brain. The blood rushed from her head, and her legs turned to water.

Dob is dying was her first desperate thought, and she screamed and then began to cry, to cry so loudly that the nurse who rushed to take care of Dob, saying, "There, there, my little man, you've just rolled over on one of these wires and set if off; now let's just move you a bit," motioned Derek to take Eve away, and he slid his arm around her, half supporting her as he eased her out of the nursery and maneuvered her through the nearest door, one that led into a large supply closet. He closed the door after them so Eve wouldn't be subjected to the curious stares of passersby.

"Oh, God, Derek, I thought he was dying. I don't want him to die!"

"He's not, Eve. He's gaining weight, and he's better every day," Derek said desperately, trying to figure out a way to tell her that the danger was mostly in her own mind. Because Dob *was* better; the doctor said so.

But Eve was hysterical, pushing him away when he tried to hold her against his chest so that he had to grab her wrists and force her back against the gurney that was stored in the room for emergencies and wrap his arms around her when she began to flail wildly at him, completely out of control, so unlike Eve that he didn't know who she was.

Finally, she had no more strength left and lay sobbing against his shirt. She was so different from the calm capable person she had once been that he knew she was sick from the strain of the past weeks, that she had been living under more tension than she could take and that she needed him as much, if not more, than his son, who had others who could take care of his specialized needs.

Eve's heart drummed madly against her ribs. She wanted to run. But she was too weak to run, and there was nowhere to go. There was no place where she could be rid of the guilt over what had happened to make Dob a premature baby, where she could feel free of the constant tormenting anxiety about his future, his health.

She was a daughter, had once been a child. She well remembered being securely held in the circle of her father's arms, and she recalled with longing the days when her mother had been alive and would smooth her hair to comfort her at all the odd little moments of childhood when comfort was needed. Would Dob have that? Had she brought a child into this world only to surrender him to a life of pain and loneliness?

When she had decided to become a surrogate mother, she had thought she was helping two deserving people, Kelly and Derek. But the way it had turned out, she was saddling Derek with a lifelong responsibility that perhaps he even now did not really want, and she had produced a child who could not yet survive on his own.

He needed machinery and medicine to survive, and if he made it, then what? Was his life going to have the quality that Eve had been so sure of in the beginning, when everything had looked bright and optimistic, before Kelly's accident, before Dob had been born too early? Would it have been better to have had the abortion?

"Eve," Derek said as from a distance, and her name echoed and reverberated inside her head. He was so much stronger than she that she knew that there was no point in fighting anymore, in fighting any of it. She stumbled against him, and his arm was beneath her knees, swinging her up on the soft padded surface of the gurney. Her arms were around his neck, and she was sobbing into his shoulder, tears dissolving into the impeccable navy-blue silk of his tie. He was murmuring "hush" and brushing her hair back behind her ear and dabbing at her streaming eyes and nose with a soft towel from one of the shelves.

His fingers soothed her, stroked delicately at her hair, traced the jawline between ear and chin, until she stopped sobbing and the tears ran silently down her cheeks. His little finger caressed her collarbone beneath the blouse she wore, the bone so fragile and birdlike. He kissed her eyebrows and gave her a hand to hold. She couldn't stop herself from gripping it tightly, hanging on to his strong fingers as though they were some kind of anchor to reason. Holding his hand comforted her somehow. How could she have hated him only moments ago, Derek, who had been so kind, who cared so much? She was an ungrateful wretch; she didn't deserve him. Why didn't he leave her here in this awful supply closet and go away? The tears stopped, and her eyes drifted closed, shutting out the glaring overhead fluorescent tubes, shutting out Derek's worried face, leaving her in blessed darkness.

"Eve," he said, knowing that she had no strength left to fight, that all the fight in her had dissolved in guilt and misgivings. He smoothed her cheek reflectively, watching over her as he would watch over a child, as he would watch over Dob. Eve needed him. Eve needed him as much as Dob, maybe more. And he could help her because he had faith now, because he knew that Dob was going to survive and was going to get out of this hospital and go home to the Myers Park house. Where Derek would be waiting and where Derek hoped that Eve would be waiting, too.

"You were there for me when it was my darkest hour," he said, his voice no more than a whisper. "You took care of me, and you made sure no harm came to my child. Do you know how grateful I am to you for that? Do you?" He didn't know if she heard him; her chest rose and fell evenly, and she lay perfectly still. He thought she had fallen asleep on the gurney, exhausted by the mental and physical strain of the past half hour. But even if she were asleep, perhaps she heard him. And so he kept talking to her, because he wanted her to know.

"If you had listened to me, Eve, I would be alone now. Utterly alone. Without Dob. Without you. I didn't know what that would mean to me at the time. I thought that without Kelly my world had ended. I loved her so much, and I felt so sad that I hadn't been the kind of husband I should have been. You showed me that my life could go on, Eve, and I can never thank you enough for that. Never, never. And so, darling Eve, I will take care of you now."

Her eyelids fluttered, but they didn't open. Derek pressed a thumb along the long swanlike whiteness of her throat; her pulse throbbed steadily against it.

He dropped a kiss on Eve's right temple, and her grip tightened on his hand.

"It will be all right," he told her firmly. And he meant those words as he had never meant anything in his life.

"GET HER AWAY from home, from the hospital from all the reminders of what she considers her failure," Dr. Perry said, running a hand through his white hair until it stood on end like ruffled feathers.

"Her father lives in Wrayville," Derek said. "Eve could go there, I'm sure."

"Good. Send her. Don't let her visit the baby in the hospital for—oh, let's say at least a week."

"She'll worry," Derek said with certainty. "She'll see this as a banishment of sorts, as if it's her fault she went to pieces and so you sent her away."

Dr. Perry shot Derek an incisive look. He nodded his head. "She might. But she needs time to pull herself together in a place where she won't be seeing Dob three times a day. She's tearing herself apart with this insistence on going in to see him so often when there's really nothing she can do to help him."

"If you'll talk Eve into it," Derek said, "I can take her to the mountains. I have a cabin there. Aunt May could come with us, even Eve's father if he would like, and his friend Nell, and it would be a support group for her. All the people who love her gathered around, and she would feel that love and concern. We can be in touch with the hospital and with Dr. Ellisor by telephone every day, and we could be back in the city in a couple of hours if necessary."

"Dob is doing very well according to his pediatrician. He weighs over four pounds now, and he may be well enough to go home at the end of the week. And as for Eve, don't worry. I'll talk her into this mountain vacation of yours." Dr. Perry regarded Derek thoughtfully. "It sounds like the best medicine in the world for both of you," he said.

"I WISH YOUR FATHER could have come," Derek said conversationally as he skillfully steered the Corvette around a huge pothole in the dirt road on the outskirts of the Pisgah National Forest in the Great Smoky Mountains. "Your friend Doug assures me that your dad feels no hard feelings over your pregnancy anymore."

"Mmm," Eve said listlessly, staring out at the bone-bare winter branches flailing at the scudding gray sky overhead. Her hands lay inert in her lap, like two fallen birds. The sight of her usually animated hands lying so still tugged at Derek's heartstrings.

"I'd like to know your father," Derek went on. "Worked in a textile mill all his life, did he?"

"Mmm," Eve said again, not at all interested in talking. Each revolution of the car's wheels took her farther away from Dob, as if she wouldn't be leaving him for good soon enough, and now they had made her leave for a whole week. She didn't have the strength to fight it, though, and Dr. Perry had been adamant. She would not be allowed to see Dob, so why not let Louise pack her bag? Why not let Derek bundle her into the car and take her on this godforsaken trip into some wintry mountain wilderness? At the last minute, Aunt May came down with a cold and couldn't go along, but Eve suspected that it was less the cold's fault than the fault of Derek's cabin, which didn't have a television set and where Aunt May

would miss the upcoming kidney transplant operation on
Love of Hope.

Damn, why wouldn't she talk to me? Derek de-
spaired, gripping the wheel tightly in his hands. He
turned suddenly into the deeply rutted road that wound
up the mountain to the cabin, hoping that his neighbor
had followed Derek's directions to open the place up, do
whatever needed to be done to the fractious plumbing
and make sure the fireplace flue wasn't blocked by a
bird's nest or something.

Smoke snaked upward from the high stone chimney,
Derek noticed with satisfaction when they reached the
clearing. "Good old Farley," he said to Eve. "He's never
let me down yet. Look, he's got a fire going in the fireplace for us." He eased the Corvette to a stop next to a
stack of fresh firewood.

"Come on," he said to Eve, assisting her unresisting
figure from the Corvette. "Got to get you inside and
warmed up. Aunt May made me promise to make sure
you ate something hot as soon as we got here. Are you
hungry?"

Eve regarded the gray cedar-shingled structure and
shook her head. "No, I'm not hungry. Not at all." The
place was big enough—huge, in fact. The Langs always
did everything on a grand scale. A mountain cabin,
Derek had told her. This place was a mansion. You could
house three or four families from Cotton Mill Hill in this
place.

"What's wrong? Don't you like it?" Derek looked
genuinely disturbed. He wanted her to be happy. It was
touching, really.

"It's—it's lovely," she said lamely, taking the steps
heavily, as though each was a major obstacle. Derek's
hand remained at the small of her back, guiding her. At

the door he dug a key out of the pocket of the shearling jacket he wore and inserted it in the lock. Eve stared down at the flagstone porch beneath her boots. Little pockets of snow nestled in the corners. Fresh snow covered the sloping front yard. Beyond, she saw leafless deciduous trees and a bank of evergreens. There were no close neighbors.

"Here we are," Derek said, ushering her inside. He flipped a light switch, and a wagon-wheel lamp overhead threw the place into a mellow glow.

He set her bag down on the bottom step of a sturdy staircase and rubbed his hands together.

"Now for something hot," he said, raising his eyebrows inquiringly. He smelled of the cold, of the outdoors, of woodsmoke from the chimney.

"I really don't—"

"I promised Aunt May," he said. He slid an arm around her slim shoulders and drew her through the hall, through a large dining room, into a huge kitchen. "Even if it's only hot tea," he began, rummaging in a cupboard.

"Hot tea would be nice," she said when she realized that he wasn't going to give up until she ate or drank something. Anyway, it would give him something to do. He seemed so nervous, and what were the two of them going to do, rattling around in this big place by themselves all week? She wondered dully if she could get by with retiring to bed and pulling the covers up as high as they would go and not coming out for seven whole days. Or ever, preferably.

"Milk?"

"What?" She tugged herself into the present time and place.

"I was asking if you wanted milk in your tea," he said patiently.

She shrugged. "It doesn't matter."

"Milk, then. That's what I'm having. That's the way my grandmother always drank her tea. Must have been the English influence. Did I ever tell you my grandmother was English? Well, she was."

Eve sat down on a cane-bottom straight chair that Derek pulled up to the scarred kitchen table for her.

"I forgot to take your coat! Here, Eve, let me get it for you." When she didn't stand up, he lifted her hands from her lap and pulled her up. He unfastened the buttons for her and slipped the coat off her shoulders. She stood unresisting, like a child, sinking back onto the chair when he left the room to hang her coat in the hall closet.

"I make tea the English way, you know," he told her as he set the kettle on to boil. "Just the way Grandmother taught me." A glance over his shoulder told him that Eve's face was pinched and white and that she couldn't have cared less about his grandmother. She barely looked up when he set the cup of tea in front of her.

"Go on, try it," he encouraged with a friendly smile. He had to keep up the conversation. They couldn't just sit here staring at each other. He couldn't allow her to drag him down into the emotional depths where she was; it was his job to keep her mind off Dob any way he could. To make her hopeful, to pull her out of this awful depression. And so he talked, asking her questions, but not too forcefully, telling her little bits and pieces about himself, but not too intrusively.

And it worked, if only a little. She favored him with a bleak half smile once, exposing her quirky bicuspid, and he almost fell out of his chair in relief. He had been telling her about a prank he and some buddies had pulled back in his high school days; they had unfurled a roll of pink toilet paper all over the red maple trees in the neighborhood fuddy-duddy's yard. He supposed that her view of him—the ultraconservative Derek Lang—didn't jibe with the picture he was painting for her. But the tiny smile made him hope that somewhere inside this bare husk of a woman was the Eve he had known, the Eve he loved.

He carried her suitcase upstairs and showed her the room she would occupy; it was a cozy guest room rusticly decorated in frilled unbleached muslin curtains and an antique pine canopy bed surmounted by a huge feather bed covered in red-and-white striped ticking. The floors were bare oak, and an immense fireplace banked with glowing embers dominated one wall. Framed embroidery decorated the walls; some of it was in poor taste—fat little girls wearing sunbonnets so you couldn't see their faces, a pig inexplicably embroidered in bright blue—but some of it was very pretty. All in all, Derek found it the most cheerful bedroom in the house.

"So I've shown you the bathroom. Don't forget, now, that the bathtub faucet handles are reversed; the cold one is the hot-water faucet, and the one labeled hot is really the cold. My father had a hard time finding any local fellows who could do plumbing work when he built this place, with the result that the plumbing here leaves a lot to be desired. Anyway, is everything okay?"

"Um-hmm," Eve said listlessly, staring out the window at the snow. It was so white, so quiet, so peaceful. A peaceful, quiet place. She wanted to lie down and sleep, to sleep for a long, long time.

She felt Derek's strong hands on her shoulders. He turned her around to face him, and his eyes searched hers. He wanted something from her, she thought wearily. He wanted something she couldn't give him.

"Well, then, I'll leave you alone for your nap." His hands dropped from her shoulders, a gesture of defeat.

She nodded, staring at his face, at his neat eyebrows, at his blunt nose. She knew that face now. It had become part and parcel of her life, and soon she would have to say goodbye. Thank God she no longer felt anything. Thank God she was numb. Because if she felt anything, if she allowed herself to feel, she would only hurt inside.

Eve crawled into bed and burrowed deep into the thick warm feather bed. She didn't bother to take off her clothes or put on her nightgown. She didn't even think about it, because she was beyond thought.

All she wanted to do was sleep. And sleep. And sleep.

Chapter Twelve

Derek let her sleep, and she slept more than fourteen hours. He looked in on her once before he went to his own room that evening, saw that she was sleeping peacefully and stole away without waking her. He reminded himself that she was not only suffering in Dob's behalf, but she was also still recovering from a difficult childbirth.

He awakened early, before she did. He knew this because he lay in bed, listening for sounds of her moving about. But he heard none, so he got up and showered and shaved in the little bathroom adjoining his bedroom, wondering if she were lying deep in her feather bed and listening for sounds of him.

"Good morning," he said to her, ready to start anew when she finally appeared in the kitchen.

"Good morning," she replied, not smiling. She wore a wraparound wool skirt of Wedgwood blue with a white sweater. She had regained her figure since having the baby, although her breasts were fuller, rounder. But her stomach was flat beneath the front wrap of the skirt. As always, she looked neat and precise. Her hair was a glossy black cap hugging her head. The nape of her neck beneath the short, sleek hair appeared white and vulnerable.

"I'm putting together a breakfast for us," he told her cheerfully. "Not as good a breakfast as Louise makes, of course, but I'm pretty good at whipping pancakes together from a mix. How many pancakes can you eat?"

He was looking at her expectantly. Eve shrugged and shook her head. "I don't know."

"If I can eat six, you can surely manage three, don't you think? I've got real Vermont maple syrup. I dug an unopened tin of it out of the pantry. Kelly had a thing for real maple syrup ordered from Vermont, not that watered-down sugar water they sell in the supermarket."

"You came here with Kelly?"

A spark of interest; that was good. And it didn't hurt to talk about Kelly anymore, the way it had in the beginning, when the very utterance of her name felt like a dagger piercing his heart.

"I came here with Kelly often, especially in the first days of our marriage. She loved the mountains."

"Did she," Eve said, but it wasn't a question. It was more of an observation.

"Look, do you think you could set the table? You'll have to find the plates and cups and silver yourself, because I'm not sure where everything is. I haven't been here in a couple of years."

Obediently, Eve moved to the cupboards, opening and closing them like an automaton as she tracked down the requisite supplies.

She didn't feel Kelly in this house at all; everything here seemed so impersonal. "Kelly didn't pick out these dishes," she said when she was setting them on the woven place mats. The dishes were ugly brown-and-yellow pottery, chipped and worn.

"No, those are left over from when I was a boy. They're pretty old, I guess, and probably came from the local pottery, which tried to make a go of it and failed. This place wasn't Kelly's and mine, you know. It belonged to my parents. We came up here every summer when I was a kid, and occasionally in the winter. Then, after their divorce, I inherited it."

"But you don't come here?"

"Well, not anymore. Before Kelly's miscarriage we came often." He wondered if he should be talking about this; perhaps, considering Dob's premature birth, miscarriage was an uncomfortable topic for Eve. But he felt no compunction about speaking of what had been a sad time in his and Kelly's life. It had happened so long ago that it was part of the past. He thought of Kelly and everything concerning her with a strong feeling of loving nostalgia. Eve had been right about that, too; time was a great healer.

"Oh" was all Eve said. The topic was closed, so maybe she didn't like to be reminded. He'd have to feel his way very carefully, try not to tread ground that would make Eve retreat even more into herself. Since the support group he had envisioned for Eve hadn't materialized when her father and then Aunt May couldn't come, he would have to be her support group. He was well aware that one person could hardly take the place of two others, but he intended to try.

Eve managed to eat two pancakes and to sip some canned grapefruit juice, but Derek couldn't persuade her to eat any of the little sausage links he had prepared.

When he was through cleaning up the kitchen, he went into the big living room and found Eve sitting in a rocking chair by the window, staring out. She rocked slowly to and fro. In the white north light from the window, her skin shone so translucent that he saw a tracery of blue veins at her temples.

"What shall we do today?" he asked her, rubbing his hands together.

She swiveled her head and looked at him, wishing he didn't look so enthusiastic. She didn't want to do anything. She wanted only to sit here and rock and watch the snow, avoiding all thought.

"I don't care," she said politely, and then returned her attention to the outdoor scene.

It would be easy to become exasperated, he said to himself, raking his fingers through his hair and standing undecided for a moment. Then he turned abruptly and sat down on the floor in front of the coffee table where someone had long ago started piecing a dusty jigsaw puzzle together. The mindless fitting of the pieces would require no creativity or thought. He would work on the puzzle, pointless as it seemed, because he could talk to Eve while he did it. He didn't know what would get through to her; he only knew that he had to keep talking to her, trying to make some impression on her, giving her something to think about when she refused to think.

And so he talked about his boyhood and asked questions about her childhood as he worked on the puzzle picture of a red covered bridge.

Eve responded when he asked her about her Greek heritage; evidently she was proud of it. He asked her about Tarpon Springs, and she told him about her vacations there. She even ventured information about her grandmother's recipe for honey cake, and he told her she should teach Aunt May how to make it. For some reason, Eve seemed to shrink inside herself at the suggestion. Just when he thought he had established a connection between the two of them, she fell strangely silent again, answering him with monosyllables and staring out the window.

That night after she had gone to bed, he stepped out on the front porch and stared at the silver-white sickle of a moon holding the sky in the curve of its arms. He wondered if the reddish-colored body near it could be the planet Mars. No, not Mars. It must be Venus. He'd never been much good at astronomy. Something skittered through the underbrush, and he tried to think what kind of animal would be abroad on a night like this, when the ground was covered with snow and the air so cold.

He would like to bring Dob here. He could imagine it someday, his son following him into the woods, his own old field glasses slung around the boy's neck, and he'd enjoy pointing out the different birds to Dob, who would love bird-watching as much as he, Derek, had loved it when he was a kid. At night they'd figure out the constellations together. They'd camp out, too, just beyond the clearing. Derek wondered if his old tent was still usable. He'd have to get it out and see. And there would be family picnics in the summers, with cold fried chicken and deviled eggs and ripe red tomatoes from the mountaineers' gardens. He and Dob and Eve.

But that was in the future. First Eve would have to snap out of this depression. He wished he had taken the time to get to know her better before the baby had been born. He had resolved to do that, to find out what kind of life she was used to living, to find out where she was from, what she liked to do. But he hadn't thought of it until it was too late. And now, when he needed to know Eve in order to help her, he didn't know her very well at all.

Oh, why didn't I insist that Aunt May come with us? he agonized. Whatever else bothered him about the lady,

Aunt May was good for one thing: filling in silences. And there were so many of those between him and Eve. Why wouldn't she talk? Why wouldn't she talk to him?

There was nothing to do, he thought unhappily, but to keep at it.

But the second day was like the first, and the third like the second. Eve remained heavy with depression and unresponsive to him or anything he suggested. The only times she ever rallied was when he called the hospital for the daily progress report on Dob, and afterward she sank into lethargy again. And she slept for such long periods of time that secretly he worried that she was physically sick as well as mentally exhausted.

Eve awoke on the fourth day and went down to breakfast as usual.

"Good morning," Derek said as he always did. He was inexpertly lining up bacon slices in a frying pan; his big hands looked so clumsy at the task! Something stilled inside Eve. She had taken Derek for granted, and in her zombielike state she had not recognized his efforts. He'd talked, cooked, hauled firewood for the greedy fireplaces. She'd lived off him like a parasite—she, who had always been so independent. She was ashamed of herself.

To Derek's immense surprise, after breakfast Eve sat wordlessly down beside him and began fitting pieces into the jigsaw puzzle. He didn't comment on her presence. As he watched her with her hair swinging forward across her pale cheeks, he was overwhelmed by the clean, sweet fragrance of her. Once their hands touched by mistake, and his skin burned where her milky-white flesh met his.

After a couple of hours of silently working on the puzzle, the Seth Thomas mantel clock, which Derek had carefully wound the day before, struck noon. It startled both of them, that brassy intrusion of metallic sound.

"I'll fix lunch if you like," Eve offered, much to Derek's surprise.

"Fine," he said, his heart flipping over. It was the first time she had volunteered anything, the only time she had spoken without his speaking to her first.

Eve found a tin of tuna fish, opened it and deftly mixed the contents with mayonnaise. Derek brewed tea, covertly watching Eve and admiring her grace of movement.

When they sat down at the old kitchen table to eat, Eve was startled to find that Derek was staring at her.

"Is the sandwich all right?" she asked quickly.

"It's fine," he said, but he continued to watch her. She chatted with him, and although she was not by any means loquacious, he sensed that she was trying hard to open up and be some company for him. Good; maybe she was feeling better. He would think of something to keep them busy this afternoon. He had come to the conclusion that Eve's constant brooding wasn't good for her.

After lunch Derek stood up and stretched and said ever so casually, "Would you mind coming down to the basement with me, Eve? I need you to hold the flashlight for me while I poke around down there." He held his breath, waiting to see if she'd continue being communicative or if she'd sink back into her all-too-familiar listlessness.

To his immense relief she nodded her agreement, and he handed her the big flashlight to carry. They descended the steps carefully.

"No telling what's down here," he cautioned. "I haven't ventured into this basement since Kelly and I replaced the old furnace with electric heat. Careful, there's a cobweb!'' and he brushed it away with his fingers before it could trail across her face.

"It's a big basement," Eve said.

"It sure is." Derek nudged at a cardboard box with his toe. "Wonder what's in all these boxes." He bent over and looked. "Oh," he said on a note of surprise, "it's all my old Hardy Boys books. I remember reading those. I used to bring a shopping bag full of them up here every summer."

"I read Hardy Boys books when I was a kid," Eve told him. She was making an effort to rouse herself from her lethargy. It was difficult, but Derek, with his constant encouragement, was clearly trying to ease her way back to normalcy. She wanted to meet him halfway.

"I would have pegged you for Nancy Drew," he said grinning. "Or Judy Bolton."

"Oh, I read those, too." She managed to grin back.

"Train the light on this corner, Eve," he told her. He tugged at a large bundle.

"What are we looking for, anyway?" she asked, her curiosity aroused in spite of herself.

"My tent."

"Your tent? You're not planning on a camping trip in this weather, are you?"

"Heavens, no. In the future sometime. Now where could it have gone? I know it's down here somewhere."

Eve circled the light around the basement. It fell on an object hanging on the wall.

"There's something we could use now," she told him. "A sled. Why don't you wait and look for the tent some other time?"

"My old sled!" Derek said in amazement. "I wondered where that was."

"And all the time you told me you didn't know how to play in the snow," Eve said.

"Well," Derek said sheepishly, "I had forgotten. And now, there's old Rosebud."

"Rosebud? Your sled is named Rosebud?"

"I saw this movie once," said Derek. "*Citizen Kane.* And he had—"

"I know. A sled named Rosebud."

"I guess I should have been more original. But at the time it seemed like the perfect name for my sled. Of course, I didn't get to use it much because we hardly ever had snow. But I did love that sled."

"I wish you would find the tent," Eve said with a sigh.

"You're getting tired, aren't you? You should have said so. Here," he said, taking the light from her, "I'll finish this. You go upstairs and rest."

"I'm fine," she objected. "Really." But he noticed that she was shivering, and he urged her ahead of him up the steps.

"I can get the tent later. In fact, it probably isn't any good anymore, anyway. When Dob is big enough to go camping, I'll let him help me pick out a new tent."

"You were looking for the tent for Dob?" Eve said with a woebegone expression on her face. They stood in the kitchen now, facing each other in the too-bright daylight.

Derek nodded. He wished she wouldn't look that way, so vulnerable. It was his mention of Dob; she always looked that way when he spoke of his son.

"It's time to call the hospital," Derek said gently. "They'll give us a progress report on Dob."

Her face lit up all at once. "Is it time? Oh, good."

So Derek dialed the hospital's number and managed to catch Dr. Ellisor there. He passed the phone to Eve. And when she talked to Dr. Ellisor, Derek's heart softened at the glow shining within her deep, dark eyes. *She loves Dob so much,* he thought with wonder, amazed that she loved this child, who was, after all, no child of hers.

But then, being male, he couldn't imagine it, harboring another human being within his body, breathing for it, eating for it, until you thought of it as part of yourself. And then having to part from it in the painful process of childbirth and, in Eve's case, having to leave it in the hospital when it was time to go. Eve had been through so much; no wonder she was not herself. He kept forgetting what she had suffered.

"Dob's taken an extra ounce of formula, Derek," Eve said with barely suppressed excitement after she replaced the receiver in its cradle. This *was* good news.

"That's great. That's wonderful." Derek beamed down at her.

Her expression faded to wistfulness. "I wish—" And then she stopped and stood forlornly staring into space. He knew she wished she had been there, had been the one to coax him to take more at his feeding.

"I know," he said, yearning to take her in his arms. "Say, Eve, we can't be there, but let's celebrate. Let's drive down the mountain and have dinner someplace. How about it?"

"But—"

"I won't take no for an answer. Anyway, I'm tired of eating things out of cans."

She sighed softly. "It's nice of you, Derek. But I just don't want to go out. You go; I don't want you to stay because of me. I can heat up a can of soup or something."

He would not surrender her to inertia; he refused to let her talk him out of it.

"Wear something pretty," he told her impulsively when she started reluctantly up the stairs to change clothes.

"But I don't have anything pretty," she said, and then her cheeks flushed.

He had forgotten; she'd worn nothing but maternity clothes for months. "Then wear something comfortable," he said gently, and he watched her as she walked up the stairs, her legs slim beneath her skirt.

He should give her some of Kelly's clothes. But no, that wouldn't be right. Anyway, they wouldn't fit Eve. Kelly had been bustier, slimmer-hipped. He could hardly remember Kelly's size; how strange it was! He could only think of Eve, the narrow shoulders, the sturdy hips, the slim legs. He'd love to see her wearing bright colors—coral, jade green, crimson, aquamarine. Eve should have new clothes of her own.

She appeared wearing a beige sweater dress with a turtleneck; it was fuzzy, as if made of lamb's wool or, less likely, cashmere. He could tell it wasn't new, but the light behind her limned her in gold so that her figure appeared to be haloed. Her earrings were simple gold discs flashing beneath the arc of hair at her cheeks. He thought she looked beautiful.

He took her to a restaurant called the Juniper Inn near the Blue Ridge Parkway. The restaurant was in an old house and was renowned for its good food. When Eve didn't seem to know what she wanted to eat, he ordered for her with confidence.

After the wine arrived, he held his glass up and waited for her to raise hers. She did, a bit hesitantly. He had never seen her drink wine or anything alcoholic before; she had been pregnant as long as he'd known her.

"To Dob," he said softly, because he knew that was the only thing Eve would want to drink to.

"To Dob," she murmured, and when she tried to pull her eyes away from his, his sheer force of will prevented her.

"Derek?" she whispered, setting her glass on the table. The wine sloshed back and forth; her hand was unsteady.

"What would it take to make you happy, Eve?' he asked her gently.

"For Dob to be well," she said with feeling.

"He's going to be," Derek said. "My son is a survivor, Eve."

Eve looked somber. "If only I hadn't gone out in the snow that day—" she began.

"No," Derek interrupted. "We both have enough to feel guilty about. I could have stopped you from going out. I should have been there when you went up the steps, not running over to get fresh snow for snow ice cream."

"But you—"

"The point is, Eve, that either of us could feel guilty about that day. And yet Dr. Perry has said that he doesn't think that the fall had anything to do with your going into premature labor. Don't you see? We could go on hating ourselves forever if we wanted to. We could blame ourselves for Dob's being premature, but it won't do any good. I ought to know. I blamed myself for years for Kelly's miscarriage. And my guilt did more harm than good in the long run. I should have let go of my guilt and been a better husband for Kelly when I had the chance." His eyes burned into her.

Eve traced a circle on the tablecloth with one finger. She raised troubled eyes to his. "I don't know how to get to where you are," she admitted. "You've grown through that setback, you've forgiven yourself, but the guilt I feel is like a net trapping me. I know there's a way out, but I can't find it. I just keep floundering around in my thoughts, wishing... wishing..." She could not go on.

"I'll help you find your way," he said. "If you'll let me."

She only stared at him unhappily.

And yet it turned into a pleasant evening somehow. Not just for him but for her, too. He made a deliberate attempt to cheer her, calling upon his considerable repertoire of repartee. The wine relaxed both of them until Eve actually laughed once at something he told her about work, and he thought that his work would be something they could talk about, not just now but during the next few days. His eyes lingered on her mouth, the lips curved upward for once, and he was struck with the thought that it was a passionate mouth, and at that moment he wanted to kiss her very much.

He hesitated when they said good-night at the foot of the stairs. He longed to sweep her into his arms and had an absurd picture of himself carrying her up the stairs like a movie hero, but that was ridiculous. This was Eve, practical, down-to-earth Eve, and she was sad, and he was sorry, and when he kissed her, it would have to be real, not a replay of something he once saw in a movie.

But she surprised him. She lifted one hand slowly and touched the palm of it to the lean plane beneath his cheekbone, curving her hand to fit. Her hand trembled, and for a moment he thought about actually sweeping her up into his arms, but he couldn't move when he looked deep into her bottomless brown eyes and saw the tenderness in their depths.

"You are a good friend to me, Derek," she whispered, and his heart lightened, because he hadn't known what he was to her, and friendship was a start.

And then she was gone, moving swiftly upward, leaving him to stare after her, feeling breathless and hopeful and so much in love with her that his heart ached.

DEEP IN HER WARM FEATHER BED, Eve remained wakeful. She closed her eyes, only to find that they sprang wide open again to stare into the darkness. She tossed; she turned. She could not find a comfortable spot.

She would have been a fool not to know what was wrong with her. It was Derek, Derek Lang. She felt close to him, closer than she ever had to any other human being, even her father, even Doug.

Well, was that so surprising? They had been through so much together—first Kelly's death, then finding their way back to each other. Not that finding their way back to each other had been for their own comfort; Derek had taken care of her out of guilt, and she had accepted his care because she had the welfare of the baby at heart. She had hoped that Derek would come to want the baby eventually, and that had happened, thank God. And then there had been the heartbreak of poor Dob's being a preemie and therefore at risk, and they had shared that pain. Derek had been so kind to her. It was only natural for her to feel grateful to him.

And yet . . . and yet. The way Derek's soft gray eyes beamed comfort over dinner, the compassion he felt for her and which he took no pains to conceal. The *liking* she felt for him, for the person he was.

He'd spoken to her so kindly in the restaurant tonight. And slowly, slowly, what he had said began to pierce her consciousness. If he, Dob's father, did not

hold her accountable in any way for what had happened
to cause his son's premature birth, if he didn't hold himself responsible, then perhaps she could let go of her own
overwhelming guilt. And yet when she thought of poor
little Dob and all the needles and machines that he had to
endure in order to stay alive, it was hard not to blame
herself. Still, she knew in her heart of hearts that Derek
was right—blaming herself didn't help anyone, not Dob,
not Derek and certainly not Eve Triopolous.

Derek had comforted her with his words. When they
had said good-night at the foot of the stairs tonight, she
had longed for Derek to comfort her even further by
gathering her in his arms. She'd wanted nothing more,
just his sweet, warm, gentle comfort.

Was that so odd after everything they'd been through?
After all, they were the only ones who could understand
the pain of seeing Dob in the intensive-care nursery. It
was only natural for them to turn to one another in their
need.

But Derek was Kelly's husband. Eve had loved Kelly.

Derek had loved Kelly, but Kelly was gone.

Derek had kissed Eve once.

She imagined his kissing her again, his lips sure and
smooth against hers, so silky as they trailed from her lips
to her neck, to the space between her breasts and then
beyond. To join her body to his would be the pinnacle of
sharing and giving, the ultimate expression of—but what
was she thinking? With difficulty, she pulled herself back
from her thoughts and made herself think rationally. Or
as rationally as possible, anyway.

With wonder, she admitted to herself that she could
love him so easily. *Love.* She whispered the word into the
darkness, unfamiliar with the set of it on her lips. A

beautiful word, one that opened its heart in acceptance and closed its eyes in peace.

Love.

The word eased her into a jumbled sequence of scenes, all mixed up and yet somehow too clear. Derek, his mouth warm upon her lips. Her lips reaching up, up, toward his, and the sweetness of his mouth. His hands upon her body where they had never been before, feeling natural and right. Her legs entwined with his and murmuring his name over and over until it became a moan in her throat. The heat in her breasts, cooled by his kisses. Finally, his head pillowed on her shoulder, his hair against her cheek. Sleeping, the two of them, together.

Love.

She whispered the word in her dream, and then she slipped into a deep, deep sleep.

THE PHONE RANG shrilly early in the morning before he woke up, and Derek lurched out of bed, momentarily confused, before shrugging into his robe and running downstairs where the only telephone was.

It was Maisie Allen, his secretary, on the line.

"Just a few points to clear up on that contract for the new mill," Maisie said, and he was so relieved that he sagged down onto the couch nearby. He had thought it was the hospital calling. He had thought something had happened to Dob.

And Eve had, too, for she appeared at that instant, pulling on the familiar old bathrobe over her nightgown, her eyebrows winging upward, startled.

"Dob?" she whispered urgently, her face tense with strain. "Is it Dob?"

He slid his hand over the mouthpiece and smiled reassuringly. "No," he whispered, "it's my office."

Her shoulders slumped in relief, but when she turned to pad away on her bare feet, he caught her hand in his free one and would not let it go until she sat down on the arm of the couch next to him.

"Fine, Maisie, I'll agree to that. Sure. This has dragged on for the better part of a year now, and I just want to get it over with. Yeah. Okay, call me if you have any questions." He hung up.

"I'm all right," Eve said tremulously, pulling her hand away.

"Are you?" His eyes searched her face.

She inhaled a deep shaky breath and attempted a smile. "Yes."

"Let's have a cup of coffee. Or tea. We've both had a scare."

"All right."

He noticed her bare feet again. "You'd better go put on some slippers."

She smiled. "I will. You know those old black corduroy ones you didn't want me to wear to Oktoberfest? I still have them."

He grinned at her, remembering that day with fondness. It was the first time he had felt good, *really* good, after Kelly died. "I'll have the water boiling before you get back," he said, getting up and heading for the kitchen.

When she returned, he noticed that she had run a brush through her hair and that her face had a fresh-scrubbed look. She competently poured the tea he had brewed and sat down across from him, the old black corduroy slippers peeping out from beneath her long robe. There was a sense of familiarity about sitting across a breakfast table from her now; the ease of it warmed and heartened him.

"Actually, that phone call was about a new mill Lang Textiles is acquiring," he told her. He wanted her to be interested in his work; he had made up his mind to talk about it when she seemed ready to talk.

"Oh?" she said. "So how many mills do you own now?"

"Twenty-two," he said with satisfaction. "Eleven of them acquired since my father retired."

"So many!"

"One thing I learned at Harvard Business School is that you either grow or stagnate. I'd rather grow." His eyes sparkled at her; she was captivated by his dynamism when he spoke of his work.

"And where is this new mill of yours?"

"Wrayville," he said. "That's where you grew up, isn't it?"

Oh, what had he said wrong? He didn't like the white line around her lips or the way she had clamped them shut, nor did he like the way her dark eyes narrowed.

"Yes," she said shortly, dropping her eyes to her teacup. "I grew up in Wrayville."

"And your father worked in a mill most of his life, right? He worked at Wray Mills, then?"

"Yes," she said, whispering the word, her head in a whirl. She had never in all this time dreamed that Derek's company would be the one to buy Wray Mills. She should have guessed, she supposed, but so many other big names in the textile business had been mentioned as rumors swept Wrayville that she had never given Lang Textiles a thought.

Her stomach did a dive, turned over. This man, Derek Lang, who sat across from her and who was her friend—this man had the power to right the wrong done to dozens of textile workers in the past and to make the future of present workers free of the crippling brown-lung disease! Did he know the working conditions at Wray Mills? Did he care? He was a caring man—she knew that—but she also knew that he was a hardheaded businessman who needed to make a profit because he still felt a need to prove himself worthy of his inherited position.

Should she take him into her confidence? Should she tell him about the workmen's compensation claims waiting for him when he finalized the takeover of Wray Mills?

She shoved back her chair. "I—I think I'll get dressed now," she stammered, fighting for composure and avoiding Derek's eyes. She almost overturned the cane-bottom chair in her haste to get away.

Derek's gray eyes reflected hurt and rejection. But Eve couldn't stop to think about that; she needed to be alone. She had to think about other things. About what to tell Derek—if she should tell him anything—about the effect the Lang Textiles' takeover would have on the claims she had worked so hard with Doug to file, about—oh, about all sorts of things.

She had retreated from the real world long enough. Now she had been yanked back into it by Derek's revelation, and the shock of it bent her mind, overshadowing her anguish over Dob and her grief at having to give him up.

Running upstairs, fleeing to the privacy of her room, she knew that she couldn't afford the luxury of self-pity for Eve Triopolous any longer, not when the quality of life for hundreds of mill workers was at stake.

What should I do? she agonized, sinking down on the edge of her bed. *How much should I tell him?* Questions hurled themselves back and forth in her mind as she searched her soul for the right answers.

It was at least two hours before Eve appeared before Derek, who was in the living room halfheartedly working on the jigsaw puzzle. He didn't understand why she had fled, especially when things were going so well between them.

He looked up to find her standing quietly beside him. She was tastefully dressed in a long-sleeved dress the color of burgundy; it had a stand-up ruffle at the neck instead of a collar. She carried her small suitcase in one hand.

Eve's velvet-brown eyes met his directly. He rejoiced to see that she looked like the Eve he remembered.

"I've decided," she said in her clear firm voice, "that it's time for you to meet my father."

Chapter Thirteen

Wrayville in winter hunkered spare and bleak in the shadow of Cotton Mill Hill. Weak January sunlight glinted off the dirty windows of the two-storey brick building that dominated the scene, and a chill wind whipped around the corners of street after street of identical mill-village houses.

In the middle of Nell Baker's block, children with runny noses played in the street. They ran away at the car's approach and stood wide-eyed on the curb, staring at Derek's Corvette. One of them yelled something derisive.

"Here it is," Eve said suddenly. "Fourth house on the right." Derek slowed his car to a stop in front of the white frame house.

He shot her a dubious look. "Are you going to tell them I'm the new owner of the mill?"

"No," Eve said. "Since there's been no public announcement, they won't know yet. If your name is connected to the mill, it will seem like just another rumor. To Al and Nell, you'll just be Derek, Dob's father."

Derek felt ill at ease, but he could see that Eve did not. She sailed confidently up to the front door and knocked.

The door swung open to reveal a round, ruddy-cheeked woman wearing glasses with silver frames.

"Eve!" The two women embraced, and Derek felt even more awkward than before.

But Eve turned to him quickly and drew him forward. "Nell, this is Derek."

Nell smiled an uncertain greeting as she ushered them into a minuscule living room. It was tiny, but the furniture had been polished to within an inch of its life, and the blinds at the windows were raised to let in the maximum light.

"You'll want to see your dad right away," Nell said with an inquiring look.

"Yes," Eve said.

"Vernon's gone to the barbershop, and your father's out on the back porch watching television. I'm so glad I had the porch closed in last summer; it's made a wonderful TV room. Al stays out there most of the time. Thank goodness for the sports network. Al and my other boarder both love it."

Al, resting in a reclining chair with a plaid blanket over his lap, looked up as Eve paused in the doorway. On the television set in the corner, men in baggy shorts ran back and forth on a hardwood basketball court.

Derek's first impression of Eve's father was of a sick, elderly man. But Eve's father wasn't elderly; she had told him that he was only sixty-two! And these days, that wasn't old. It wasn't even retirement age. But hadn't she said her father was retired from Wray Mills? Or had she said that he used to work at Wray Mills? Derek couldn't recall.

Al tried to struggle to his feet, but Eve put a restraining hand on his shoulder.

"Don't get up, Dad," she said gently. Nell quietly turned down the volume on the TV set. The men continued running around on the basketball court; without the sound, the game looked like pointless scurrying.

"I—I—" Al said, and then began to cough. Finally, the cough subsided into an agonizing wheeze that punctuated every breath. But Al held up his hand to shake Derek's, and there was a welcoming light in his brown eyes, which were so like his daughter's. Derek gripped Al's hand with his customary vigor, but he realized too late that his grip was too much for Al, whose hand lay within his, lacking the strength to do much more than make a futile effort at a proper handshake.

Derek did not know how to react. He knew, of course, of Eve's father's resentment toward him for the part he had played in employing her as a surrogate mother. And yet he knew that with time and because he had taken care of Eve and had been kind to her, her father's resentment had faded into acceptance. Still, Derek felt some embarrassment at his part in what Eve's father had so long considered the immorality of her situation. He had assumed, in the light of his discussion with Eve at the Juniper Inn, that Eve wanted him to meet her father in order to exorcise that part of her guilt, in order to put it behind her, as he, Derek, had urged her to do.

But perhaps that wasn't the reason at all.

"You're feeling well, Evie?" her father was asking.

"Very well, Al. The few days in the mountains helped."

"And the little fellow?" This question was directed to Derek.

"He's doing fine. He's eating well and may come home from the hospital soon."

Al nodded, his energy spent.

"Have you had your flu shot this year, Al? You know how important that is."

"I carried him to the doctor for it myself," Nell said, peeking around the door from the kitchen.

"She did," Al said with a smile. "She's a right pushy old gal, if you want to know the truth."

"Aw, Al. Now don't go telling Eve how much I bully you. Besides, if it weren't for me, you wouldn't be working in Doug's office. And you like working there." Nell appeared bearing a tray with a coffeepot and four cups. She handed cups around and disappeared into the kitchen before reappearing with four plates of fudge cake.

But Al couldn't eat his and only waved it away. Eve left it sitting on the end table near him. Al coughed again; Derek tried not to listen and looked blankly at the men on the television screen. The men ran off; cheerleaders in short skirts danced on. It seemed wrong somehow, cheerleaders shaking pom-poms in this sickroom. For that's what it was, all right. This man was very ill.

"Do you have your inhaler, Al?" Eve asked anxiously.

"He's got it. It's right there in the table drawer," Nell assured her. She frowned. "He does need a new refill, though."

"We can get it for you before we leave," Eve said quickly with a look at Derek, who confirmed her words with a nod. "That way you won't have to go out in the cold, Nell."

"That's real sweet of you, Eve." Nell smiled her thanks.

The cake was good, and Nell was pleasant. But the hour dragged on and on for Derek in the light of his realization that Eve's father was a chronic invalid. Why hadn't she told him? She had never mentioned anything to that effect.

Finally, blessedly, it was time to leave. Eve bent and kissed her father goodbye. Al tried to get up again, but this time Derek urged him not to. His coughing seemed to have left him exhausted. In spite of himself, Derek looked back over his shoulder one last time before he left. Al's lined face was sallow and weary, and he lay limply in his recliner chair.

"I'll be back with your medicine in a few minutes," Eve called back to Al. "Just as long as it takes us to run down to the drugstore on the corner."

Derek said nothing when they were in the Corvette. He followed Eve's directions to the drugstore.

"Come in with me?" she asked.

"Sure," he said, although he didn't understand why she wanted him to.

He followed her down the long row of merchandise to the pharmacist's section. They waited while the pharmacist, an old friend of Eve's, filled Al's prescription.

"Come here," Eve said, tugging Derek toward an alcove near the cash register. She pointed to a machine. "Do you know what that is?"

Derek shook his head. All of this was beyond him; what point was Eve trying to make?

"It's a Liberator," she said. "It weighs eighty-four pounds. It provides oxygen for people who can't breathe well. See that clear tubing? It allows the patient to move no more than twenty feet away from the machine. If the patient has to go out, for instance to church or shopping, he has to carry a portable liquid oxygen set." She looked Derek squarely in the eye, sizing up his comprehension. "That's what my father has to look forward to," she told him bitterly. "That will be the next step for him. He'll have to rent a Liberator so he can breathe, probably that very one.''

''Here you are, Eve,'' the pharmacist said, stepping out from behind the partition. ''Al doing okay?''

She managed a smile for the pharmacist, whom she had known all her life. ''He's about the same, Charlie. Thanks.''

Derek followed Eve out of the store. Her purpose was now clear.

''Your father has brown-lung disease, doesn't he?'' They stood outside on the pavement now; wet black leaves blew against their feet and stuck to their shoes like soggy leeches. But Eve didn't move. She stared up at him, almost defiantly.

''Yes, he does. He worked in the card room at Wray Mills for thirty-eight years.'' She bent her head against the wind and stuffed her free hand deep in her coat pocket, walking swiftly ahead of him to the car.

He opened the door for her and went around to the driver's side. Then he threw the car into gear and drove slowly back to Nell's house. He watched Eve as she ran quickly up to the front porch and handed the medicine quickly through the front door. She waved cheerily, called something encouraging to her father and ran back out to the car. She brought a fresh-air smell with her when she folded herself into the seat beside him.

Derek stared at her. He looked hollow-eyed, like someone in shock.

''Well?'' she said.

''I don't know about you, but I think I'd like to stop somewhere for a drink,'' he said heavily.

IT WAS A ROADHOUSE on the outskirts of town, a working-class hangout, but Derek stopped, anyway. There was a dearth of customers; the only cars in the parking lot were a dilapidated old Dodge sedan and a rusty pickup truck with two hunting dogs flapping their tails back and forth as they nosed against the tailgate.

Inside it was dark and gloomy. On the jukebox a woman wailed a somebody-done-somebody-wrong song. None of this mattered to Derek. He only wanted to sit down across a table from Eve and let her help him sort out his feelings about what he had just experienced in Wrayville.

They ordered—for Derek, his customary bourbon; for Eve, a glass of water. She wanted to be at her clearest and sharpest for this conversation.

"I've never met anyone with brown-lung disease before," Derek said. Above the round table where they sat, a Miller beer sign winked sporadically on and off, victim of a faulty light bulb.

"The people who suffer from byssinosis are usually poor and uneducated. They're not people who travel in your circles," she told him matter-of-factly.

"I suppose not," he agreed. His eyes were dark and troubled in the flickering light from the sign.

"I'm fully aware that some people deny that brown-lung is a disease," she said carefully. "I know that two people can work side by side in a dusty room and one will develop symptoms and one will not. There's an individual variability in response to the cotton-dust irritant. And nobody has yet figured out how a patient gets to the point where the disease is irreversible chronic lung disease. But no one who has seen the effects on mill workers over a period of many years can say that the cotton dust in the mills doesn't play a part in the disease's development."

"But a lot of brown-lung patients are smokers," Derek said. "Who can say that tobacco didn't cause their disease?"

"My father never smoked. Neither did Nell Baker's husband." She sipped at her water. "Oh, Derek, I have to admit that today was one of my father's bad days. He has good days; he has bad. But we can't expect him to ever get much better. His disease is irreversible according to the doctors."

"Why didn't he transfer out of the card room when he began having respiratory problems?"

"In the old days, you were happy to have a job. You didn't tell management where you wanted to work. You worked where they sent you. And as you know, there was no union at Wray Mills to stand up for workers' rights. Tell me, Derek, have you ever been inside a cotton mill? If you have, you must know what the working conditions were like twenty years ago, ten years ago. And even now." The sputtering light from the beer sign lit her face in all its earnestness.

"I went with my father once," Derek said, "to a mill over in Cherry Grove. I was only about ten years old, but that was part of his training of me as a future textile magnate—to take me to the mills when he went. And I followed Dad into the mill and saw the workers moving around in this haze of thick white lint with the machinery making an awful noise all around them. I was intimidated by all of it, to tell you the truth. I asked my father how the people could work under those conditions. Lint was everywhere—under the looms, in the workers' hair, heavy in the air like a blizzard of cotton dust. And Dad laughed and said the lintheads got used to it."

Eve's eyes flashed fire, and two red spots appeared high on her cheeks. "Used to it! They got sick from it!"

She leaned closer over the table. "The dust was everywhere. They couldn't get away from it. My father used an air hose to blow the lint off him every night before he left the mill, but he still had to keep his work clothes in a separate closet so that the dust wouldn't get all over his good suits."

"I knew that Wray Mills hasn't complied with the law in cleaning up their plant," Derek conceded. "That's something we investigated before buying. But I had no idea there were any brown-lung sufferers. They didn't tell us that."

"I know," Eve said angrily. "They deliberately concealed the information. They 'lost' my father's claim after he filed it two years ago when brown-lung disease was diagnosed and he had to quit work. And when I objected to their treatment of him and when I refused to hand out statements to the press that Wray Mills was taking steps to comply with the cotton-dust standards set down by the state labor department, I was fired."

"Fired!"

"Yes, fired from a very good public relations job. Why do you think I hired myself out as a surrogate mother? I'd been unemployed for months."

"You needed the money," Derek said woodenly. "I read it on your application."

"Yes, I needed the money to support my father."

"My God." Derek stared at her as though she were a stranger. He'd realized he didn't know everything about her. But he'd felt close to her, had experienced the ease of friendship with her, had thought he knew *something* about her, and yet now he felt as though he hardly knew her at all. He could not have imagined the pressures Eve Triopolous had faced, and to think that he had added to them when he had insisted on the abortion made him feel sick and angry with himself.

He motioned to the barmaid for another drink. She poured it and brought it to them, all twitching hips. They sat silently until she slinked back behind the bar.

"I want you to know, Eve, that Lang Textiles has a history of bringing each of its mills into compliance with the law. We're a big company, and it's a huge capital expense, but we can afford the air-filtration equipment and new machinery it will take to clean up Wray Mills."

She studied him. The corners of his eyes fanned with creases she had never noticed before. "Wray Mills has taken advantage of every appeals procedure available under the law in order to stave off compliance," she told him. "In the opening room, workers are breaking open bales of cotton in air six times dustier than regulations allow. The most that's ever happened after an inspection is that the labor department fines the mill five hundred dollars and gives them a year to comply. You're saying that you're going to change this?"

"You're damned right I am," he said through clenched teeth. The beer sign flared brightly as if in approval of his words.

And Eve believed him.

"We'll use remote-control bale openers at Wray Mills," Derek told her. "In every plant where we've installed air-filtration systems and remote-control bale openers, not only has the machinery reduced worker exposure to cotton dust, but productivity and the quality of the product have improved."

"And the workers? People like my father who have brown-lung claims? There are at least twelve people with valid claims, thirteen counting my father. I helped fill out the claim forms myself."

"You?"

"Yes, me. I spent Mondays working with Doug Ender in his office. We ran a brown-lung hotline. I donated my time, and Doug took time out from a busy practice to donate his. We canvased Wrayville by telephone. I filled out forms. We threw out the people who were faking it because they wanted free benefits."

"You and Ender? When you were living at my house?" This news astonished him. Now he knew where Eve had gone on Mondays, why she was never there when he arrived home from work.

Eve nodded her head once, twice.

He stared at her, finally comprehending. And he comprehended more than her passionate advocacy of the rights of workers to work in a clean environment, more than her championship of brown-lung claimants. He comprehended the uncompromising high standards of Eve Triopolous and her stubbornness when confronted with what she considered wrong, whether it was the failure of a mill to comply with regulations or the shunting aside of a hearing-impaired old woman or—abortion. In a world that could be ugly, Eve never compromised her convictions. She had always been, to his knowledge, faithful, loyal, moral—and kind.

He looked at her soberly, and when he spoke, his voice was calm.

"This fellow Ender. Is he important to you?"

She considered this, and Derek found that he couldn't breathe.

"He's an old friend, and very dear to me. But we're not romantically involved, if that's what you mean." She spoke candidly, and there was a ring of truth to her words.

"That's what I mean, all right," he said, draining the liquid in his glass. He locked his eyes with hers, knowing he had never been so relieved or so happy in his life.

"Let's get out of here," he said, rising from his seat and tossing a large bill on the table.

He couldn't resist pulling the plug on the maddeningly erratic beer sign before they left.

THEY HAD TO PASS the hospital on their way back to Myers Park. Eve glanced at him as they approached it.

"Derek?" she said softly.

He swung the car into the hospital parking lot. "We'll go up to the intensive-care unit," he said. "We'll try to see Dob."

Dr. Perry had ordered Eve not to see Dob for a week, and it hadn't been that long yet. But Derek felt sure that if Dr. Perry could see Eve now, he wouldn't object to her visiting Dob, if only for a few minutes.

Derek and Eve stood side by side in the elevator on the way to the intensive-care unit, suddenly self-conscious together. A new tension existed between them, and they both knew it. Eve sensed what Derek was thinking, and her heart pounded in her chest. She knew him well enough by now to know what he wanted. Did she want the same thing? Was it *right* to want it? Was the affection she felt for him really love, or was it something else?

The nurse on duty outside the intensive-care nursery glanced up from the charts spread out on her desk. She was someone they knew from all their previous visits, and she smiled with pleasure when she saw them.

"Derek. Eve. You've chosen a good time to come." She stood up and beckoned. "Follow me."

Through the window they saw an aide sitting in a rocking chair, holding a bundle wrapped in a blue-and-white checked flannel blanket, and she was holding a bottle in her hand.

"It's Dob," Eve breathed, recognizing the unmistakable shape of Dob's head, the sparse tuft of brown hair on his head.

"Would you like to feed him?" the nurse asked with an inquiring look at Eve. "We've taken him off the tubes. He's taking all his nourishment by mouth."

"I—I—"

"You'd better put on a gown and a mask," the nurse said, producing one of each. "You, too, Daddy." She handed a similar outfit to Derek.

Once properly garbed, they entered the nursery. The aide wordlessly stood up and handed the bundle over to Eve. Eve's heart swelled with love; her chest felt so full that it hurt. Dob wriggled; he moved his legs restlessly, and his tiny seeking mouth rooted for the nipple so recently removed from it.

Eve sank down in the rocking chair, cradling Dob against her breasts, and inserted the nipple into Dob's mouth. With a sigh of pleasure, he began to suck at it, his eyes, gray and curious, fixed steadily on Eve's face.

Her own eyes filled with tears of happiness. There was no way she could have imagined the euphoria of holding Dob in her arms, to feel again bound to him as she had felt when he had still been a part of her.

His cheeks had filled out, and although they weren't plump, he was no longer wrinkled. His skin was pink and rosy, and someone had combed his hair into a peak down the middle of the top of his head. He was more than a bit of raw tissue; he was real, he was beautiful, he was *Dob*. He was a miracle.

His eyes drifted closed as the round cheeks worked at the nipple. A thread of milk ran out of the corner of his tiny rosebud mouth. Derek reached down and wiped it away with a corner of the blanket. Derek's face was absorbed, and in a quiet way, joyful. But Derek would never be bound to this baby the way Eve was. Never.

"Do you want to hold him?" she asked softly, glancing up at him.

Derek shook his head. He smiled tenderly at the two of them.

"No, not this time," he said gently. "I'd rather watch the two of you together. I've never seen a more beautiful scene."

His eyes touched her heart with gladness, and they did not speak to each other again. There was no need to talk. One heartfelt look said everything that needed to be said between them.

No one was awake at the Myers Park house when Eve and Derek tiptoed through the back door. Aunt May didn't expect them back for a few more days; anyway, it was late, and Aunt May usually retired early.

Nevertheless, Eve felt like a criminal sneaking up the stairs hand in hand with Derek.

"I don't want to leave you," he said outside her bedroom door. His hands rested lightly on her upper arms, and she found herself inclining toward him so naturally that she saw no point in stopping.

Her forehead met his chin. He put a finger beneath her chin and lifted her face until he was looking full into it. The wing-swept eyebrows, the straight, sharp nose, the high cheekbones and her eyelashes, so short and dark. All were breathtakingly familiar and yet much too unfamiliar. He drifted his fingers across her features, committing them to memory so he could recall them and the way they felt whenever he chose. And then she lifted her mouth to his, the lips slightly parted, and he slid his arms around her, delighting in the rightness of it, the perfection of it.

His mouth met hers, and he was touched that her lips trembled beneath his, but they didn't tremble for long, because then everything was sure and honest, and their lips together felt right and familiar even though they had only kissed once before.

Eve's doubt melted away as Derek's lips explored hers, and happiness surged through her so that she was able only to think, *Yes, yes!* as she returned his kiss with joyful abandon. After all they had been through, after their sharing of grief and guilt and joy, after circumstances had so irrevocably blended their lives, how could she ever leave this dear and wonderful man? She couldn't.

Derek pulled her tightly against him, so tightly that he felt his heart beating in unison with hers, speeding up, urging them on, racing toward what they both knew was the inevitable result of their passion. This night, they could not be apart. It was as simple as that.

His lips released hers, and he looked down at her to see tears glazing her dark eyes. Without a word he opened the door to her room and drew her inside, closing the door softly behind him.

"Eve, I want you to know I love you. This isn't merely a—"

She placed a quieting finger across his lips. Her voice was warm and rang with a new confidence. "I know. And I love you. It's just that at first it didn't seem right. I couldn't be sure if it was real, and if it wasn't real, I couldn't admit to it, but now I'm sure, Derek. Very sure."

He smiled at her in the dark. "And so am I. We've shared so much. So much, Eve," he said and his head bent to hers again, absorbing her in a kiss that took her breath away.

When finally they broke apart, he slid his hands around to the buckle of her belt.

"May I?" he whispered.

Slowly she nodded. He unfastened the belt, then moved his hands around to the tab of the long zipper at the back of her dress. When he tried to slide it, it wouldn't budge.

"Oh," Eve murmured. "It gets stuck on the ruffle sometimes." She lifted her hands and found the tab, and his hands remained over hers as she tugged it loose. Then he slowly edged the zipper slide down and down, past her waist, over her hips until he felt the silkiness of the undergarment beneath.

Eve shrugged out of the dress, letting it puddle into folds on the floor. She stood before him, pale and white, in her slip.

He eased the straps over her narrow shoulders and kissed her shoulders one by one. Then he shimmied the slip down around her hips, letting his hands rest there for a moment as he captured her lips in a kiss, then allowing the slip to fall around her ankles.

She wore a bra that crowded her breasts, still swollen from childbirth; she had had a shot after the delivery to dry up her milk, because she would not be nursing Dob, but her breasts remained full and round. Derek knew, he understood, and he was gentle as he unhooked her bra, removing it before touching her reverently and then pressing his lips to each dark peak, one by one.

And then he slid her panty hose downward, and she gracefully lifted one leg and then the other as he knelt at her feet, and when he stood up again, she stood before him completely naked and free, and he caught his breath at the absolute beauty of her in the light from the street lamp outside the window.

Silvery marks marred the smooth white skin of her newly flat abdomen. Carefully, tentatively, he caressed one with an experimental finger.

"These?" he whispered.

"Stretch marks," she breathed, aroused by his touch. "From Dob."

"They won't ever go away, will they?" His voice sounded anxious.

"No." Her eyes on his face never wavered. "But it doesn't matter." Suddenly she felt elated; she had borne this man's child, and she was proud of it.

He knelt again and gently kissed each stretch mark. She closed her eyes against the sweet torment of her desire for him.

He stood again, holding her loosely within the circle of his arms. "It's too soon after the baby to really make love, isn't it?" he asked her gently, kissing her earlobe as he did so.

"Yes," she murmured, not at all embarrassed. She felt no modesty or shame with him, none at all. "But we can—"

"I know," he said, lifting her in his arms and striding to her narrow bed. He laid her carefully there as though she might break, and his eyes caressed her as he took off his clothes, too.

She lifted up the sheet and blanket for him to come to her, and he laid down beside her, absorbing her warmth, the softness of her body, the pleasure of their skins touching. He drew her into his arms and murmured her name over and over into her fragrant hair.

"I love you, Derek," she said, her lips hungry for him, hungry for all of him.

"And I, you," he said unsteadily. Newly wise in their love for each other, they knew better than to say all the words, so in this time and space they spoke no more of their love. The peace enveloping them was as pleasant as their caresses, as soothing and as meaningful as their love itself. With a passion so tender that Eve thought her heart would break with the joy of it, Derek made love to her until their exhaustion overcame their euphoria, and finally they slept, entwined in each other's arms.

When the morning sun broke through the trees, Derek reluctantly slipped away to his own room.

"Because," he said lovingly as he sat on the edge of her bed to kiss her goodbye, "for your sake, I want to keep up appearances for Aunt May. Until we get married, that is. Will you, Eve? Will you marry me?"

For a moment he was afraid. What if she said no? Because of Kelly, because they were from different backgrounds, because of a hundred and one reasons why he wasn't good enough for her. And he wasn't good enough, not by half.

Eve smiled and reached up to pull him down to her, sliding her arms around his neck. "Yes," Eve replied, her voice thick and warm. "Yes, my darling. I'll marry you. As soon as we can."

Chapter Fourteen

Eve Triopolous married Derek Lang in March in a short private ceremony at the home of the groom. Her father, looking spiffy in his best suit and coughing very little, attended the wedding with Nell Baker, who wore a new lavender dress for the occasion. Aunt May, who was touchingly overjoyed, donned her best three-and-a-half-inch rainbow-striped high heels with her teal-blue suit, and she even bought a new battery for her hearing aid so as not to miss any of the ceremony. Doug Ender was there, and Derek's friends, the Kleinsts and Jay Stanley, came, too.

Also in attendance was Derek Robert Lang, Jr., sleeping peacefully in an heirloom cradle under the bay window in the living room with Louise standing by in case he awoke.

"He's supposed to sleep through the ceremony," Eve said nervously, glancing at her wristwatch as she and Derek took their places before the judge in the living room with their guests looking on. "He just finished his feeding."

Indeed, Eve had almost been late for her own wedding when Dob spit up all over her wedding dress. Fortunately, she had another one equally as appropriate, so she exchanged apricot silk for eggshell lace and thanked Derek for being so insistent on buying her everything in sight the day he took her to Montaldo's to outfit her with a trousseau.

"Well," Derek had said, adjusting his tie one last time and then turning to her with a smile on his face. He kissed her adoringly on the tip of her nose, admiring once more the geometric precision of her haircut, short in back and longer on the sides. "That just shows you how good it is to have a plan. And an alternate plan, of course."

She beamed up at him. "Just be sure to let me in on what the plan is from now on, will you? It helps." It still rankled that he hadn't told her earlier how much he loved her. Because then she wouldn't have thought all the things she had thought, that she would have to leave Dob, that she would have to leave Derek. And maybe she never would have become so depressed that she went utterly to pieces.

But of course Derek had made up for it. He told her he loved her every chance he got. And she thought she would never hear it enough, even if he told her every five minutes for the rest of her life. Which he had laughingly threatened to do as he offered his arm to escort her down the stairs to the ceremony.

"And will you, Derek, love her, comfort her, honor and keep her in sickness and in health—"

Why, he already has, Eve thought.

"I will," Derek said, and his eyes upon her face shone with commitment and love.

"To have and to hold from this day forward, for better for worse, for richer for poorer, in sickness and in health, to love and to cherish, till death do us part." Eve's eyes, shining with happiness, never left Derek's face.

Above them, Kelly smiled in the gold-rimmed portrait over the mantel. It was as though she blessed them in their union.

Derek drew Eve tenderly into his arms and kissed her gently on the lips. And she clung to him, overwhelmed with happiness.

From the cradle beneath the window came a low whimper and then a long wail.

"Oh," Eve said, pulling away from Derek. "I thought he'd sleep through it. He always takes a long nap after his afternoon bottle." She hurried to the cradle and picked up the crying baby. "There, there, Dob," she soothed, patting him on the back. "It's all right. Mama's here."

"Champagne in the dining room for anyone who's interested," Derek said, and with a comforted Dob reposing in Eve's arms, they all trooped in for a toast proposed by Doug Ender.

"To Derek and Eve and Dob in their happiness," Doug said, holding his glass high. Everyone raised a glass of Derek's favorite Dom Perignon to his lips, and Derek beamed at his wife and son.

Louise passed dainty sandwiches and petits fours on which she and Aunt May had collaborated, and a cornered Doug listened patiently to Debby Kleinst's glowing description of her unmarried sister.

"I told Derek," Aunt May declared earnestly to an interested Nell Baker, "that the only thing I could possibly miss my soap opera for was this wedding. Did you see the last episode of *Love of Hope*? The hockey player told Susan about the computer hackers who penetrated the bank records, and—"

"I'm sending in a consultant to determine what measures are necessary at Wray Mills to bring it up to standard. I'm prepared to spend as much as necessary to clean up the air in the next few months—"

"Evie, you look so pretty. And the baby's a cute little fellow, isn't he? You know, it's nice to have a grandchild. It really is. I wish your mother—"

"Psst, Eve, come in here. I haven't told you I loved you since before the ceremony. It's been at least half an hour. Do you have any idea how much I love—"

"Derek, stop it! Aunt May or somebody will walk in any minute, or Louise asking if we want something to eat!"

"What do you think, Dob? If your mother won't kiss me, I'll have to kiss you. Come on, son; come to Daddy," he urged, and Derek eased an open-mouthed Dob into his own arms and stood beside the cradle, gazing happily down at his son. Then he planted a kiss on the baby's small forehead.

"Look, Eve, he smiled! He did! He has Kelly's mouth. Remember I told you that one day in the hospital?" Derek sounded genuinely pleased.

Eve gazed at her son. "Kelly's mouth but definitely your nose." And Dob *was* smiling. Definitely smiling, his eyes crinkling with mirth.

Derek laid Dob gently in the cradle and watched as his son energetically bicycled his legs. Then, after several moments of exercise, Dob yawned widely and sighed as his eyes drifted shut. In a time span as brief as the blink of an eye, he had fallen asleep.

Hand in hand, Eve and Derek watched their small son. "You know," Derek said with a glance out the window, "it's almost time for Aunt May's pansies. See the little green sprigs in the flower beds? Remember she planted them in the fall to bloom in the spring?''

"Yes," Eve said, recalling the very day. "I wondered how those fragile little plants would ever weather the winter." To be honest, she had worried then about how *she* was going to weather the winter, how she'd manage to leave the baby behind when spring came, because at that time that was what she had hoped for, that Derek would keep the baby. Then she had never dreamed that he would keep her also. Well, the pansies had weathered the winter, and she had, too. They were both stronger than they looked.

"I love pansies," she told Derek. "They're my favorite flower. I sat beside a bed of pansies the day I saw your ad for a surrogate mother in the newspaper. I've always thought I was like a pansy. Not flashy."

He studied her face, so dear to him now. "I like that. You *are* like a pansy. And they used to be called heartsease. You've eased my heart, Eve. Ever since you came back."

She turned within the circle of his arms and rested her head on his chest. She closed her eyes and let the sweet comfort of his embrace enfold her. She felt so safe, so happy, and the feeling made up for everything that had happened in the past.

"I'm never going to leave you again, Derek. Never."

"You'd better not. It isn't in the plan. And in this case, there's no alternate plan, either."

Eve lifted her head and smiled at him, revealing her quirky bicuspid, and then they laughed together and after one last quick but heartfelt kiss, the two of them hurried arm in arm to join their wedding guests.

And in his cradle, Derek Robert Lang, Jr., slept on, blissfully unaware for the time being that his life, his existence, his very *being*, was a true miracle of love.

Harlequin American Romance

COMING NEXT MONTH

#141 THE STRAIGHT GAME by Rebecca Flanders

E. J. Wiley looked at the man across her desk—one Colby James.
He claimed to be an itinerant sailor and dockworker.
Honoraria Fitzgerald called him her long-lost son and heir to her
San Francisco fortune. E.J. didn't know who was right—she only
knew he was her fantasy.

#142 WINTER MAGIC by Margaret St. George

Even as Teddi watched the icy flakes falling from the warmth of
the ski lodge, her drying throat constricted her breathing. It had
been six years since she'd seen her family and friends—and
snow. But it wasn't until her eyes lit on the indomitable
Grant Sterling that she knew returning to Vail was her greatest
mistake.

#143 A FAMILY TO CHERISH by Cathy Gillen Thacker

More than anything Christy Shannon wanted this family.
Orphaned and now widowed, she couldn't understand why her
husband had run away and denied his relatives. Until she visited
the Texas ranch and met his brother, Jake. Jake opened his
home to Christy, but he swore she'd never uncover the shocking
incident that was the brothers' secret.

#144 A CLASS ABOVE by Carolyn Thornton

Squawking roadside chickens, rundown pickups and circling
buzzards. It wasn't exactly what she expected when she
accepted the challenge of this hitchhiking contest. For risk was
Tara Jefferson's middle name. But little did she know that when
she hitched a ride with pilot Marcus Landry he'd be taking her
on the adventure of a lifetime.

Can you keep a secret?

You can keep this one plus 4 free novels

Readers rave about Harlequin American Romance!

"...the best series of modern romances I have read...great, exciting, stupendous, wonderful."
—S.E.,* Coweta, Oklahoma

"...they are absolutely fantastic...going to be a smash hit and hard to keep on the bookshelves."
—P.D., Easton, Pennsylvania

"The American line is great. I've enjoyed every one I've read so far."
—W.M.K., Lansing, Illinois

"...the best stories I have read in a long time."
—R.H., Northport, New York

*Names available on request.

WORLDWIDE LIBRARY IS YOUR TICKET TO ROMANCE, ADVENTURE AND EXCITEMENT

Experience it all in these big, bold Bestsellers— Yours exclusively from WORLDWIDE LIBRARY WHILE QUANTITIES LAST

To receive these Bestsellers, complete the order form, detach and send together with your check or money order (include 75¢ postage and handling), payable to WORLDWIDE LIBRARY, to:

In the U.S.
WORLDWIDE LIBRARY
901 Fuhrman Blvd.
Buffalo, N.Y.
14269

In Canada
WORLDWIDE LIBRARY
P.O. Box 2800, 5170 Yonge Street
Postal Station A, Willowdale, Ontario
M2N 6J3

Quant.	Title	Price
_____	**WILD CONCERTO**, Anne Mather	$2.95
_____	**A VIOLATION**, Charlotte Lamb	$3.50
_____	**SECRETS**, Sheila Holland	$3.50
_____	**SWEET MEMORIES**, LaVyrle Spencer	$3.50
_____	**FLORA**, Anne Weale	$3.50
_____	**SUMMER'S AWAKENING**, Anne Weale	$3.50
_____	**FINGER PRINTS**, Barbara Delinsky	$3.50
_____	**DREAMWEAVER**, Felicia Gallant/Rebecca Flanders	$3.50
_____	**EYE OF THE STORM**, Maura Seger	$3.50
_____	**HIDDEN IN THE FLAME**, Anne Mather	$3.50
_____	**ECHO OF THUNDER**, Maura Seger	$3.95
_____	**DREAM OF DARKNESS**, Jocelyn Haley	$3.95
	YOUR ORDER TOTAL	$_____
	New York residents add appropriate sales tax	$_____
	Postage and Handling	$___.75
	I enclose	$_____

NAME _____

ADDRESS _____ APT.# _____

CITY _____

STATE/PROV. _____ ZIP/POSTAL CODE _____

WW-1-3